Mindset of Murder

A Bekbourg County Novel

by Sherrie Rutherford

VENCIN Publishing

Venice, Florida

Bekbourg County Novels

Mindset of Murder

Valley of Murder

Pathos of Murder

Bookends of Murder

ISBN: 978-1-7345992-3-7

Library of Congress Control Number: 2021912185

VenCin Publishing

Venice, Florida

iv

Acknowledgments

To Larry—a mainstay in my *Acknowledgments* because of his support and dedication in making the Bekbourg County series possible. Thank you, my love, for all you do to encourage my writing.

To Gary Steinhilber and Pat Goetz for their continued support and diligence in imparting their knowledge and insight as readers.

To family and friends, whose cheering for my next novel inspires me as I write each new chapter in the Bekbourg County mysteries.

To Clarissa Thomasson, my editor, for her guidance.

To Cross Ink, Corp., for cover design.

To all the people who read my novels.

Mindset of Murder

A Bekbourg County Novel

By Sherrie Rutherford

Chapter 1

Spring 1967

Number 91 was a regular west-bound through-freight manifest train that ran from Wheeling, West Virginia, to Cincinnati, Ohio, and it was running late. Number 91 had departed Wheeling two hours later than usual, but they were making good time as they approached Bekbourg, a small town in southeast Ohio about mid-point between the two cities. The engineer, Cecil Davis, lived in Bekbourg—as did his fireman, Jules Leroux. They typically commuted together to Cincinnati to catch this roundtrip train run. The brakeman, Bart Fedders, was new. It was only his third run, and Jules was trying to impress him with his command of railroad lore as he and Bart sat on the left side of the engine cab.

"You know, you're probably getting tired of my stories, but one of the best happened right up here around the curve that we're coming to."

Jules Leroux was a third-generation railroader—his father and grandfather had both been engineers. With four years of experience under his belt, Jules was training to become an engineer. Bart liked Jules well enough, but he yearned for some quiet time, if only a short respite. Bart tried to change the subject, "Shouldn't we be slowing down? Why does Cecil have the train at full throttle?"

Jules didn't hesitate to express his knowledge, "It's called stretch braking. As you get ready to slow down, you throttle up to stretch out the train. Just watch the old pro. He's not called 'smooth as silk Davis' for nothing. We're trying to make up time. You'll see. He's the best at this."

Bart was dubious as his wide eyes shifted between Cecil and out the front of the engine cab.

"But let me tell you the story about this bend up here." Jules was not to be deterred. "Back in the 30's, my grandfather, Ruben Leroux, was on a run one foggy night coming through here. That was back in the steam-engine days. My grandfather was the engineer, and he couldn't see too well up ahead due to the steam and the fog. So the fireman, Casper Finke, was looking out the side window to check on the signal. My grandfather was a little hard of hearing, and of course those steam engines made a lot of noise. Cap Finke, that was his nickname, saw something in the curve. He later said it looked like

2

the tracks were covered with snow or water, but he couldn't tell what it was. When they got about a hundred feet from it, he realized what it was. It was a herd of hogs that had gotten loose from a local hog farmer.

"He tried to scream at my grandfather, but all my grandfather could hear was 'hogs,' and he didn't know what that was about. As they made it through the hogs, he heard ole Cap Finke screaming 'OOOHHHH!' My grandfather looked over and saw all this blood and gore where Casper's head was supposed to be. My grandfather put the train in emergency, because he didn't know what had happened. He thought Casper had been partially decapitated. Casper wouldn't stop screaming. Once my grandfather was able to bring the train to a stop, he saw Casper in a panic trying to wipe all that blood and guts off him. It was the damnest mess. The engine was covered with hog parts. To make matters worse, the farmer came running up to the engine cursing and screaming and threatening to kill my grandfather for killing his hog herd."

Just then, Cecil yelled, "You boys stop jawing. Looks like something's in the middle of the track up there."

The brakeman, Bart Fedders, already distressed after hearing the hog story, frantically searched out the window. Cecil suddenly threw the train in emergency and leaned on the horn. Jules shouted, "Looks like a man on the tracks!"

Cecil shrieked, "Oh my God!"

Chapter 2

Spring 2004

Holding the phone, Kim Conner, the sheriff department's administrative assistant, listened to the agitated farmer's wife screeching about a culprit letting the goats loose. At the same time, Kim watched with curiosity the man waiting for Sean's return. He'd sit a short time and then pace to the window or door, and then sit again. It was hard to place his age, but Kim figured mid 50's. His medium length gray hair revealed a reddish tint from a younger age. He was wiry, but firm— medium height. Nothing about him made her wary, but his alert green eyes were hard. She wondered if he was from Sean's military past; his khaki pants and light-weight jacket suggested military, but more than that, there was a self-assuredness, a swagger, about him.

After assuring the farmer's wife that a deputy would be promptly dispatched, she once again offered, "You sure I can't get you a cup of coffee, or maybe a bottle of water?"

He looked up at her, "Okay, maybe some water."

Kim had just handed the man a bottle when Sean Neumann, the sheriff of Bekbourg County, walked in. He started to speak to Kim when he spotted the man, who stood and faced Sean. For a moment, neither man spoke as each took in the other. Finally, the man asked, "Is there somewhere we can talk?"

"Let's step in here," Sean directed as he showed him into the small conference room.

Despite the passage of twenty years, Sean recognized Flynn Taggart, a convicted murderer.

"I guess you didn't expect to see me," Flynn said in an attempt to break the ice.

Flynn was leaner than Sean remembered, and his rugged facial features had been chiseled into sharp angles outlining hollowed cheeks.

When Sean didn't respond, Flynn made another attempt, "So, you're a sheriff. How long did you put in?"

Sean found his voice. "Twenty years. I suffered injuries that prevented me from continuing what I was doing, so I retired."

"I understand that you were with an elite investigative division. Didn't surprise me when I heard that. You struck me as smart and dedicated—although I saw little of you on my case."

"Why don't you tell me why you're here?" Sean's piercing brown eyes telegraphed suspicion.

"Okay, Sean. I'll get to the point. I didn't kill Caroline Montgomery. I can't get those twenty years back, but I can damn sure live out the rest of

5

my life—but not until I find the bastard who framed me."

Sean furrowed his brows.

"You were a grunt, Sean, carrying Keaton's cases, but I watched you. Hell, I watched everyone. My life hung in the balance. But you, there was something gnawing at you about the case."

Sean looked at Flynn. Sean's memory flashed back to one of the first court martial cases he had been assigned to after joining the military police. Sean never spoke to Flynn during the criminal investigation or court martial. He was little more than a lackey during that investigation. Donald Keaton was the lead investigator. In fact, Keaton had been the only investigator for a while after his assistant had been pulled to handle another case. Sean was assigned shortly before the trial started, after most of the leg work had been completed. Sean was surprised to hear from Flynn that his reservations had been that transparent as he observed the trial from behind the prosecutor's table.

"Not going to respond?" Flynn tilted his head. "Huh. Good for you, Sean. You wouldn't give anything away in a poker game today. Look, I'm going to lay it on the table. I got out a few months ago and hired a retired JAG who practices civilian defense. He looked you up for me. He said I'd need to find evidence if I had any hope of having my conviction overturned. I know you had doubts. I need a starting point. That's why I'm here. What do you know? What questions or reservations did you have?"

Although Flynn had aged, twenty years in prison had not diminished his brashness. Sean remembered the younger man who took the witness stand in his own defense. He was a decorated Marine. Unlike other defendants who took the witness stand, Flynn's testimony actually helped his case. It just wasn't enough to overcome the evidence found in his car and his lack of alibi.

"Have you thought about asking Keaton?"

"Oh yeah. He was *first* on my list. Too bad the SOB's dead."

"What about the JAG who defended you? Have you contacted him?"

"Hell, no. My new attorney might, but I don't plan to talk to him. I never could figure if he didn't know his butt from page two or if he was scared shitless of rocking the boat. You were on the investigative team. That's why I'm here."

"What do you think happened?" asked Sean.

"Caroline Montgomery was a beautiful woman. Only a dead man wouldn't notice her. That SOB she was married to didn't attend to business. He was gone a lot. You know the saying, 'when the cat's away, the mouse will play.' She sure did her fair share of playing."

Sean narrowed his eyes. "You were an officer, Taggart, and she was an officer's wife."

"Hell, I knew that! Believe what you want, but I tried to steer clear. But hell! I only had so

7

much willpower when it came to a smoking woman like that. I thought we'd have a hot round or two, and that'd be that. I even told her I didn't want any entanglements. Same with her, she told me. Those were the ground rules."

Sean looked skeptical, "As I recall, you'd been seeing her longer than was needed for 'a round or two.'"

Flynn ran his hand down his face. "Got in over my head with that one. Like quick sand." He shook his head, "I tried to cool things, but she'd call. Damnit, I knew we were playing with fire, and we both sure as hell got burned."

"Burned, my ass!" Sean bellowed as he slammed his hand on the table, "She got more than burned. She got killed."

Flynn stood so fast, the chair careened into the wall. "I know that, damnit!" he shouted. He walked over and looked at the vacant wall as if studying a picture. His voice calmed. "It's not the same thing, I know, but I spent twenty years of my life in a shithole for something I didn't do."

Sean watched the man. Twenty years had not robbed him of his determination.

"The scarf she was strangled with was hidden under your car's front seat. You were sleeping with her. You expect me to believe you didn't kill her?" Sean certainly wasn't about to swallow Flynn's story hook, line and sinker.

"Why would I be here, Sean, if I was guilty? Before you say it, you're thinking I'm after the pension, and you would be right too, but whoever killed her is out there somewhere, unless the SOB is dead. With my luck, he might be, but he needs to pay if he's alive, and by damn, I'm going to find him."

The silence allowed the tension to pass. Sean studied Flynn. It seemed unlikely, but what if he was telling the truth? "Why didn't you end it?" Sean asked.

Flynn blew a long breath and returned to the chair. "I should have. Here's the thing. Those damn ground rules got flushed down the latrine somewhere along the way. I felt a stirring for her, which should have sent me running to the farthest reaches. She got to me in a way no one had and in no way that I wanted." He paused. "But the hell of it is that she told me she loved me. I didn't want that, and I told her so."

"What'd she say about that?" asked Sean.

"She said she understood—that she just wanted it to last until it didn't."

Sean watched Flynn closely as he made his next point, "That was Keaton's theory of the case— that you wanted to end it and she threatened to expose the affair, which would have ruined your career."

"That pompous SOB," Flynn's eyes narrowed. "He lied through his teeth. I had never met the man before the shit happened, but he was damn determined to screw me."

"Any idea about who would have killed her—*and* framed you?" That was the part of the story that fell apart for Sean. Why frame Flynn? From what he gathered, there weren't many suspects, so why would someone go to the trouble of framing Flynn? Had Flynn made some enemies?

Flynn jerked his attention to Sean. "Let's get this straight. I didn't kill her. Yeah, there were some guys who preferred I go to hell, drop dead, and other anatomical-impossible feats. Even had a fight with a couple along the way, but I can't say that any of them would kill a woman just to see me deep-sixed. My theory is that someone wanted her dead and knew about us and framed me to get the authorities off the scent."

"Any specific people?"

"Well, one was Hutch McAlistair. He was her squeeze before me. Best I could tell, that SOB Keaton never even sniffed in his direction."

"Why would he kill her?"

"He didn't take it too well when Caroline dumped him. That was a short time before we started our play dates. I didn't know anything about it until one night we were at a honkytonk out in the boonies where I didn't think we'd be seen. He was civilian, so no harm with him being from the base, but he'd seen her. When we left, he followed us outside. He'd had a few too many and made a scene. I told her to go back inside, and he started to follow. I grabbed his arm. She ran on inside, because I was yelling for her to. I taught ole Hutch some manners. Afterward, I wanted to know what the hell that was all about. Caroline told me that he kept calling her and wouldn't leave her alone even though she told him to. She never mentioned him bothering her again, so I assume he stopped, but maybe he didn't.

"Keaton kept harping that it was a crime of passion. Hell, that would sure fit the bill for Hutch if he still had the hots for her and couldn't take rejection. Sounds like a suspect, and why not frame me for kicking his ass?"

"Have you talked to your attorney about him?"

"Yeah. He said he would locate him and he might hire a PI to check him out. Hell, even Caroline's husband could have decided he'd had enough of her screwing around—didn't seem to me Keaton looked at him."

"He was out of town, Flynn. In D.C."

"Yeah, but maybe he hired someone?"

Sean was silent before he said, "I'm not sure I can help you, Flynn. I don't know what you expect me to do."

"Sean, I didn't kill Caroline Montgomery. I've spent twenty years in prison for a murder I didn't commit. All I'm asking is for you to think about the case. What was it that caused you to have questions? I just need something that can get me started on this investigation. I don't want to put all my eggs in the Hutch McAlistair basket and have that blow up. If there's somewhere else to look, that's what I need to know."

When Sean didn't respond, Flynn continued, "I'm going to stay in town a couple of days while you think about it. Here's my number. Think about it."

"Where are you staying?"

"At that dinosaur joint just north of town." Sean knew the old run-down, single-story motel with a large green dinosaur prop out front.

Sean remained sitting as Flynn stood. Realizing that Sean wasn't in the mood to be hospitable, Flynn opened the door and left without looking at Kim or Alex, who had heard the yelling between the two men. Alex walked into the conference room, "Everything all right, Chief?"

Sean nodded and stood, "Yeah."

"I heard the shouting," Alex continued, curious. Alex was Sean's assistant.

"I'm not surprised. I played a minor role in an investigation that resulted in that guy being sentenced to twenty years for killing a woman. It was a shock seeing him."

"Who is he? What did he want?" Alex asked.

"Flynn Taggart. He says he is trying to find the real killer and thought I might have some information."

"You believe him, that he is just here to see if you have some information?"

Sean looked at Alex, "I don't know what to believe."

Sean returned to his office and sank into his chair. He remembered the case well. At the time, Sean was stationed in Fort Leonard Wood and had gotten the temporary assignment to go to Camp

Lejeune to assist Donald Keaton in the investigation. Most of the investigative work had been completed, but Sean handled follow-up matters for Keaton and the prosecutor. What struck him was the speed at which the case had been handled. Keaton and the prosecutor had treated it like an open-and-shut case. Certainly, finding Caroline's scarf under the front seat in Flynn's car, which forensics concluded was used in her strangulation, was damning. Flynn couldn't establish an alibi. Even so, it was the quickest murder court martial Sean ever saw during his tenure with the Marines.

Another oddity was Keaton's handling of the case. When Sean arrived to assist Keaton, he took the case file to his office and was going to review it. The secretary must have notified Keaton, because Sean had just started his review when Keaton walked in and took back the file. "I need to check a few things. I'll get this back to you as soon as I can." Sean never had the chance to review witnesses' statements, forensics or any of the records.

One thing Sean had seen in the file was the name, Fritz Marlow, who had initially assisted Keaton in the investigation but early on was transferred to another base to handle a different case. Once the verdict was announced, Sean was transferred back to Missouri and any questions or doubts he had soon faded as he plunged into other investigations.

As he reflected back, he realized the speed of the trial and Keaton pulling the file would not help Flynn at this late date. However, something about the current situation did cause unease. Sean did not think Flynn held a grudge against him for his part in the investigation, but he wondered if Flynn knew that Simon Montgomery, Caroline's husband, now lived in Bekbourg.

Chapter 3

"Okay guys." Lilly tried to keep the frustration from seeping into her tone. The video class project was important to Lilly. She wanted an A in the course, and not only that, the top three videos in the class would premier in Bekbourg's newly-renovated downtown theater where the community was invited to view students' art exhibits, including the video class movies. Lilly gave her all to her studies, but communications and video production were her passion. Her advisor at Schriever High School, Annalee Carter, had seen Lilly's talent and arranged for her to assist a teacher the previous summer in creating a syllabus for a new video production class. In that class, students would learn the finer points of filming and editing videos along with the opportunity to obtain "in front of camera" experience. Even though she had already been accepted into the renowned communications and journalism college at the university in nearby Athens, Lilly had pride in her work and hoped to win first prize in the video category.

Given Jake's lack of interest and the acrimony between Claire and Brian, she was having doubts about her team's ability to produce that video.

"We only have a few weeks to get our video topic approved, scripts written, costumes gathered, and deciding the locations, as well as filming and editing the video."

Looking accusingly at Claire, Brian repeated, "Well, we can start by ruling out something mushy."

Claire glared back, "Huh! What's wrong with doing a love story or something romantic?"

Before Brian could fire back, Reid jumped in, "I like doing something about aliens from outer space." With a gleam of mischief, he eyed the school's star running back, "Jake there could be the king alien who we defeat."

Claire and Brian jerked their heads toward Jake, who had on earphones. Brian muttered, "Yeah, the way to defeating the alien king would be to disconnect those wires from his life pack."

Claire giggled.

"I've got an idea." Brian looked hopeful. "What about a movie about zombies or a horror movie?"

Claire shook her head, "Ugh! No way am I going to do a scary movie. I don't even watch them."

They were getting nowhere. So far, Jake hadn't uttered a word—had not even bothered to acknowledge their presence. Lilly knew him because he was in her senior class, but they had only had two classes together during their time in school. The other three were juniors and, as far as Lilly knew, never played sports. Since he hung around with athletes and cheerleaders, the three juniors warily viewed him as an aberration, especially since Brian and Reid, who were medium height and could almost pass as brothers, looked like junior high kids next to him. This time next year, Jake would be playing football on scholarship at a university in northern Ohio.

Their teacher had randomly assigned students to each "Video Production Company." Lilly had worked with Reid the previous semester in a related class, but she had never had classes with Claire or Brian. Right now, she needed to try to get Jake engaged, because their class grade depended in part on everyone being a participant in the project. "Jake, do you have any ideas for our video?"

When he continued to listen to his music through his earplugs, Lilly waved her hand to get his attention. He finally looked at her, and she repeated her question with more volume. He pointed at his headphones as if to tell her he could not hear her. Claire jabbed her finger at his headphones and then mimicked the action he needed to take to remove his headphones. In no hurry to remove the head piece, he held it away just enough to hear. "Huh?" he wondered why Lilly was talking to him.

Claire narrowed her eyes, but Lilly was more patient, "Do you have a suggestion for our movie? We could do a documentary, something about an historical event around Bekbourg, or a mystery of some kind."

He looked at the four, and as he put his ear phones back in place, said, "A football movie won't work."

Claire rolled her eyes. Brian's head slightly shook, "He's no help."

After silence permeated the group, Claire spoke up, "I might have an idea." She explained family lore involving her great-great grandparents."

"Gads! I ain't doing anything about *looovve*," Brian huffed.

"It's not just about *loooovve*. It's about a mystery," Claire's eyes sparked.

Lilly liked the idea, but she needed to get Brian and Reid on board. Then, hopefully Jake would go along since he had rightly concluded that their group couldn't pass for athletes, particularly football players. While she was slender and about 5'6", she wasn't an athlete. Claire was short and pudgy, and Brian and Reid were both skinny. "Maybe we can use Claire's idea but also include your two ideas," Lilly said looking at Brian and Reid.

"I don't see how that's possible." Brian looked doubtful.

Reid asked, "What are you thinking, Lilly?"

Lilly thought for a minute and then began to formulate an idea. The four discussed it, and soon enough, they had a plan. Lilly waved again at Jake. He slowly removed the headphones, "Yeah?"

"Does this storyline work for you?"

He mumbled, "Whatever."

Claire narrowed her eyes at him. "I bet he doesn't even know what it is."

Lilly was relieved they had a story. "I'll get this written up and submit it to our teacher. In the meantime, let's get started on the script. Claire, you and I will work on that. Reid, why don't you and Brian work on the locations we can shoot the scenes. Be sure to include Jake, too."

The two boys looked skeptically toward Jake as he stood, "Gotta be somewhere."

After he was out of earshot, Brian muttered, "How did we end up with a jock on our team?"

Claire added, "He's going to be useless."

Lilly urged the group forward, "It'll be okay. Let's talk about the costumes."

Chapter 4

Cheryl Seton spent the first fourteen years of her life in Bekbourg before her mother whisked them to Cleveland to escape a scandal involving her grandfather. Cheryl, an investigative reporter, had recently returned to the small southeast Ohio town to investigate a murder of five family members but also to seek answers into what had really happened in the murder for which her grandfather pled guilty. In the process, she met the handsome deputy who was now the sheriff and decided to stay. Soon, Cheryl and Sean were engaged to be married, and she had recently bought the local newspaper, the *Bekbourg Tribune.*

Cheryl ushered Joy Shuler into the conference room. "Please have a seat, Mrs. Shuler."

"Thank you. This coffee hits the spot. I want to begin by telling you how much I enjoy reading about the cold cases you have investigated in the region. I am a high school English teacher, and while I certainly enjoy drinking tea and reading the classics, murder mysteries are my favorite."

Smiling, Cheryl asked, "How do you know about my stories living in Cincinnati?"

"For several years now, I have had the *Tribune* mailed to me, so that's how I know about you buying the paper and your investigations into the old murder mysteries." She took another sip of her coffee and continued, "Which brings me to why I am here. I really don't know much about the situation. I was only seven at the time, and Hogan, my brother, was eighteen. Despite the age gap, we were close. Most big brothers wouldn't want their little sister tagging along, but he wasn't like that at all. When his friends came over, he didn't mind if I hung around." She smiled when she added, "Mom miscarried twice before I was born, so I guess he was glad I made it."

Cheryl smiled.

"Spring of 1967 was when it all happened. Hogan was a senior in high school and had been dating a girl, Rylee Flowers. She was a junior. They planned to get married when she graduated from high school."

Joy opened a folder. "I found a few pictures of her with Hogan in a box of photos as I was going through the house. I guess Mom or Dad must have taken the pictures. You will see that she was a pretty girl. What I remember was that she laughed a lot and was peppy. She loved petting our dog, Bingo."

Joy sighed. "I don't know a lot about what happened, but from fragments of conversations I overheard at the time, Rylee died. I think Hogan maybe had something to do with it, but on the same night, Hogan was killed by the train hitting him. I wish I knew more. Mom and Dad were overcome with grief. What I remember is that soon after the burial, they decided to move. We moved during the summer, and I started school in Cincinnati that fall. Mom has an older sister, who still lives here, and she would come visit us sometimes. I remember once when Aunt Milly came, I overheard Mom tell her that neither she nor Dad believed it was true what the police told them. Aunt Milly suggested they have the case investigated, but Mom told her it was too painful, that she just couldn't go through anymore. I never knew what that meant."

"You mentioned an aunt who still lives here?"

"Yes. In fact, I'm going to see her after I leave here. Her last name is Couture. Milly Couture. Do you know her?"

Cheryl grinned, "Our landlord is a retired school teacher—Kye Davis. She and Milly and two other retired teachers play bridge."

Cheryl detected sadness as Joy recounted how her parents used to play bridge with Milly and her husband, but after Hogan died, they never played bridge again.

"When did you last see your aunt?" Cheryl asked

"It's been years. I always meant to drive over, but one thing led to another. Dad died of a heart attack a few years ago, and then earlier this year, Mom was moved into a facility that cares for patients with Alzheimer's." She sipped her coffee.

"Since then, I have been going through their house, and that's when I came across the box of pictures of Hogan. I would like to find out what happened. I thought this might be something you would be interested in looking into."

"It does sound interesting. I will see what I can find out. Can I hold onto these pictures? I'll keep them safe and return them to you."

"Of course. I also have two boxes in my car. One contains Hogan's personal effects like trophies, his bible, pocket knife, things that were in his bedroom. The small box has things dad found when he cleaned out Hogan's car before he sold it. Dad wasn't in a hurry to go through it. After the police returned Hogan's car, it sat in our yard until we moved. I can bring the boxes in for you to look through if you're interested."

"I'll walk out with you so you won't have to make another trip in."

After Joy left, Cheryl looked at the two cardboard boxes—one an old shoe box and a larger box. Cheryl wondered what it was that Joy's parents thought should be investigated.

Chapter 5

When Cheryl first came to Bekbourg to investigate the murders, she met Lilly Vargas, a high school sophomore at the time, and her mother, Elena. Lilly was working part-time at Max's bistro helping to support her and Elena. Elena was a recovering addict, but thankfully, she had stayed clean. Elena worked at Bri's B&B, but Cheryl knew Lilly worried about her mother relapsing.

Lilly was a senior at Schriever High School and had been accepted into the communications and journalism program in nearby Athens. At first, she was hesitant to accept—even though she had received a fully-paid scholarship from Mary Zimmstein's local foundation, "Bekbourg Gives." Lilly had concerns about leaving her mother, but everyone close to Lilly and Elena rallied around them to encourage Lilly to pursue her dreams. Although Lilly was shy when Cheryl first met her, she had blossomed into a mature young woman with a great deal of potential. Cheryl had taken her under her wing and, after acquiring the newspaper, hired her part-time. Lilly was thrilled with the opportunity because of the experience working for a newspaper offered in her planned college major.

Cheryl walked to Lilly's cubicle, "Hi, Lilly. How are you doing?"

"Hi, Cheryl. I'm fine. Is there something I can help you with?"

Cheryl smiled, "As a matter of fact, there is. A woman who lives in Cincinnati came by to see me today. She was born here in Bekbourg and had an older brother. When he was eighteen, he was killed by a train. His name was Hogan Slater." Lilly jotted down his name. "The sister's name is Joy Shuler." Lilly was taking notes. "Anyway, she said her parents were devastated and soon after the incident, they moved to Cincinnati. She was much younger than her brother, and because her parents never talked about the accident, she never knew much about his death."

"When did this happen?" asked Lilly.

"Spring of 1967."

Lilly's eyebrows shot up. "Wow, that's a long time ago. Why did she call you?"

"Her parents were suspicious that the police didn't investigate it more thoroughly, and she thought I might be interested in looking into it as one of my cold cases."

"Cool. That's exciting."

"Yes, it is. She found some old family pictures that had been packed up and decided it was time to see what she could find out. I was hoping you could locate the articles in our archives."

"Of course. I'll get started on this right away."

"Thank you. How's your video project going?"

Lilly sighed. "I know teachers like group projects, but it can be frustrating if everyone is not committed."

Cheryl smiled, "Well, it's good experience, because you learn how to deal with people, which will follow you throughout life."

"I know that's true, but it can sure be challenging," Lilly ruefully replied.

Cheryl laughed.

Cheryl arrived home to find Kye returning home with Buddy. The Chocolate Lab bounded for Cheryl as Kye released the leash. "Such a good boy," Cheryl cooed as she stooped to rub his head and ears as his tailed whipped from side to side. "Hi, Kye."

"Hi, Cheryl. We had a nice walk." Sean and Cheryl rented one side of the duplex from Kye Davis, who they thought of as family. When they were away, Kye cared for Buddy.

"Sean is working late tonight. Would you like to join me for dinner?"

"Of course, my dear. I made some chocolate chip cookies earlier and was going to bring them over for you and Sean. I'll go get them and be right over."

Most people around Bekbourg knew Kye, because she had taught them English during their junior year at Schriever High. Sean said that she was one of the best teachers he ever had, a sentiment echoed by many around the county.

After they were settled down for dinner, Cheryl told Kye about Joy's visit and that Milly Couture was her aunt.

"Oh me. I remember all that terrible business like it was yesterday, but it's been thirty-seven years ago. It tore us all up. Hogan and Rylee were students at the high school when it happened."

"What do you know about it?" Cheryl asked.

"Well, dear, Hogan was a handsome young man, and a sweet boy. He played football, but he wasn't a standout like your Sean. He had lots of friends, and he and his parents were active church members. Such a fine young man. Rylee was a student of mine when the tragedy happened. She was a cheerleader and popular with the other students. Although, let me just say, in my class at least, school was not her top priority."

Cheryl nodded her understanding.

Kye took a bite. "Some students are like that. Anyway, Rylee was found dead in the wooded area near the park. The authorities speculated that someone hit her hard enough to knock her down where she hit her head on a sharp rock. She died there of her injuries before they found her."

Cheryl poured them some more lemonade, and then Kye continued, "Anyway, the night that Rylee died was the same night that Hogan was killed by the train. What makes it so bad, Cheryl, is that Cecil was the engineer on that train. He said that the body was on the track, and despite putting the train into emergency, there was no possible way to stop. He blew the horn, but Hogan just laid there." Cecil was Kye's husband who had since passed away.

"Oh, that is terrible."

"Yes, dear, it was. Cecil was so upset about it that he talked about retiring early. He had to take some time off. It bothered him for years, and I don't think he ever got completely over it." Kye paused while she sipped the lemonade. "I take it that you are considering looking into it as part of your 'cold cases' series?"

Cheryl chuckled. "Yes, I asked Lilly to review our archives and see what is there."

"Well, dear. I know some people who you may want to talk to."

"Let me grab a pen and paper."

Once Cheryl was settled, Kye started her list, "Milly, of course, but I should tell you that she has difficulty hearing, so be sure to talk loud. Then the football coach who recently retired, Clyde Jackson. If Cecil was still alive today, he could tell you first-hand about the train accident, but I would talk to Jules Leroux. He was on the engine with Cecil."

Kye changed subjects, but after she left, Cheryl couldn't get her mind off the teenagers' deaths. She decided to see what she could learn from the police reports.

Chapter 6

Simon and Skylar Montgomery, Harvey Bennett and his guest, Becky Werner, and Noel Fischner, a county commissioner, dined in Bekbourg's finest, the GilHaus. Built in 1912, the grand hotel's regal presence across from the courthouse commanded notice as one of Bekbourg's landmarks—even though the hotel's lodging operations had ceased decades earlier. The hotel was structurally sound, and its neglected exterior gave a false impression of the beauty and nostalgia of the restaurant inside. Encompassing most of the hotel's first floor, the GilHaus' opulence offered early 1900's grandeur with its crystal chandeliers sparkling across white tablecloths, crystal goblets and china. Cream and gold wallpaper offered solace to the darker furnishings of hardwood floors, ornate chairs and rich, but worn fabrics.

Alcohol flowed freely as the men boasted of financial triumphs and notable acquaintances. The two women feigned interest as they drifted in ruminations—one considering possible benefits from a relationship with the man posturing for a land development, and the other anxiously consumed with the impending separation from her husband. Skylar Montgomery fought nausea as she heard his boasts of lucrative ventures and liaisons, some of which pushed the envelope of credibility.

The last place Skylar wanted to be was here. She could care less about the land deal the three men were discussing, and she barely knew Becky Werner. Her thoughts drifted to her mental checklist. She knew she was taking the coward's way out, but that was the least of her thoughts. Thank God the weather looked good for the weekend. Barring inclement weather, Simon never missed the tee-time. She had a short window to get everything done. She would leave as soon as he left and drive to get the rental truck.

Until this plan came together, one of her long lists of grievances was that he didn't want her to bring any of her furniture into his condo when they married. He wanted every furniture piece to match with symmetry—matching end tables had to have identical lamps. She was content with, in fact preferred, an eclectic look. He tried to dissuade her from bringing any of her possessions when she moved into his condo. She had insisted on keeping a few of her cherished pieces, but they had been relegated to corners and inconspicuous places. Now, given her plan, having few personal possessions worked in her favor. She trusted Danny Chambers from whom she was renting the truck. Other than her clothes and a few small personal items, and the furniture, there wasn't much to load. As soon as they finished, she would drive him back to his station and start driving toward D.C. She did not want to be in Bekbourg when Simon returned from playing golf.

She glanced at her husband. God, how could she have been so stupid not to have seen how rigid and controlling he was before they married? She was not a slob, but she could live with books laying around, clothes waiting to be put away, and dishes sitting in the sink. She finally drew the line that he was not allowed in her dressing and bathroom area, but that did not deter him from chastising her for not putting things away in the rest of the house. She barely contained hysterical ranting every time she heard, "Skylar, a place for everything, and everything in its place," as he was "cleaning" up after her.

Maybe their marriage could have survived if she had held firm on her feelings, such as the furniture she wanted to keep, places she wanted to visit, keeping her car, and the biggest of all—not moving to Bekbourg. When she expressed her opinion, it just fell on deaf ears. He made decisions, and she succumbed rather than endure his monotone droning on and on about the "logic" of his decision.

She could also never live up to his standard in dress—even though her hair was kept styled, her makeup looked professional, and her clothes and accessories were fashionable. Just tonight, he insisted she iron her light-weight wrap before they left for dinner. Unless he was working outside or

31

exercising on the equipment in their basement, he was immaculate in dress. She felt sorry for the cleaners. If his slacks weren't perfectly creased or his shirts crisply starched, he insisted they redo the pieces free of charge. His shoes were shined spotless, and his sports coat was flawless. She had never known him to miss shaving twice a day.

Just thinking about everything made her tense. She knew Simon wouldn't be happy with her lack of conversation during dinner tonight, but she didn't care. She felt she was hanging on by a thread. She just had to make it until she was in that truck heading east, and then she knew she was free. She would call him once she was in D.C. and tell him the marriage was over. To say that he would be displeased was an understatement, but he'd eventually get over it. She had a job lined up at the pentagon, and he wouldn't do anything that would appear like he was making waves there.

Her musings were jolted when she recognized Simon's patronizing tone aimed at her, "Skylar, dear, Harvey asked if we are enjoying living in Lake Shore." Harvey Bennett, President and owner of Bekbourg Enterprises, had developed the large gated residential and golfing development where they lived.

"Oh, I am so sorry, Harvey. I have been fighting a migraine, and my attention is not what it should be."

Becky, Harvey's date, interrupted, "Are you okay? Is there anything we can do?"

"Thank you, Becky. I am managing fine," Skylar apologetically smiled, "except for not being as attentive as I should. But, to answer your question, who wouldn't love living there. I especially love the natural weave of the amenities among the residences. It is a beautiful development."

Harvey smiled, "That's what I like to hear. I want all my homeowners to be happy. Your home is on the far end of the lake, away from the golf course. I take it that has not been a disappointment?"

Simon jumped in, "Skylar and I value our privacy, so that piece of property had our name on it," he chuckled. "It's easy enough to take the golf cart to the course."

Becky asked, "Skylar, do you golf?"

"I'm afraid not. It just never came natural to me. I play tennis, and the courts in Lake Shore are really nice."

"Skylar is also a swimmer. She enjoys swimming in the lake," Simon added.

"I like seeing people enjoying the lake," Harvey said. "During warm weather, the lake is busy with swimmers and people canoeing. Another benefit is the close proximity to the state park. That has been a big selling point to people looking to buy in Lake Shore. Speaking of which, Simon, I'm hoping I have whetted your appetite about investing in my new development, 'Lake Meadows.' Your track record for profitable investments has me convinced you're the right partner for this venture. All my sources tell me that the state is ready to commit to the conference facilities at the Peatmont State Park, which just enhances our development. Prospective buyers are lining up for this."

"I can certainly see the interest in having a weekend home or cabin so close to Lake Peatmont and the state park. You say the total development is four-hundred acres?"

"Not quite four-hundred. Celeste and Collin Steinsen own two-hundred acres that is on the western part of the development. I am in talks with them to purchase one-hundred-sixty acres, which will make it three-hundred-sixty acres as currently planned. I'm also talking with the property owners to the east, and over time, my goal is to purchase that and roll it into this development."

"What about the thirty acres that Kye Davis owns? Is it part of the development?"

"Yes. Mrs. Davis has agreed to sell the property—as a legacy to her husband's family, who owned the property for generations. I'm going to name the park and main road after him."

"Good to hear you've reached a settlement with the Steinsens and Davis, but what about the legal issues surrounding the property, and wasn't Nickolas Garrison, the former county commissioner, somehow involved?" asked Simon.

"That's all in the rearview mirror. I can put your attorney in contact with mine. He'll answer any questions, but the bottom line is I bought out Nickolas Garrison's interests in this development as well as some of his other property holdings. I own one-hundred percent of the property in this development—or will once I finalize the purchase of the Steinsen and Davis parcels, which are in the bag."

Simon had met Harvey when he was visiting Bekbourg on a personal matter. Deal-making was in Simon's DNA, and Harvey's mention of seeking investors in his newest residential development in Bekbourg had captured his attention. Simon could see right off that having a development for weekend and vacation homes adjacent to the state park would be a gold mine. People from Columbus, Cincinnati, Athens and other cities would be drawn to the idea. Without further consideration, he decided to move to Bekbourg. He had grown up here, and Skylar was from here as well. He figured she would be content to move back, and besides, her sister lived here.

Unfortunately for Simon, an investment had gone terribly wrong, and he had recently found himself teetering on financial ruin. He did not know how much longer he could go before things started closing in, but if he could get into this investment with Harvey, he thought he could postpone a calamity and then work himself back from the brink. He just had to play his cards right. He knew being a retired brigadier general made his stock as a potential investor very attractive to Harvey, which was elevated given that his family had been prominent around Bekbourg. Simon didn't want to appear over eager, but time was of the essence in getting into something that would start yielding a return. He took a drink from his scotch, and as he lowered it, asked Harvey, "Do you expect those legal matters to be wrapped up soon?"

"I expect that to wind down any day now," Harvey confidently replied. "The feds tried to pin me with knowing about the Thompson's planning and reporting, but hell, let's face it, how could I have known that public funds were being used and profits were underreported. They were in charge of the county, not me. Pauline Kaufmann, the county treasurer, was responsible for the tax sales. In the end, they had no proof against me. I paid the back taxes they claimed I owed just to get past it. It's all settled. There are no liens or claims on any of this property."

Simon looked at Noel Fischner, who was the newest member of the county commission. "Are you also planning to invest?"

Noel glanced at Harvey, "I would like to, but the timing's not right for me. This guy here," he tilted his head toward Harvey, "is a rainmaker."

Harvey jumped in, "I asked Noel to join us this evening so you can hear from him that this project is going to have the commission's support. You needn't worry about delays with applications and permits. No red tape. Right, Noel?"

"That's right. This development will be good for the county just like Harvey's Lake Shore development has been. The property tax revenues alone justify our approval, but weekend residents will support our area businesses in big ways, and those businesses are well aware of that. You won't run into any roadblocks with the county."

"Simon, if you're interested, I'd like to introduce you to a couple of business partners who have invested in several of my other developments. They will be private backers. They are interested in a status update, so I've arranged to meet them in Columbus this coming weekend. If you're interested, it would be an opportunity for you to meet them and hear more about the project. We can drive up on Thursday. We'll plan on dinner Thursday night, a meeting Friday morning and then a round of golf Friday afternoon, and dinner Friday evening. We can have some breakfast before we head back on Saturday." Harvey looked at Becky, "I haven't mentioned this to Becky, but if she and Skylar want, they can come along and shop or whatever while we meet and play golf."

Skylar couldn't believe this stroke of luck. Hopefully, the truck would be available on Friday, and Danny could drive it to the house Friday afternoon after she got home from volunteering at the foundation. She would get everything packed while she waited on him, and he could help her load the truck. Maybe she could stay at her sister's Friday night and then leave early Saturday morning. She might even be in D.C. by the time Simon returned from Columbus.

Becky glanced at Skylar whose eyes had widened. Skylar seemed to forget she was holding a wine glass, which slipped to the table.

Miraculously, the near empty glass contained the sloshing liquid. "Uh, I'm sorry. That is very considerate, Harvey, for you to invite me." She looked at Becky, "I would enjoy very much spending time with Becky, but I can't make it this time. I have plans. Every Friday, I volunteer at Mary's foundation." She looked at Becky, "Becky, let's touch base soon and plan something."

Becky agreed, "Harvey, I'm with Skylar that this sounds like a fun-filled weekend, but I too need a rain check. I've got plans with my daughters."

Skylar gently exhaled.

"Yeah, I know these women have busy schedules. What about you, Simon? Are you interested in attending? We could drive up together if you like."

"I'm in, but I'll plan to drive separately."

"Good. Then it's a plan. I'll get you information on the hotel and the itinerary. Everything's on me."

Chapter 7

"Hey, Nat," Skylar yelled to her sister.

Natalia looked concern as she approached Skylar. "What are you doing here? Has something happened?"

"Let's go sit in my car and I'll tell you," said Skylar as she headed toward her car. "I didn't want to take a chance that Luca might overhear our conversation." Luca was Natalia's husband.

Natalia was a cashier at the Shopper's Pavilion, a big box store in Bekbourg. "Was it busy today?" asked Skylar as they walked to Skylar's newer model Cadillac.

"Not too bad. I can't talk long. I need to get home and fix dinner."

Once they were settled, Skylar told her about Simon going out of town with Harvey Bennett. "I called Danny. Unfortunately, I can't get the truck as early as I hoped because it's not due back until later in the afternoon, but at least I won't be pushed to get it all loaded as quickly as I had planned during Simon's golf game."

"Is Danny still going to be able to help you load everything?"

"Yes. He's such a sweetheart. Sally got lucky with him."

"You could even get things packed after he leaves on Thursday. I know you want to help Mary Friday morning with that big project, and that way, you won't have to push yourself to pack."

"I thought about that, but I don't want to take a chance. Columbus is only about an hour-and-a-half drive. Just to sleep in his own bed, I wouldn't put it past Simon to drive home Thursday night and then drive up early Friday morning. It's okay. I can get it all packed."

"So, you're going to get up early Saturday morning and leave?"

Natalia knew the look on Skylar's face. Sure enough, Skylar said, "Nat, I was hoping I could spend the night at your place. After I'm packed, I just want out of there. Besides, I don't think he would drive home after the dinner that night, but if he did, I don't want to be there."

Natalia was uncertain, "I don't know, Sky. I don't want to make Luca angry by asking."

Skylar frowned with aggravation. "God, Nat. It's your house too."

"Please, Skylar," Natalia exhaled.

"Okay, okay." Skylar looked out the front window. "We both ended up with jerks, Nat. I know you don't want to talk about this, but I'm getting out, and you should, too."

"Skylar, you know I can't. I wish you would drop it. Look, you're leaving soon. Let's not talk about it anymore."

"But you wouldn't have any problems finding a job in D.C. You can stay with me until you find a job. It's a great place to live and so many museums to see. You love things like that."

Natalia's eyes were downcast as she fumbled with the strap on her purse. Skylar watched her, hoping she might give in. Natalia didn't look up, "We've been through this, Sky. I don't want to leave him. He's just going through a hard time. He hates not having a full-time job."

Skylar ran her hand through her hair. "Yeah, I guess. I'm worried about you. Are you doing okay?"

"Yes. The other day, my boss asked if I'd be interested in training new hires. I told him I would."

"That's good news. I guess Luca still doesn't like you working."

"I didn't tell him about that." Skylar started to protest, but Natalia tried to sooth Skylar's intolerance, "It's okay, Skylar. As long he doesn't have a job, he doesn't say too much about me working."

"You told me you like working, Nat. Even if he gets a job, you shouldn't give up your job."

Natalia changed the subject, "Let's not worry about me, let's worry about you. You have lost too much weight. The stress cannot be good for you."

"I'm fine, sort of," sighed Skylar. "Listen, forget I asked about spending the night. Heck, once I get everything loaded, I can just take off and head to D.C. I can always find a place to spend the night if I get tired."

Natalia shook her head, "Oh no. You can't risk it. I'll talk to Luca."

"No, really. It'll be fine."

"Okay." Natalia moved to open the door. She reached over and hugged her sister. "I gotta go."

Chapter 8

Cheryl stopped by Lilly's cubicle to say hello and catch up. As they talked, Cheryl asked her how the video project was progressing.

Lilly smiled, "It's going okay. Mrs. Janacek approved the project. Claire and I finished the script, and the team is meeting tomorrow after school to schedule our video shoots. The guys have scoped out the different places where we will shoot the video."

"How many are in your group?"

"Me and four others. Reid Mondy is a true techie and will do most of the filming and editing. Since everyone has to play a role in the film, Brian McCrosky will help some with the filming. He's a techie too. Claire Linmund is the other junior." Lilly grinned, "She's a taskmaster. I can't really say the same for Jake Garland."

Cheryl's brows furrowed, "Mmm. That name sounds familiar."

"It would. The *Tribune* wrote about him every week during football season."

Cheryl nodded, "Of course. He was the star running back for the team. He even got a scholarship to play in college."

"Yes."

Cheryl's smile tilted to one side, "So I take it, he's not much into the project?"

Lilly shook her head, "I don't even know why he took the class. I guess he needs the credit to graduate, but he's got to participate or our project will be penalized."

"What does he think about your storyline?"

"I don't know."

"I see. Well, if you can dial into something about the project that interests him, he might surprise you. To be that good a football player, he obviously has determination and a strong work ethic."

As Cheryl returned to her office, she didn't envy Lilly. Getting everyone on a school project to carry their weight could be trying if they were not motivated.

The last class for the day had just let out, and Jake's friends, Jorge Perez and Gabe Palmer, caught up with him in the hall. "Hey, Jake, want to go toss around the football?" asked Jorge.

Jorge was tall and a talented receiver. Gabe was the squad's largest defensive lineman. Both had been recruited to play football at Division 2 colleges. Schriever High School had long populated colleges and universities with football players. Its storied program included several state championships, but this year had been a disappointment for the team and the community. The school's beloved Coach Clyde Jackson, who had brought home multiple state championship trophies over his years as head coach, had retired before the season started, and his long-term assistant was named as his replacement. Despite the quality of football talent, this year's team had not even made it to the regionals. Everyone hoped that the new coach would do better next year, but many around the community had their doubts.

"Can't, man. Got something else I've got to do."

"What's more important than football?" Jorge joked. "Other than maybe a girl. Huh. Give man. Who is she?"

Gabe and Jorge were grinning, waiting for the scoop.

"I wish. I've got to meet with my video team. Shit. I wish there had been some other class I could have taken during sixth bell. I ain't into that shit. Besides, I'm on a team with a bunch of nerds. Well, Lilly's not really a nerd. It's just that she takes this stuff serious."

"You're kidding, Bro," smirked Gabe. "You're going to a meeting on a class project after school? And you're turning down tossing football with yours truly?" He pretended to turn serious when he elbowed Jorge, "Man, we better kick it into gear on our video project. We can't let Mr. Football here and his nerd friends win."

Jorge shook his head with a determined look, "No way are we going to let them beat us out of first place."

"What are you jerks talking about?" Jake asked with suspicion.

"You don't know?" Gabe grinned.

When Jake didn't deign to respond, Gabe's smirk grew larger. "I can't believe you don't know this shit. It's probably a good thing you're on Lilly's team. I bet she knows what's going on." Gabe needled more when he looked to Jorge, "Shit, I was disappointed when Bro here didn't get in our video class, but maybe it's not a bad thing. Hell, he don't even know what's going on. We are *sure* going to beat his ass in the competition."

"You got a good point, Gabe," Jorge playing along by shaking his head, faking a solemn expression.

"Knock it off, assholes. I ain't heard of a competition. You guys are jiving me."

Both Gabe and Jorge started laughing. Jorge said, "It's really too bad you're not in our class. We could've convinced Mrs. Janacek to put us all on the same team. The top three videos will show at the summer's art night and then the one that wins best video, *which will be ours*, gets a dinner at—drumroll—GilHaus, Bekbourg's finest. I can already taste that big, juicy steak. How 'bout you, Gabe? Have you decided what you're going to eat?"

"Hell, yeah. The biggest steak they have with fries and a baked potato."

Jake shook his head as he started to walk away, "You guys ain't going to win shit. You don't know any more than me about that shit."

He heard as he started to walk away, "Yeah, baby, but we know about football, and that's what our video is about. We're naturals. We'll probably get Oscars."

Jake waved dismissively and shook his head. He still heard them laughing as he rounded the corner.

Claire glared as she handed Jake his copy of the script. "You're fifteen minutes late."

He didn't acknowledge her as he took the copy and sat toward the back of the room away from the others. Brian continued talking about the locations they had decided on. "We've got it all figured out except for where Anton hides the jewels."

"Okay, well, let's talk about the script and then we can figure something out," suggested Lilly. "I like the locations."

Claire was steamed at Jake for being late but at least he didn't have his earbuds in. After outlining the storyline, Lilly said, "So, here are the parts. Claire will be Esther's granddaughter, Katarina, and also play the part of one of the robbers. Reid will be our cameraman but also play one of the robbers."

"Wait a minute," interrupted Reid. "Why do I have to play a role? I know how to operate the camera. No one else here does."

Brian piped up, "I know how to operate a video camera."

"Not the ones the university donated to our video program. These are super high-tech."

"Guys, wait. Let me explain. Reid, according to the rules, everyone has to have an appearance in the film itself. We all know your expertise with filming. That's why I listed you as our main cameraman, but we have to have another camera person when you're on film. Brian knows more than any of us," she looked at Jake to see if he knew something about filming. When he remained silent, she continued, "so, you and Brian can work together to make sure Brian knows what he needs. Okay?"

Lilly could tell Reid wasn't happy about sharing the filming, but he shook his head.

"Okay, now, Brian is going to play three parts."

"What?" howled Brian.

"They're short. It will be fine. One is Esther's father, Herr Krause, and then Katarina's fiancé, Russell. The third is the handyman villain."

"Wait! The villain shows up in the graveyard when my fiancé is with me trying to find the jewelry. He can't be both parts." Claire looked at Lilly.

"Right. In this shot, Brian will play your fiancé, and since Brian and Reid are about the same size, in this one place, Reid will play the handyman. I will film."

"You know how to operate a video camera?" Reid asked Lilly.

"I've used older cameras, but you can show me on the new one." When Reid didn't comment, Lilly continued, "I'm also going to be the director and Esther's ghost." Lilly silently hoped Jake didn't object, "Jake, you're going to be Anton Seiter, which means you will also play his ghost."

"No way, man. That's one of the biggest parts. Give it to one of those two," he said looking toward Brian and Reid.

"We have to have each of them running the camera at different times during the shooting. Unless you want to handle the filming, that's the part you have to take." He shook his head. Lilly was not going to be denied. "It's a great part for you, Jake. You can see by reading the script that it's the biggest action part. You're great at that. That's why everyone around school calls you, 'Mr. Football.' It will be fine. I think we have a really good shot at winning first place. The script is good. Claire and I spent a lot of time thinking about the roles. Reid really knows a lot about videotaping and editing."

Silence descended, everyone holding their breath to see if Jake would go along with the ideas. Finally, Lilly prodded, "You okay with this, Jake?"

He glanced at the others, who were looking at him. Not at all happy but not finding a way to refute Lilly's logic, he grunted, "Fine. Shit."

"Okay, good." Lilly internally breathed a sigh of relief. The others similarly seemed to relax. "Now, we need to decide on where the jewels get stashed."

Brian offered, "Reid and I couldn't think of a place. You all need to decide."

Lilly and Claire looked at each other trying to think. Jake spoke up. "What about the old Shiloh Ridge graveyard? It's got those old tombstones, and it's pretty much deserted." His features relaxed, which was the closest he ever came to smiling, "Seems like a good place for a ghost to hang out."

The others jumped on the idea, "Great idea. Yeah, that works. Sure."

Reid was particularly enthusiastic, "We can get some great shots there, especially as it gets dark. This camera is supposed to have the ability to film real clear even in low light."

"Great!" Lilly was especially encouraged that Jake had been the one to make the suggestion. "Now, everyone needs to find his own costume. Maybe your parents have something. Just remember, except for Claire's Katrina's and her fiancé's clothes, which are contemporary, everything needs to look old."

"What about the ghost? Am I supposed to wear a sheet?"

Everyone looked back at Jake. Lilly laughed, "No, I'll give that some thought. Try to find some clothes you won't mind ruining if my idea doesn't turn out so well."

He nodded.

50

Lilly was encouraged. "Good discussion, guys. We've made some real progress. One more thing: since it is supposed to be years apart between when the robbers chase Anton through the cemetery and when the jewels are discovered, which is when Anton is a ghost, we'll do two separate shootings at the old Shiloh Ridge Cemetery. Let's do our very first shooting at the cemetery when Anton is still living and hides the jewelry. It may not be very noticeable, but when the jewels are finally discovered in the cemetery, that will be one of the last shoots. Maybe the trees will be blooming more and give the appearance that it's two different time frames."

"Do you really think a few weeks is going to make that much of a difference?" scoffed Brian.

"Well, if you shoot at different angles and use the shadows, it might. Every little bit of change will help," said Lilly.

"Yeah, I can experiment with some of the special effects as I edit things. We will make it work," said Reid.

"Bring your costumes for the filming of when Herr Krause confronts Anton," reminded Lilly. "We might find a good place for that near the graveyard. Anything else before we go?"

No one said anything. As they were gathering their things, Jake asked, "You think this is good enough to win first place?"

Lilly thought for a minute, "Yes, I really do. It's based on a true story—Claire's great-great

51

grandparents. The ghost parts are fictional, but I think people will like the supernatural twist. We know the camera work will be fantastic," she said nodding toward Reid and Brian, "and I have no doubt that the acting and everything else will make the film. Does everyone else agree?"

Claire was the first to voice her support, and then Reid and Brian each nodded. Reid said, "Thing is, Jake, with Lilly being the director, we're bound to win."

Lilly started to respond, but Jake stood to leave, "Good, 'cause winning's what's important to me."

Chapter 9

Flynn was restless. After spending twenty years in prison, he craved the outdoors. After talking with his attorney this morning, he decided to drive around the local back roads. He observed that Bekbourg was a hodgepodge of old and new, past and present. Large corn and soybean fields were interspersed with once productive farmland overtaken with forests and undergrowth. Abandoned houses and mobile homes populated areas not yet claimed by newer developments. Bekbourg had once had a bustling economy with factories and a vibrant downtown. Like much of the Midwest, industries had dried up or closed, and Bekbourg's economy had been in decline. However, the railroad's presence had proven an asset in keeping some of the area businesses viable, and thanks to a retired railroad executive, C.P. Traylor, the railroad had recently been saved from closure.

Several years ago, the town's leaders and businesses had embarked on an initiative to grow local tourism. Because of the city's proximity to large urban regions, natural resources like lakes and rivers and a large state park, the tourism strategy had proven quite successful. While challenges still plagued Bekbourg, similar to other rustbelt communities, it was growing in terms of new businesses and people visiting or moving to the area. While some of the downtown buildings remained vacant, new retail establishments had spruced up the old buildings and brought prosperity. An example of the new entrepreneurial spirit was a husband and wife team, Bri and Max, who had relocated here over ten years ago. They opened a stunning B&B, formerly a boarding house, and a chic coffee and bistro establishment next door. Bri had been elected Bekbourg's mayor in the recent election. While Flynn had not met Bri, he had been in the bistro a few times and liked Max and the bistro's ambience.

Max seated Flynn, poured coffee, and treated him to a complimentary scone. He sat along a back wall, where he could distance himself from people and the activity around him, and enjoyed sipping coffee and being part of a normal lifestyle he had been deprived of for so long. As he drank coffee and enjoyed the pastry, his thoughts drifted as they often did to his life. Other than establishing his innocence, he had no goals or ambitions. He was in his mid 50's adrift on a raft heading toward a waterfall or beach, he wasn't sure which. He didn't really care as long as he cleared his name. He supposed he should be grateful for the small inheritance from his mother. That provided the where-with-all to retain the lawyer and cover basic living expenses, but that would not last forever. He did not need a lot to live on—being confined for twenty years had conditioned him to be a minimalist. Establishing that he did not kill Caroline was his number one objective, but getting his pension reinstated would sure be welcomed. He supposed he could find work, but doing what? Hell, who would want to hire a dishonorably discharged Marine, who so happened to have served twenty years for murder?

How his life had changed. All he had ever wanted was to be a Marine. His talents and skills were noticed early on, and he soon found himself training for the Special Forces. Being a member of the force recon took him into dangerous reconnaissance missions in hotspots all over the world. The civilian world remained unaware, but the Brass knew of his contributions and successes.

The most daring occurred soon after the Iranians captured the United States Embassy in 1979. One of the United States intelligence agencies had a vital source who bridged a life as an Iranian businessman with Iranian government contacts. When the U.S. embassy fell, he managed to flee with his wife and two young children to a "safe house" in a remote village where they hid. Once the initial upheaval from the revolution lessened and more order was restored by the revolutionaries, the U.S. agency was concerned that the Iranian revolutionaries would span out and search houses, even those that appeared vacant or deserted, looking for traitors. Equally concerning was that locals would become suspicious and alert the revolutionaries. The U.S. government wanted their contact and his family extracted before he was discovered. Flynn and another member of the specialized reconnaissance force were sent into Iran to validate the information they had about the man's location and devise an extraction strategy. The mission was deemed high risk on U.S. forces—who needed to go undetected and avoid casualties. With Flynn and his partner's attention to details and the logistics of the advanced planning, the daring rescue was a success.

He was a Major when he was transferred to Camp Lejeune to train recon special forces and had been stationed there for about a year when he was arrested for the murder of Caroline Montgomery. Until Caroline entered his life, women came and went with little notice. Even with Caroline, he was leery of anchors, but he couldn't bring himself to cut her loose. She was fun and vivacious, but the hook had been a vulnerability she kept mostly hidden. He discerned her shield and took on the challenge, implicitly anointing himself protector of what she hid from others.

As he sat sipping his coffee at Max's bistro, he retraced these thoughts that had replayed themselves thousands of times during the last twenty years—along with his futile attempts to divine who was responsible for Caroline's death. Movement from across the room drew his attention as two men rose from a table and headed toward the exit. One saluted Max as they disappeared through the door with Max nodding, "See you soon, Brigadier." Flynn stopped breathing and squeezed his eyes shut to draw on his recollections. When he opened them, he assured himself he was not hallucinating. Casting aside the shock, he stood and headed toward Max.

"Want a coffee to go?" asked Max.

"No, I've had enough for the day, but thanks. Say. I was in the Marines, and I thought I recognized that man who just left."

Max continued to slide the evening menus into the sleeves. "Could be. He's a retired brigadier general."

"His name wouldn't happened to be Montgomery, would it?"

Max looked at Flynn and chuckled. "Well, it is a small world. Yeah. He grew up here, and after he retired, he moved back."

"Some coincidence," muttered Flynn.

"Next time he comes in, you want me to pass along your name?"

"Naw. He probably wouldn't remember me. I was a lower rank. Enjoyed the coffee."

Flynn looked both ways on the street, but Simon and his companion had vanished. Simon Montgomery had not changed much over the years. He was about six-feet tall with a broad chest that tapered to an offsetting slim waist and long legs.

His face was broad, and his thick ears were pronounced as the expanse of his tanned forehead rose to meet the military-cut hairline. Except for deeper wrinkles and silver hair, time had been relatively generous to Simon.

Seeing the man was a shock. But most pressing was learning why that SOB Neumann didn't tell him Montgomery lived in Bekbourg.

Chapter 10

Cheryl saw Milly standing at the door when she walked up. Milly, a tall woman, had short curly snow-white hair, and her freshly applied pink lipstick matched the flowers in her sweater.

Her loud voice carried as she ushered in Cheryl. "Come in, come in, Ms. Seton. Kye has talked about you so many times—I feel like I know you. Of course, I read the *Tribune* from cover-to-cover every morning. Now, let's have a seat. I've made some fresh coffee and these ginger cookies I just got out of the oven. I hope you like ginger."

"Some of my favorites. This is so nice of you. You have a lovely home."

"Why, thank you. I do my best. When you're my age, there is only so much you can do, but I try."

Cheryl spoke loudly and pronounced her words with distinction so Milly could read her lips. "Kye told me you were a high school teacher. What did you teach?"

Milly's eyes were sharp and focused on Cheryl's lips. "Math."

Milly fancied having company, and they talked about a number of things before Cheryl turned the topic to Hogan and Rylee.

"That was horrible. My sister was never the same after Hogan died. She and her husband always thought there was more to the story, but they just couldn't bring themselves to follow up."

Milly talked about how Hogan's mother loved that he and his friends liked to hang around their house. She kept extra food and refreshments so they could make themselves at home. Hogan and Rylee were planning to get married after she graduated. He wasn't going to college. Hogan's father was a lineman and had arranged for him to start a job with the local utility company after he graduated, which would have been a fine career. Hogan was aware he might get drafted, so they wanted to marry as soon as she graduated from high school in case that happened.

Milly frowned, "I think what haunted my sister the most is that the police theorized that Hogan and Rylee were having an argument and that he struck her. When he realized she was dead, he committed suicide by train. Everyone knew the train ran through here each night." Milly paused. "My sister dwelled on something, and it seemed strange to me. That night, Hogan and his parents were watching TV and the phone rang. Hogan jumped up and answered it. After he hung up, he told them he needed to run out, but he shouldn't be long.

Hogan's mother never knew who called him. She told the police about the call, but they never followed up with her."

Cheryl next talked with the former high school football coach. Coach Jackson was an assistant coach at the time, but he remembered Hogan. He echoed what she had heard from others that Hogan was an outstanding young man. He discussed how Hogan worked hard in the weight room and during practice, and even though he was not a starter, he maintained a positive attitude and played hard when he was in the game. "He didn't have that fierce competitiveness or killer instinct football players sometime have, but he put in the extra effort, and that goes a long way." He did not know Rylee, but he knew there was a girlfriend.

"Cheryl, I coached a hell of a lot of years, but that really affected me. When I heard the police conclusions, I thought, 'that can't be right.' Some things in life don't add up, and that sure was one of them."

Chapter 11

Cheryl sifted first through the contents of the larger box that Hogan's sister had brought. Greeting her when she opened the cardboard flaps was a folded letterman's sweater. Before laying it aside, Cheryl gingerly checked its pockets. She pulled out a couple of Little League football trophies and miscellaneous Cincinnati Reds baseball cards. She was surprised to find his wallet intact, which contained a ten dollar bill and four singles. The wallet's plastic photo slips held Rylee's class picture; a picture of Joy, his little sister; and his driver's license. She found his high school ring, which must have been returned by Rylee's family. A bible and baptismal and confirmation certificates were among the possessions. She took her time looking over each remembrance, thinking how each marked a milestone in Hogan's life. When she was finished, she looked at Hogan's mementos spread across the table and pondered the life he had led as well as the future stolen by his untimely death.

She next turned to the shoe box, which contained items Hogan's father had found when he finally cleaned out Hogan's car before selling it.

She studied the road map, but nothing looked unusual. There were a couple of random church bulletins, a brochure from Peatmont State Park, movie theater ticket stubs, and a pair of sunglasses. From her findings, Cheryl deducted that Hogan's father could not bring himself to throw anything away, but simply took what he found and deposited it in the shoebox. The exception was that he had removed the car key from the Ford key ring, leaving what appeared to be a house key. An unusual loose key sparked Cheryl's interest. It had a larger-than-normal oval-shaped top with two letters and a number stamped on one side. A thin circular ring was intertwined through a hole at the top of the key, which may have once had something attached. This key was heavier than the house key attached to the key ring. *Why wasn't this key also attached to the key ring and what was it for*, she wondered.

The police report on Hogan and Rylee's deaths left more questions than it answered. When she told him what she had found, Sean was as perplexed as Cheryl. "Honey, I agree with your assessment. It doesn't look like the department did much in the way of investigation. Jack Rhodes, the assistant sheriff at the time, handled the investigation. The ME's report confirms what Kye said: she was struck hard in the face and fell and struck her head on a rock, which caused her death."

"The surprise was learning that she was three months pregnant," Cheryl said. "Neither Kye nor Milly mentioned that. I think they would have said something if they knew."

Sean agreed. "There would be no reason not to tell you. You said the coroner determined that neither Rylee nor Hogan had drugs or alcohol in their systems?"

"That's right. It would have been difficult to find evidence of foul play on Hogan's body, but the ME concluded there were no gunshot wounds or anything resembling stab wounds. Interestingly, I didn't see notes of any interviews other than Cecil Davis, the train engineer, and the other two men in the cab, Jules Leroux and Bart Fedders."

Sean frowned, "They should have interviewed people who last saw both of the kids and anyone who might have known she was pregnant. The incomplete nature of the investigation raises questions. There may be a logical explanation, but this occurred while Randall Thompson controlled things around the county."

"You think he had something to do with these kids' deaths?" asked Cheryl.

"I wouldn't rule anything out when it comes to Thompson. Could have been a favor for a crony."

"I'm going to look into this further. There may not be anything to it, but there's enough to raise my suspicions."

Sean grinned, "The beautiful reporter's mind never sleeps."

She smiled. "Kye mentioned Jules as someone to talk to. I'm going to give him a call."

Sean arched his eyebrow, "Now don't let that Frenchman charm you."

They both laughed. "You stand alone in that regard," she teased as she blew him a kiss.

Chapter 12

Always the gentleman, Jules seated Cheryl before he sat. Cheryl had interviewed Jules on a prior case. Jules prided himself on his French heritage, although some of the railroaders questioned just how much French linage there really was. He was courtly in his speech and mannerisms. He tucked his napkin in at his collar as he perused the table to ensure the salt and pepper shakers and ketchup bottle were present. Cheryl mused to herself what the expectations were at a family diner like Frau's, which had been around since the 40's and hosted a jukebox, laminate table tops, aged melamine dishes, and paper napkins.

Jules was a locomotive engineer, who carried a wealth of information about railroad stories and history. "Ms. Seton, the lunch specials are a chicken Caesar salad and a hamburger platter, but the fair Anita will bring a menu if you wish."

"The Caesar salad is perfect, Jules."

When Anita showed up with the water pitcher to fill their glasses, Jules promptly advised her of their luncheon choices. The waitress knew

Cheryl and Jules were both coffee drinkers and hustled away to bring coffee.

"Now that we've got that out of the way, please tell me how I can help you," urged Jules.

Cheryl told him that she was looking into the case in the spring of 1967 when Hogan Slater, a senior in high school, was killed by the train. She told him that Cecil Davis was the engineer.

"That is true, my dear. He was, and if anyone could have stopped the train in time, it was Cecil. I was on the engine that night. I remember it as clear as day. I was Cecil's fireman, which means I was the assistant engineer. There were three of us on the engine that night. Bart Fedders was a new-hire. He was the brakeman."

"Would you start from the beginning?"

"Of course. We were on a run from Wheeling, West Virginia, to Cincinnati. As we made our approach into Bekbourg, we came around the curve at the road crossing. Cecil saw something on the track. At first, we didn't know what it was, because it wasn't moving."

"How could you tell it wasn't moving?" Cheryl interrupted.

"The light on the engine is very bright. It shows up *everything* on the track ahead. We could easily see something was on the track. Cecil cranked down on the horn and never let up at the same time he threw the train into emergency."

"What happened then?"

"As we got closer, we were horrified to see that it was a person. It was impossible to stop in time, but when we did, the conductor called the dispatcher who called the local police. They showed up and saw the remains and took our statements. We had to cut the train and pull the cars forward so the coroner could collect the body. They inspected the train and everything. It took about six hours before we were cleared to head on in to Cincinnati."

"You said the body wasn't moving before the train hit it?"

"No, it wasn't. We could see that. Let me tell you, Cecil never let up on the horn until we were past the body, and that is some event hearing a train's horn going like that. The boy never moved. I saw in the newspaper a couple of days later that they decided the young man had committed suicide. Cecil wondered about that because generally if someone wants to commit suicide, they just step out in front of an oncoming train. They don't lay down on the track and wait."

"Did anyone ever ask for your opinion?"

"No, the police never talked to any of us after that night."

"Why do you think Hogan would have just been lying there still like that?"

Jules paused. "Well, he could have been passed out drunk, or unconscious, or dead."

An ominous shiver ran up Cheryl's spine, because the coroner's report concluded that Hogan did not have drugs or alcohol in his system that night.

Chapter 13

"Can I help you, Sir?" Kim asked.

"I want to speak with the sheriff," his lips firm with resolve.

"Okay. Please have a seat, and I'll tell him you're here. I'm sorry I didn't catch your name last time."

"Flynn Taggart."

The first time he entered the police station, Kim could not ignore the man's potency—a caged tiger pacing along the confines. Today, that vigor was ramped into something combustible. Whatever this was about, she expected there would be another round of shouting. Unlikely, but possibly, she could ebb his seething, "Mr. Taggart," she attempted humor, "we have the best police station coffee around. Can I get you some?"

He paused, keeping his anger siloed for Sean. With no give in the hardness in his face and firmness of his lips, he accepted her offer.

After handing him a cup, Kim went and tapped on Sean's door. Her look signaled something was up, "Sheriff, Mr. Taggart is waiting to see you." She mouthed, "Maadd."

Sean nodded, "Thank you, Kim. Tell him I'll be out in a minute."

There was only one thing Sean could think of that would give Flynn the red ass. *Damnit. Why couldn't he have left town without seeing the Brigadier?* he wondered as he stood.

Flynn was leaning against the wall sipping coffee when Sean walked into the reception area. Sean was not deceived by his relaxed posture. "Flynn, let's have a seat in here," he motioned Flynn in the conference room ahead of him.

Flynn shoved forward. Sean could sense the cauldron boiling as Flynn's lips nearly disappeared and his eyes squinted. Sean closed the door to mute the coiled eruption.

Not bothering to sit down, Flynn demanded, "What's you game, Sean? I thought you were someone I could trust. I came here to ask your help. What the hell? You sit there all smug and don't bother to tell me the Colonel is living here? Hell, I guess he made it to Brigadier—that's what I was told anyway. You and him partners around here in the social dance?" Flynn gritted between teeth.

Sean tried to diffuse the tension and held his eyes, "No games, Flynn. Yeah, the Brigadier lives here, but we don't circulate in the same circles. Anyway, I saw no reason to tell you. It has nothing to do with looking at a twenty-year-old case."

"The hell it doesn't!" Flynn's lips firmed. "That SOB could have had her killed."

"You got to be kidding! You really think the Brigadier hired someone to kill his wife?" Sean shook his head. "Look Flynn, even if he did, how does him living here now matter?" Sean pushed back.

Never taking his eyes off Sean, Flynn paused and finished off his coffee with a long swallow. "It's a matter of trust, Sean. I thought I saw something in you back then, integrity, and someone who stood up for the truth. I'm not going to stop until I find who killed Caroline." He crushed the paper cup as he resolved, "No way in hell did I kill her or have anything to do with her death."

He tossed the cup in the can as he charged out. After Sean returned to his office, he pushed back in his chair. *What a damn mess. Hell, even if he was innocent, finding the killer now would be like finding a needle in a haystack. Besides, exactly how am I supposed to help?* A disconcerting thought suddenly hit Sean, *What if Flynn already knew the Brigadier was here and barging in here just now was a ruse? If so, for what purpose?* Sean raked his hand through his sandy colored hair that had started to gray. *Damn, why do I have the feeling that things are getting ready to get a whole lot worst?*

Sean and Cheryl were walking Buddy around the park. Cheryl laughed at the Lab's vigilance for squirrels and birds, teasing Sean that he should hold tight to the leash as Buddy lunged toward a scurrying squirrel. Sean grinned and held up the leash to indicate they were of like minds. Cheryl told Sean about her conversation with Jules, but his "Mmms" and "Unhuhs," signaled his disengagement. As they headed home, Cheryl took his arm and leaned into him, "Sweetheart, is something on your mind?"

He looked down into the glowing eyes of the five-feet, ten-inch tall beautiful and successful woman and grinned, "I didn't mean for it to show. I hope I haven't spoiled the evening."

Cheryl looked into the eyes of the man she loved. He had grown up in Bekbourg. After spending twenty years in the Marines, he had returned to an unfaltering notoriety for being the quarterback who powered the local high school to a state football championship victory. He was recognizable for sure, standing six feet, four inches tall. Being his fiancé, Cheryl knew there was a compassionate man behind the face from which youthful handsome looks had given way to a weathered maturity. In contrast, colleagues and criminals alike saw a man who was relentless and formidable in the pursuit of right and justice.

Cheryl squeezed his arm tighter, "Of course you haven't, but I couldn't help but notice that you seem pensive. Is it something you want to talk about?"

Sean told her about Flynn's two visits and the murder investigation involving Simon Montgomery's first wife. He also explained his frustration about not being able to help Flynn. "I felt like a heel today for not telling him Simon lives here and also for not being able to help him, but I don't see what I can do."

"I agree with why you didn't tell him about Simon, but I also know my 'law and order man,'" she chuckled as she nudged him.

He laughed. Cheryl had a way of lifting the weight. "You do, huh?"

She giggled and nodded.

"Okay, you got some ideas?" he smiled as he watched Buddy check out the fire hydrant.

"I get it that it's not really your place to get involved, but maybe if you could talk to someone who might know something about the case and pass on whatever you learn, you would have tried to help. Who knows, maybe that will be enough to get Flynn moving on his investigation."

Sean leaned over and kissed her head. "When we get home, I'm going to show you how lucky I am to have such a smart woman to solve my dilemmas."

Cheryl's eyes were bright, "Oooo. Let's hurry. Come on, Buddy. Let's run."

They took off laughing and jogging as Buddy galloped beside them with his tongue lolling and his happy face on full display.

Chapter 14

As Cheryl slept curled up beside him, Sean considered options on how he might do as Cheryl had suggested and find someone who *might* give Flynn something to work with. He finally landed on an idea that at least would open the starting gate. He didn't hold much optimism, but at least he could say he had made a good faith effort.

The following morning, he called Tanner Bradford, who had been his commanding officer when he retired from the military. Tanner had been disappointed when Sean was forced out of the special criminal investigative branch due to the injuries suffered in a violent ambush. Sean was one of the best investigators on his team, and when Sean fell on hard times after his retirement, it was Tanner who flew to Key West and brought him back to Bekbourg to recuperate.

"Well hell, Sean! Couldn't believe it when my assistant told me you were on the phone. How does being sheriff suit you?"

Sean smiled. He could picture the short, stout bulldog of a man with the flattop sitting perched on the chair's edge in crisp uniform dress. "It's just fine, Sir. How have you been?"

"Up to my ass in alligators, but I say bring on the crocodiles."

Sean laughed. "Some things never change."

"No, they don't."

Sean and Tanner caught up for a few minutes, and then Sean said, "Sir, there is someone I would like to talk to and thought you might know how I can reach him."

"I'll help if I can, Sean. Who is it you're trying to find?"

"Fritz Marlow. He was an assistant investigator on one of my first cases. I don't know if he's still with the military."

"Mmm. That name sounds familiar, but I can't say I know him. I can look into it. Mind telling me why you're looking for him?"

"Not at all. Do you remember a case out of Camp Lejeune about twenty years ago when a Major Flynn Taggart was convicted in the death of the wife of Lieutenant Colonel Simon Montgomery?"

Silence greeted Sean until Tanner finally spoke. "Yeah, I remember that case. I never knew much about it, but with it involving two officers, the story got around. Major Taggart was having an affair with the Lieutenant Colonel's wife. She was killed in a motel, strangled as I recall, and Taggart was court martialed and convicted."

Tanner's steel trap memory never failed, Sean mused. "Yes Sir, that's the case. The lead investigator was Donald Keaton, and his assistant was Fritz Marlow. Marlow wasn't on the case very long before he was transferred to work a case in California. Keaton needed someone to do the grunt work, and me being the low man on the totem pole, I was pulled into the case toward the end to help. Flynn was released a few months ago and showed up here in Bekbourg. He is still maintaining his innocence. He has hired a retired JAG who now handles civilian defense cases. Flynn remembered me from the case and wanted to know what I might know about the case. I never got a chance to delve into the investigation, so I really can't help, but I thought Fritz Marlow might know something. If he does, maybe I can connect those two."

"I see. I can tell you that Donald Keaton died a few years ago with cancer."

"Flynn mentioned that he was deceased," Sean replied.

"You must have some questions yourself, Sean, to be willing to reach out to Marlow."

"Yes, Sir, I must, but I don't know what they are. Just a gut instinct."

"Well, that's enough, Sean. That's what I always thought made you a great investigator. You had an instinct and followed it. Let me see what I can find out, and I'll let you know."

"Thank you, Sir. I appreciate this."

Chapter 15

Alex Ogle was the assistant sheriff. Even though he was in his late twenties, he looked more like a high school student. He had thick reddish hair. He was leaning on a desk cleaning his glasses when two other deputies, Sydney Johnson and Arlo Lopez, walked into the office area. Arlo and Syd had joined the department within the past year. Arlo was the oldest, having spent time in the military. He was an outdoorsman, spending a lot of time during his youth hunting and fishing around the area. Where Alex was almost six feet tall and slender, Arlo was short and stocky. He had dark hair and—despite shaving—always had a five o'clock shadow.

On a dead run, Syd was the fastest of the three. She had attended a small college on a basketball scholarship before she decided to enroll in the state police academy. She had graduated at the top of her class. Alex and Darrell Logan, the fourth deputy, were deputies when Sean started with the department.

Arlo grabbed a cup of coffee and sat down and put his feet on the desk. After getting a cup of coffee, Syd sat and leaned back in her chair. Of the three, Arlo had the most interest in gossip. "Any word yet on when the Chief might get approval to hire a new deputy?"

Alex shook his head, "I know he's working on it. Hopefully it will be soon."

"Yeah. Is Darrell getting tired of working strictly the night shift?"

"He hasn't said anything. I know he's glad that we each take turns doing double duty. He couldn't handle it by himself with all the DUI's and fights. Other things, too."

"I'm on tonight with him," said Arlo. "Say, Alex. Kim told me about that man, Flynn Taggart, and the blow-up with the Chief. What was that all about?"

"I don't really know. I heard part of it through the conference room door—couldn't help it. Seems the Chief was green behind the ears when he was assigned to the case. Flynn was convicted of killing, get this, the Brigadier's wife and spent twenty years. Now, he's wanting the sheriff's help in trying to clear his name."

Arlo whistled, "What's the Sheriff saying about it?"

"Nothing."

"Is he going to help?"

"I don't know. It happened a long time ago. I can't see him getting involved. Not unless he thinks Flynn is right, but if he did, why wait until now?"

Syd spoke up. "This all sounds kinda suspicious to me. Flynn shows up here, and the man whose wife he was convicted of killing lives here."

Alex and Arlo looked at her. "You raise a good point," said Arlo. "But, from what Kim said, the second blowup was about the Chief not telling Flynn the Brigadier lived here the first time Flynn came in. He saw him somewhere around town."

Syd was watching as she swished the remaining coffee around inside the cup, "Still, it sure sounds fishy to me." She threw her cup in the trash. "Time to call it a day. I'll see you both in the morning meeting."

Alex stood, "I've got to get a report to the Chief, and then I'm calling it quits for the day. See you both in the morning."

Chapter 16

Always happy to receive company, Milly was delighted when she opened the door and saw Cheryl. As she served coffee, she asked if Cheryl was there to discuss Hogan.

"Milly, I read the official reports."

Milly's eyes widened, "Yes?"

"There is no delicate way to ask this."

"Go on."

"Did you know that Rylee was expecting?"

Milly's wrist dropped causing the coffee to splash on the table. Cheryl quickly wiped it up with the napkins.

"Where did you hear that, Cheryl?"

"It was in the coroner's report."

Milly was stunned, "No, I did not know that."

"Do you think your sister knew?"

Milly thought for a minute before responding, "I really don't think she did. Cheryl, you may not know this, but she had two miscarriages before Joy was born. If she had known Rylee was expecting Hogan's baby, she would have been even more devastated than she was. We were close. She would have told me something like that. Maybe no one else, but she would have said something to me."

"How do you think Hogan would have taken hearing the news from Rylee?"

Milly's eyes sharpened, "You think she told him that night, and he struck her?"

"I don't know, Milly, but it's possible."

Milly's pink lipstick smudged her cup as she sipped her coffee deep in thought. "I can see why you might consider that, but it just doesn't sound like Hogan. Hogan loved his little sister, Joy, and her hanging around him and his friends was never a burden to him. He loved kids. He volunteered with the Youth Football program and with the youth events at church for the elementary ages. My sister thought that perhaps her suffering two miscarriages may have affected him. I just can't see that he would have been upset enough to have hit Rylee. They were engaged. He was set to graduate and had a good job lined up. Also, don't forget that Hogan knew there was a real possibility of being sent to Vietnam when he turned twenty. I think he and his family would have cherished his child knowing he could have been drafted. So, no, I think if anything, he would have been happy."

"Well, what about Rylee? Is it possible that she didn't want to have a baby then?"

"But why tell Hogan?" reasoned Milly.

"Good point, unless she needed his help."

Milly paused. "I can't see that, Cheryl. They both were excited about getting married." Milly winced as she drank some coffee. "All of this comes as a surprise, but Rylee had a sweet disposition. She also helped out with the elementary age children at the church, so she appeared to like children, too. Regardless, I can't see Hogan ever striking her. He wasn't like that. He just wasn't the type of young man to do something like that."

"One other thing. I'm going to write a story for the *Tribune*. Sometimes, memories are jogged when people think back to something in the past. We could learn something."

"If there is more to learn, my niece and I both would like to know what that is."

Cheryl arranged to meet with Rylee's sister, Robyn, who lived in Bekbourg. Once they were seated in Robyn's living room, Robyn said, "So, Ms. Seton, you mentioned that you wanted to see me about something pertaining to Rylee?"

"Please call me Cheryl. You probably know that I recently acquired the *Tribune*. Hogan's sister, who lives in Cincinnati, contacted me. She was much younger than Hogan and never knew much about Rylee and Hogan's deaths. She was cleaning out her parents' house and came upon a box of pictures. She told me that she wanted to know what happened. I am looking into the matter and thought you could tell me what you know."

"God, it was so awful and so long ago, but I remember it so clearly. I was home on spring break, and Mom and I were asleep when we heard the police knocking on the door. They were looking to see if we knew anything about Hogan. They told us that he had been killed by the train, and when they informed his parents, they didn't know who might know something, so they told the police Rylee might. Only Rylee wasn't home. We thought she was spending the night with Paige, her best friend."

"Was she?"

"I called Paige's house, and Paige was in bed asleep. Her dad woke her, and she told me that Rylee wasn't there. They didn't have plans for a sleepover that night. The police were already thinking Hogan intentionally laid down on the track, so we were panicked with worry about Rylee. We didn't know where she was. We called everyone we could think of. It wasn't until the next day that they found her body."

"So, you don't know where Rylee was that night? Who she was with?"

"No, except the police eventually concluded that she and Hogan were together, they got in a fight, he accidently killed her and then killed himself."

"How *did* they locate her body?"

"She was driving Mom's car, and they found it parked in the lot there at the county park. They searched and discovered her body back in the woods."

"What about Hogan's car? Was it there?"

"Mmm. I don't remember hearing anything about that."

"You mentioned that the police thought Hogan accidently killed her. What did you think?"

Robyn paused. "Are you questioning what happened, Cheryl?"

"The articles caught my attention. I guess you call it a reporter's instinct. So, I decided to look into it further."

"I see. Well, here's what I can tell you. I was three years older than Rylee. With Dad dying like he did, Mom had to go to work. I felt Mom needed help with things around the house. I don't think Rylee particularly cared for my big sister attitude, because that meant I was keeping tabs on her. I lived at home for the first two years and attended Hillsrock Community College and then went to Athens for my third year. That was Rylee's junior year. She and Hogan started dating the summer I moved to Athens, so I only saw him a few times when he came over to pick her up on a date. Same with when I came in that year, which was about once a month. They dated almost every weekend, but I can't say I was around him enough to know him real well." She gathered her thoughts as she took another sip. "But, to be honest, I would have never guessed that he would hit her. If I'd thought he was like that, I would have insisted Rylee drop him."

Cheryl had not raised the pregnancy yet because she wasn't sure if she knew, but Robyn's next words answered that. "If there is more to the story than the police concluded, I'd like to know, so if you're going to research it, there is something you need to know. She was expecting. Neither Mom nor I had any idea. The police told us that the coroner found that during his examination."

"Do you know if it was Hogan's?"

"Why yes. They were engaged. She never dated anyone before him." She hesitated, "I mean I assume it was his. I can't imagine it was anyone else's."

"Who were her close friends?"

Robyn smiled, "Oh, Rylee had a lot of friends. She was a talkative person, but her absolute best friend was Paige Bridges. I haven't kept up with her, but she used to live in Columbus, Ohio. If there was anyone Rylee would have confided in, it would have been Paige."

"What can you tell me about the investigation by the police?"

Robyn knitted her brows, "Well, I guess I never really thought about it before. At the time, Mom and I were overcome with grief. I was able to get special approvals to complete my courses that summer, so I stayed home with Mom and we handled things best we could. But getting back to your question, we only talked to one of the deputies, Mr. Rhodes. He later became the sheriff. He's the one who came and told us they had found Rylee's body. He came back and asked us some questions, and then he came and told us about the cause of death and the discovery that she was pregnant. He wanted to know what we knew about Rylee being pregnant, and we told him we didn't know. After that, we never heard anything from him, but we read in the newspaper that the sheriff thought Hogan struck her and accidently killed her and then took his own life. Thankfully, it never became public knowledge that she was expecting."

"Do you know if anyone else knew? Or learned about it?"

"I have no idea. We never talked to Hogan's family about it. We attended his memorial, but his parents were distraught, and we never saw them again. I saw Paige at Rylee's service, but I didn't want to say anything about the pregnancy if she didn't say anything. I don't know if she knew or not, but I never heard anyone mention it. No one."

Chapter 17

Tanner called Sean and provided contact information for Fritz Marlow. He had retired from the military and was a police chief in a medium-sized town in California. Sean put in a call to him and did not wait long before he called back. "Sheriff Neumann, this is Fritz Marlow returning your call."

"Chief Marlow, thank you for getting back to me."

"I was curious when my assistant said a sheriff from Bekbourg County, Ohio, was calling, so I looked you up. You were running with the big dogs being in Tanner Bradford's division. What made you retire? You had, what? Twenty years?"

"Yep. Injuries sustained during an investigation in Kuwait ended my career."

"That's tough. So how did you end up in Bekbourg?"

"I grew up here. I didn't intend to stay more than necessary to recover, but the sheriff offered me a deputy position, and I'm still here."

"Yeah, I hear you. I put my twenty in and retired to my wife's hometown."

"You and I nearly crossed paths on a murder investigation," said Sean. "Do you remember working on a case out of Camp Lejeune about twenty years ago? Major Flynn Taggart was accused of killing the wife of Lieutenant Colonel Simon Montgomery."

"Oh, hell, yeah. I remember that case."

"Donald Keaton was the lead," said Sean.

"That's right. Good ole Ass Keaton."

Sean asked, "I take it you weren't fond of him?"

"Hell, no. The best thing that happened to me was getting transferred to Camp Pendleton. Even if the transfer happened in the middle of that investigation, I was more than ready to say good riddance to that guy."

"What can you tell me about the case?"

"Well, Flynn was having an affair with Montgomery's wife, which as you know is problematic enough. Montgomery had been stationed there for about three years. Flynn was there on assignment. As I recall, he'd been at Lejeune almost a year when the murder happened."

"Who were the suspects?"

"Well, no one really. Once Keaton found out Flynn was hitting it off with the victim, he got a search warrant. They found the scarf in Flynn's vehicle, and forensics confirmed the residue fibers found around her neck matched those on the scarf. You know the rest."

"Were you involved in the search?"

"No, Keaton handled that along with some MPs. Flynn didn't have an alibi. He said she called and told him that she was going to be late. She never called back, so he figured something came up. He claimed he started to drive to a bar, but when he ended up with a flat tire on the way, he decided to turn around and go back home."

"Yeah, I remember that testimony," said Sean. "Did you look at any other suspects?"

"We naturally looked at Montgomery, but he was out of town when it happened, so that eliminated him. Rumor was that she had a string of men she partied with. She'd be with one for a while, usually a couple of months, and then move on to the next eye-candy. The most recent one before Flynn was, let me think." After a pause, "Hutch someone."

"Hutch McAlistair," offered Sean.

"Yep, that's him. He was a civilian. Apparently, Flynn and he had words over the victim. Flynn's attorney talked to him, but all that came from that conversation was that Hutch wasn't forthcoming with an alibi followed by a door being slammed in the attorney's face. Flynn's attorney wanted us to investigate good ole Hutch. I was going to call the local sheriff's office to help out, but Ass Keaton told me he'd do it, so I don't know what he found out. I'm curious why you're asking about this," Fritz probed.

"After you were transferred out, Keaton decided he needed a briefcase carrier. I got tapped to finish out the case with him, but that wasn't too long before the court martial. Anyway, Flynn was recently released after serving twenty years. He tracked me down, thinking I could help him. He's still claiming his innocence. He's hired a retired JAG to represent him, and he wants to retrace the investigation to see if it leads to a vindication."

"I see. How can you help him?"

"I can't help him, and I told him that. The thing is, this was one of my first cases, and most of the leg work had been done by the time I was assigned, but something just never felt quite right. I can't explain it. Anyway, when Flynn showed up, I thought if I could give him something to start with, I would have helped in some small way."

"Yeah, once that scarf was found, Keaton was convinced he had the perp, and he fast-tracked the court-martial."

"Well, I appreciate you calling me back. Even if Flynn's innocent, I don't see where he can go with this."

"I agree, but shit. If he was innocent, that sure sucks," said Fritz.

"Yeah, *if.*" Sean added, "It must have been an important case for you to have been transferred in the middle of a high-profile case like that."

"You would think. Hell, I was on Pendleton's base within forty-eight hours of receiving orders. It was a domestic violence case that resulted in the wife's death. Not as sexy as a murder case involving an officer killing another officer's wife who he was sleeping with." Fritz paused, "I never knew what the urgency was in getting me transferred. When I got there, I worked alongside another investigator who had several fewer years of experience, but he had done a good job. Based on the investigative work, mostly from him before I arrived, they convicted the guy. But at the time, I was relieved to be anywhere but being under Keaton's thumb, so I never looked back."

Chapter 18

Simon, Harvey and Noel walked out into the bright spring day having just finished lunch at the GilHaus. "I'll plan to see you for dinner at six o'clock Thursday night. The others will be joining us."

"Sounds good, Ha . . ." Simon stopped mid-sentence as he looked past Harvey. As Harvey and Noel turned to see what had snatched Simon's attention, Simon thundered, "What the hell are you doing here?"

Harvey and Noel didn't know the man whose eyes were locked on Simon. Harvey turned to see red blotches on Simon's strained face as nothing short of rage consumed him.

"Is there something I can help with?" Harvey asked Simon.

Simon's anger intensified, never shifting his glower. "No."

Harvey gave Flynn another look before he and Noel melted a couple of steps back to better keep both men in their sights.

"I just want to talk to you," said Flynn.

"What the hell are you doing out?"

"I paid for something I didn't do, Montgomery. I'm trying to find who killed Caroline. I thought Sean Neumann might be able to help me. He was on the team that investigated the murder. I saw you the other day and thought you might have some information."

Simon's face turned redder. His eyes narrowed as he growled, "You SOB. You had an affair with an officer's wife. You violated the Corp's code, and you come to me asking for my help. You're scum, Taggart. Whatever time you got, it wasn't enough. They should have thrown away the key. Now, don't you *ever* get anywhere near me again."

Simon spun around and marched away, leaving Flynn standing in view of a stunned sprinkling of onlookers. Flynn didn't bother looking into their faces as he reversed course and walked down the sidewalk. Harvey and Noel were left wondering what that was all about.

Throughout the afternoon, Sean harkened back to his conversation with Fritz. Something kept gnawing at him. The Montgomery case was the only time Sean worked directly under Donald Keaton. He had been pulled from his team to assist Keaton in the waning days before the court martial. It seemed odd that Fritz was zipped off to another base for a case that, from all appearances, was being competently handled. But maybe, he was no longer needed, because when Sean was transferred in, Keaton did not need his assistance with any heavy lifting in the investigation.

Kim interrupted his thoughts, "Hey, Boss. If you don't need anything, I'm going to leave." She enthusiastically reminded him, "I'll be back ready to hit it again bright and early in the morning." Kim's cheerfulness buoyed the entire department.

"It's all covered, thanks to you. Have a good evening. I'll see you tomorrow," Sean nodded.

"Don't forget, Boss. You have dinner plans."

Sean sat up and glanced at his watch. "Yeah, I better get going. Milton and Martha invited me and Cheryl to meet them at the GilHaus. Must be one of their birthdays. It's not like Milton to miss going to Frau's for a burger. Anyway, see you tomorrow."

Chapter 19

Milton Grant had been an icon in the newspaper business in Cleveland, Ohio, where he had been an investigative reporter for forty years for *The Cleveland Presenter*. His sources and contacts spanned far beyond the Ohio region. When Cheryl joined the newspaper after graduating college, Milton recognized her talent and grit and took special interest in teaching her how to excel in investigative reporting. A few years ago, he suffered a heart attack and was compelled to pare back on assignments. When Cheryl decided to purchase the *Bekbourg Tribune,* Milton offered to relocate to Bekbourg to assist her around the newspaper. His reasoning was twofold—it kept him around the newsroom, helping a young woman he cared for like a daughter, and it gave him close proximity to Martha.

As they were dining, Cheryl smiled to herself thinking how Milton had cleaned up his act. After the heart attack, his chain-smoking had been replaced by incessant gum-chewing, but even that had dwindled since he met Martha, a lovely matronly woman who Milton adored. Since meeting Martha, his gruffness had mellowed, his shirts were commonly tucked in and his white hair more tamed.

Drew Chambers had taken over Martha's former employer's CPA practice after Owen Donaldson died. Milton and Owen had been long-time friends, and Milton met Martha when he came to Bekbourg for Owen's memorial service. Martha still worked for Drew. Cheryl asked Martha, "Have things quieted down for you and Drew now that tax season just ended?"

Martha laughed, "Thankfully, yes. This was Drew's first tax season after passing his CPA. I felt sorry for him. He is so conscientious. He'd be hard at it when I left for the evening and already at the office in the mornings when I arrived."

Milton spoke up, "Yeah, and I know he was working long hours, because Martha was putting in long hours."

She chuckled, "I don't mind at all. I enjoy my job, and working for Drew is a delight. But, I am glad to have that big push behind us."

Milton turned to Sean, "How are things going in your department. I haven't heard of any murders lately." That brought a round of laughter.

Sean dryly replied, "Not any that I'm aware of, at least." After everyone's laughter subsided, Sean said, "There is something from my military days that has cropped up."

"Oh. What's that?" Milton looked at Sean as he picked up his wine glass.

Sean told them about Flynn Taggart's visit and then his conversation with Fritz Marlow. "I know you and Cheryl have reporter instincts that drive you in your investigations. Well, there is something about this case that keeps pulling at me."

"You say this happened at Camp Lejeune?" asked Milton.

"That's right," responded Sean.

"I have an idea, Sean. It may or may not be a wild goose chase. I went to college with a man who was from North Carolina. When we graduated, he went to work for the newspaper in Jacksonville, which is where Camp Lejeune is located. I was a groomsman in his wedding there. Maybe I can track him down. It's possible he might have been around when that happened. Sometimes these local reporters have insights about things like this. Maybe we could find out something."

"That's not a bad idea, Milton."

"Okay, I'll see what I can find out." Milton grinned at Martha. "If he's still around, Martha and I could take a trip and talk with him."

"Oh, I don't want to put you to all that trouble, Milton."

Milton's grin grew, and Martha smiled. Cheryl arched an eyebrow. Something was up.

"Oh, it wouldn't be any trouble, Sean. I'd like to introduce him to my new bride, and it would add to the fun on our honeymoon."

Cheryl screeched, "What? Bride? Are you two getting married?"

Martha and Milton sat beaming. He reached over and took her hand in his. Cheryl's impatience demanded to know, "Oh, my gosh. You're engaged?" Her face was lit up with wide eyes and a huge smile. Sean smiled at Cheryl's exuberance and the happy couple.

Milton chuckled, "I guess we should tell you."

Martha eased her hand from his and reached into a pocket. She slipped a wedding band on her finger. Seeing Cheryl's mouth drop open, Milton laughed, "We're not engaged. We're married."

Through the excitement, Sean ordered a bottle of champagne as Milton explained how they had gotten married at the courthouse. "We just decided to do it, so we got our license and got married."

Martha interjected, "And, the news wasn't leaked!"

Laughter erupted again.

Chapter 20

Paige Bridges, now Paige Moore, Rylee's best friend, lived in Columbus. On her drive to meet for lunch, Cheryl thought about what she had learned about Paige. Paige and Rylee were cheerleaders and had been best friends since junior high. Paige attended Hillsrock Community College for two years and then worked as a teller at a local bank. There, she met her future husband, and they eventually moved to Columbus where he took a job.

After they were settled with their lunch orders, Cheryl told Paige she was the new owner of the *Bekbourg Tribune*. She explained how she had become interested in what had happened to Rylee and Hogan. Cheryl asked Paige what she could tell her about Rylee.

"Rylee was like a sister *and* best friend. We were basically inseparable. We were partners for cheerleading tryouts every year. Once you made the freshman team, it was pretty much certain you would make it the rest of the time. For our freshman tryouts, Rylee was determined that we make the squad. She planned our matching outfits, how we wore our hair, everything. She was like that—when she set her mind to something, she went after it. She was so pretty with her long blonde hair and had such a bubbly personality. There were some girls who were jealous, but she was like a magnet for most of girls." Paige chuckled. "She had her own entourage. She did okay in school, but that wasn't her priority."

"Did she ever date anyone other than Hogan?"

"I don't know how much Rylee's sister told you. Robyn was three years older, but a lot older when it came to maturity. When their dad died, Robyn became like an adult. She tried to shield their mom from as much stress as she could. With their mom having to go to work to support them, Robyn took charge around the house and kept tabs on Rylee. She insisted that Rylee not date until she was a junior. Rylee loved Robyn, but she was relieved when she went off to college in Athens.

"Boys liked her, the way she would smile and laugh, but because of Robyn, she didn't date until she met Hogan. You know how I told you that Rylee went after what she wanted, well, that applied to Hogan. Besides wanting to be popular, her goal was to get married as soon as she could after high school, settle down and have kids. She didn't want to work outside the home the way her mother had after their dad died." Paige laughed. "When she spent the night with me, which was often, we'd evaluate the boys. She had her eye out for a possible husband, and towards the end of our sophomore year, she decided Hogan was the one. She made a point to spend time with him at the end-of-the-year school picnic. That's how they ended up together."

"Do you think she loved him?" asked Cheryl.

Paige thought about that before responding. "I think so. I mean, she really liked being with him, and she was always talking about him. He was one of the best-looking boys in the senior class. Hogan was on the football team, although he didn't play a lot. He was popular. He was class treasurer. She loved the idea of dating an older boy, and he was willing to marry her when she graduated. He was going to work for the utility company, so he fit her dream." Paige paused. "There wasn't anyone else she seemed interested in, at least not in our class. I have to say, that's the only secret I ever knew Rylee to keep from me."

"What's that?"

"There was a boy two grades ahead of us who she was dreamy about, but she wouldn't tell me who it was. The only thing she told me was that he was on the football team. She fantasized about him from a distance. Of course, even if he had expressed an interest, there was no way Robyn would have let her date him, she being a sophomore. Rylee may have been hesitant to go after him because he was two years older for fear of looking foolish, and she would *not* have wanted to be rejected by him or ridiculed by the older cheerleaders. Sometime that spring, she told me that she had heard he was going away to school after graduation. That was when she decided Hogan was it."

"When did they start dating?"

"That summer. Robyn loosened the reins. Rylee was going to be a junior, and also, Rylee told me that her sister liked Hogan. Rylee worked her magic. They started going steady that summer. They got engaged that fall."

"So, Rylee was a junior and Hogan was a senior?"

"Yes."

"Did she and Hogan argue?"

"No, she never mentioned that. Hogan was laid-back. That was one of the things that she liked about him. We double dated with them, and she had the cute way of pouting, or just the opposite, snuggling up to tease him, so on most things, he always went along."

"You never saw him angry?"

"No, not ever."

"Was she worried about being pregnant or telling Hogan?" Cheryl asked.

Paige's mouth fell open, "*WHAT?* Where on earth did you hear that? Rylee wasn't pregnant." Paige was indignant.

Cheryl was surprised. "She hadn't told you she was expecting?"

Paige hesitated, "This can't be true. Where did you hear that she was?"

"It was in the coroner's report. She was about three months along. The police told Robyn and her mother. Neither of them knew until then."

Paige slumped back in her chair while she absorbed the shocking news. "Did Robyn say who the father was?"

It was Cheryl's time to be surprised, "Well, she assumed it was Hogan's. Why? Is there some question about that?"

Paige's look left no room for doubt as she slightly shook her head, "Look, Cheryl. I don't know what is going on, but I can tell you this. There is *no way* that was Hogan's baby. The only thing that they didn't agree on was having sex. Hogan was dug in on this. He wanted to wait until their wedding night. It was kind of a sore subject with Rylee, but she didn't want to push Hogan too hard on it."

"Are you sure they weren't intimate and she didn't tell you?"

"Oh, no. She wouldn't have held out on that. See, I had already done it with my boyfriend during the summer before our junior year, and a couple of our friends had also. We'd sit around and talk about it. Rylee acted like it was no big deal that she and Hogan were holding off, but I knew she didn't like it. In fact, after she and Hogan decided to get married, she told him that some of her friends had gone all the way, hoping to persuade him that it was okay. He told her they would wait, that their wedding night would be all the more special."

Cheryl and Paige remained silent for a few minutes, each considering what they had just learned from each other. Cheryl asked, "You don't have any idea who the father could have been?"

"No. I am floored by this. I can't believe she was pregnant. I have no doubt that it wasn't Hogan's. That much I know." She paused, "I can't believe Rylee never told me, or at least hinted."

"What about the night she was killed? Robyn thought she was spending the night with you."

"I know. She called our house late that night asking if Rylee was there, but she wasn't. Rylee had told me earlier that day that Robyn was in town and she had use of her mom's car and that she might run by later that night. She sometimes came over like that after Hogan dropped her off at home if it was an early night or if she wanted to talk. My parents didn't care. When she didn't show up, I just figured she had decided not to drop by." Even though it had been nearly forty years ago, Cheryl noticed that sorrow embraced Paige.

"Paige, I am sorry to have blind-sided you with this, but if the baby wasn't Hogan's, this raises some questions about what happened to Rylee and maybe even Hogan."

"Yes, I can see that."

"Do you think Rylee would have been upset to know that she was having a baby?"

"I would have said 'no' if I thought it was Hogan's, because school wasn't that important to her. Getting married and having children were. Now that I think about it, Rylee wasn't quite herself that spring. Even though we were cheerleaders, each year we had to try out for the next year, which was a couple of weeks before school ended. Before spring break, I suggested that we needed to think about our routine for tryouts, but she didn't seem all that interested. She was quieter than normal. I asked her if everything was okay, and she said she had a lot on her mind. We both were under the gun to get our junior English paper turned in, so I just put it off to that. I sure wished I had pushed her harder to tell me."

"Did the police ever talk to you?"

"No."

"One last question: Who were Hogan's friends?"

"Let me think. Chad Earnst and Austin Towman hung out with him a lot. Chad still lives in Bekbourg, but Austin went away to college. I believe he ended up in Cincinnati or Columbus, but Chad might be able to tell you. Cheryl, I'd appreciate it if you let me know if you find out more about this. I moved on with my life, but from time-to-time, I think about Rylee."

Cheryl assured her she would.

Chapter 21

Brian and Reid were waiting near the old Shiloh Ridge Cemetery when Lilly and Claire pulled up. Lilly couldn't help noticing Reid's newer model sporty-looking car. She knew he was from an affluent family, but he never acted superior to others. His head was always in the techie stuff. He and Brian were friends, and ever since the university had donated the new equipment to their high school, they enjoyed spending their free time in the computer lab.

When Lilly got out of the car, Reid asked, "Did you bring the video camera?" The university had recently donated ten new high-definition video cameras to their program. Being the group's director, Lilly had to check out the camera and was responsible for it. Reid and Brian had been eager to get their hands on it and experiment with its new features.

"Yeah, here it is. Guys, be careful with it."

Claire looked around, "Where's Jake?"

The boys were too absorbed by the camera to respond, so she answered herself. "Obviously not here."

A few minutes later, Jake pulled up in an older model pick-up truck and stepped out. Claire couldn't contain herself, "You're late, again." When he ignored her scowl as he approached the group, she muttered, "I bet you're not late for football games."

Lilly was ready to get things moving. "Okay, guys. Let's start with Anton whose part is being played by Jake. Anton is being pursued by the robbers—that's Claire and Reid." Lilly gave Jake a small leather bag that was supposed to contain the jewels. Brian was filming the group as she instructed everyone about their assignments.

Claire spoke up, "Brian, do you *really* need to film all this? Seems it will just make the editing take longer." Brian pointed the camera in her direction and continued filming. Claire glowered and turned away.

Lilly felt it was like herding cats. "Okay, let's all take our positions."

Jake walked up to Claire, "Here. Put this on your face to make it look like you have a beard. Otherwise, you won't look like a robber."

"What is it? Looks like a large lipstick tube."

Reid asked, "Do I need any?"

"Maybe," admitted Lilly. "I'm like Claire, Jake. I don't know what it is."

"Football players wear it under their eyes. Called 'eye black.' Keeps the glare down when the sun or lights are bright. But some wear it all over their face to make them look intimidating. She," Jake nodded toward Claire, "looks scary enough, but he could use some more," indicating Reid.

"Fuuunnny." Claire faked a smile as she squeezed the tube.

"Here, let me show you." Jake took it from her and put a small amount on his finger and gently applied it to her cheeks and chin. Looking at Reid, "Here, if you want some, put it on like that."

Jake walked back to his truck and pulled out a towel and wiped his hands and took it to Reid. Lilly was impressed. "Jake, that is a great idea. It makes them look older and more like hobos."

Claire asked, "Do you wear this stuff when you play football?"

Lilly's eyebrows nearly hit her hair line as she wondered about Claire's sometime tendency to speak before she thought. Jake didn't take offense. "Yeah, just 'cause I'm black don't mean I don't wear it."

Everyone had rehearsed their parts, and the scene in the graveyard where the robbers were pursuing Anton/Jake and him stashing the jewels went well. They were ready to film the part where Herr Krause confronted Anton/Jake. Anton was on his way to propose to Esther before being shipped off to war. The group moved to a nearby slope. Lilly thought it would be a perfect place to film the shotgun-toting Herr Krause confronting Anton. Claire was creative in turning two broomsticks into a shotgun. They went through the staging and were about to shoot when Jake said, "This doesn't look

real. I'm twice Brian's size. No one will believe that
Anton is afraid of him."

"Well, you can't shrink, and he can't grow,
so it's the way it is." Claire replied.

Jake glanced at the sky. "I've got time
before it gets dark. I've got an idea that might help.
I can be back in an hour."

"What's your idea, Jake?" Lilly asked.

"Get some shoulder and rib pads. I'll bring a
bigger flannel shirt that will fit over it. That'll give
him some bulk. He can also put on a little of the eye
black."

Claire was the one to react. "I can see that.
That's not a bad idea."

After Jake pulled away, Reid announced that
he and Brian were going to take the camera down
the hill and do some shooting where there were
more trees. They wanted to see what the video
would look like where it was darkened by trees.
They were already thinking about making another
film. "Fine," said Lilly, "just don't drop the camera,
and be back before Jake gets back. It's going to get
late, and we need to get this next scene shot."

While the boys were gone, Claire and Lilly
discussed various ideas about props and staging for
the scenes they were planning to shoot. After a
while, they heard Brian and Reid coming back up
the hill talking about how great the video camera
was. When they saw Lilly and Claire, Brian said,
"This is really a cool camera. It's not quite dark
enough to fully test its qualities in low light, but it

should work when we do our horror video this summer. The panorama feature and the lens zooming in and out are smooth. It is easy to do the 'Hitchcock' effect."

Claire asked, "What's that?"

"It's a bit complicated, but you zoom in as you step back, and it creates an interesting visual effect that makes it look like an object is coming forward," Reid explained. "We can't use it in our movie, but we experimented with it to see if it works, and it does."

About that time, Jake's truck came zipping up. He stepped out with a mesh bag filled with pads and flannel shirts. "These should help bulk up Brian."

Jake's idea was a good one. The burly old farmer, Herr Krause/Brian, looked realistic as he intimidated Anton/Jake. Jake even gave Brian tips on how to make his voice sound lower and crusty.

"Too bad we can't use your voice for his, Jake," said Claire. "Yours is the deepest of anyone I've ever heard."

Jake ignored her.

"Jake, I'm going to list you as assistant director," said Lilly. "I really like the ideas you've come up with."

Claire chimed in that she supported the suggestion, and Brian agreed. Jake said to Lilly, "You don't need to do that. Let's just get this done."

Lilly was pleased with their progress and hoped the rest of the filming went as well.

Chapter 22

Chad Earnst, one of Hogan's best high school friends, was a foreman for the Fischner Construction Company. When Cheryl contacted him, he suggested that they meet at Knucklepin's Tavern after he got off from work. Knucklepin's was a popular beer joint that had been serving patrons for decades. Chad had saved a table to give them some privacy to talk. "Thanks for meeting me here. Sometimes after work, a beer hits the spot."

Cheryl laughed. "I can relate." Cheryl asked him about Hogan and his relationship with Rylee. He told Cheryl he had never accepted that Hogan killed Rylee. Hogan was a football player, but he was not physical enough to see a lot of playing time. Chad never saw Hogan upset or miffed. "He thought she hung the moon. He was so happy that they were going to get married. He was already making plans where they would live at first. Then, once they had saved some money, he wanted to build a house."

"How did he feel about having children?"

"Oh, he was all for it. He was glad that Rylee wanted to have children right after they got married. He once told me that if Rylee was willing, he wanted to have four or five. Look. In my opinion, under no circumstances would he have done that. Hogan would never, ever hit Rylee or be violent with her. I was just a teenager myself, so there wasn't anything I could do or say to change the police on that, but no one could have ever convinced me what they said was true."

"He got a call at home the night he died. I understand he was with you earlier in the evening."

"That's right. Me, Austin and Hogan had dinner at Frau's. I was going to run by my girlfriend's house afterwards to watch a movie. I don't know what Austin was doing, but Hogan said he was going to go home. Rylee was spending the night at Paige's, or at least that's what she told Hogan, to talk about what they were going to wear to the prom."

"How did he seem that evening?"

"Just like always. Trust me. I analyzed my last time with him that night hundreds of times for any hint of anything, but I don't remember *anything* that was different."

Chad told Cheryl that Hogan's other close friend, Austin Towman, graduated from college in Cincinnati and lived there. Cheryl tried calling his home phone several times, but no one answered, not even an answering phone. She finally got lucky one day when one of his daughters answered. She explained that her parents, Austin and her mother, were on an extended trip traveling around the country in a motor home. She was collecting the mail and watering the house plants and just happened to be there when Cheryl called. They intentionally left their phones at home, so she had no way to get in touch with them. They had just talked the previous week when her parents called from one of their stops, but she didn't know if she would hear from them again before they returned. She assured Cheryl that she would give her dad the message to call Cheryl as soon as she could.

One day out of the blue, Rylee's sister, Robyn, called Cheryl and asked if she could stop by. When Cheryl arrived, Robyn showed her a box sitting on a coffee table in the living room. She explained that after Rylee's death, her mother couldn't face walking by Rylee's room and seeing all her things, so after Robyn finished her course work that summer, she went through Rylee's things. "I gave all her clothes away, but I couldn't yet part with her cheerleading awards and things like that. I didn't even look at her personal stuff. I just packed it up in boxes and put them in the attic. After you and I talked, I went in attic and found this box, which contains her diaries and some other things. It's too personal for me to look through, especially her diaries, but if you think it might help, you can borrow the box."

Cheryl took the box to her office to review the contents. The three diaries interested her most.

Chapter 23

Sean and Cheryl were home Saturday night watching a movie when his phone rang. The dispatcher told him that even though Darrell was responding to the call, he thought Sean should know that Brigadier Montgomery had called in about his wife being missing.

The bright blue spiraling lights on the cruiser guided Sean to the secluded lake house at the end of the road. Simon answered and invited Sean to join him and Darrell in the large great room that opened off the back with sliding doors to a balcony lit by outside lighting.

"Sean, I was telling your deputy that it's probably nothing, but I haven't been able to reach Skylar. She wasn't here when I returned from a business trip earlier today."

"Tell me about it."

"I left Thursday afternoon to go to Columbus on a business trip and returned today around one o'clock. Skylar wasn't here. I didn't think anything about it. I figured she was playing tennis or shopping or whatever. I tried calling her sister, but she didn't answer. I called a couple of women who she plays tennis with. I also called Mary since Skylar has been helping out at the foundation, but they didn't know anything."

"Is her car here?"

"Yes, her purse was in her car, but her phone is gone. She always keeps it with her."

"Did anything look out of place around here?" asked Sean.

"No, and there was no sign of foul play. She probably decided to go off with a friend and didn't want to call me while I was on business."

"She would not have told you if she was going out of town?"

"Not necessarily. We're both busy people. We don't keep close tabs on each other. That's why it was probably premature for me to call you like this." Simon furrowed his brows as a thought occurred to him, "Someone I didn't think to call was Becky Werner. She might know something."

"Becky Werner?"

"Yes. Harvey Bennett and Becky recently started seeing each other. The other night when we were dining, Harvey brought up the business trip and invited Skylar and Becky to tag along and shop or whatever. Maybe one of them reached out to the other and they decided to go somewhere. I don't have Becky's number, but maybe you or your deputy could check with her. I assume you know her?"

"I will contact her. Mind if I have a look around?" Sean asked as he surveyed the rustic furnishings.

"No, not at all. The master suite is off to the right, and the two guest rooms are that way," Simon pointed to a doorway leading away from the kitchen and dining room. "The stairway," which opened to the downstairs, "leads to my office and the game room. You'll find the garage there."

Except for the blinds in the bedrooms, there were no window treatments. For the most part, the upstairs furnishings were weighty dark wood and brown leather upholstery. The stone fireplace anchored the sitting area in the great room. A heavy dining table and eight bulky chairs consumed the dining area. The fully stocked built-in bar suggested the couple enjoyed entertaining. Except for a landscape painting hanging in the dining room, trophies from hunting expeditions accented the walls.

"Who hunts?" asked Sean.

"I do. Skylar is revulsed by the sport."

As Sean surveyed the house, he felt as if he were a prospective buyer touring a house already vacated by the owners. He moved into their bedroom. Skylar and Simon each had their own private quarters off the master suite. Finally, Skylar's private bathroom and closet area gave respite to the hollowness he felt from the rest of the house. There, he saw a feminine sitting area with two upholstered chairs, a small table, and some flowering plants in front of a window. The soil was dry and needed watering. A small curio held an opaque blue vase and a glass paperweight encapsulating a sketch of the pentagon.

In the bathroom, an array of lotions and makeup filled the countertop along with a hairbrush, comb and hairdryer. Used towels hung from hooks. Nothing was damp, which confirmed she had not recently been here. Clothes were carelessly hung and shoes randomly discarded in her closet. He peered inside an overnight bag, which was empty. The withering plants and dry towels evidenced she had not been around lately, but if she had left for a trip, why leave all her makeup and hair necessities?

Except for a wedding photo of Skylar and Simon on the fireplace mantel, Sean saw no other personal pictures until he made his way to the lower level. The walls were filled with Simon's citations, awards and photos detailing his military career. Mirroring the upstairs, a row of sliding doors looked out over the lake, and a large TV sat along one wall. Off to the far side was a pool table, and another wet bar filled out the corner. Pushed off in another corner was a cedar chest holding a contemporary stained-glass lamp.

In the three-car garage, Sean saw two cars: a black Cadillac SUV with the license plate, "BrigG1", and a black Cadillac sedan, license plate, "SkyM1". Sean felt the hoods on both vehicles, but neither had been recently driven. He looked inside Skylar's purse. An anti-anxiety prescription bottle was laying on top of her wallet. With a handkerchief, he looked to see that the bottle was about half full. Nothing suggested her whereabouts.

While Sean searched the house's interior, Darrell surveyed the outside. The three men were now standing in the living room. Darrell had not seen anything unusual. Nothing was amiss in the shed, and a canoe was tied to the dock. He did not see standing water in the canoe or on the dock.

Sean told Simon that he would follow up with Becky and Skylar's sister and that if something didn't turn up soon, he would open a formal investigation.

Since Becky lived nearby, Sean decided that would be his first stop before driving to Skylar's sister's home. The interior lights were on and a luxury sedan was parked in the circular driveway. Gary, Becky's estranged husband, owned a large and prosperous dealership in Bekbourg, but the business nearly went under when he was arrested and convicted for his involvement in a cartel-run drug operation. He was now serving time, leaving Becky to run the dealership and raise their two teenage daughters. Through grit and vision, she had managed to not only save the dealership from bankruptcy, but had made it profitable once again. She had vowed to keep her daughters in the home where they lived when Gary was arrested, and they still lived there.

Sean heard heels clicking on the floor as the door chimes were fading. Despite the passage of time, Becky was still a stunning woman. She had been one of the most popular girls in high school. The girls admired her boundless personality, and the boys enjoyed her flirtations. During their junior year, she set her sights on Sean. Their relationship rocketed with intensity and circled in a stratosphere of youthful attractions and affections. Then, after graduation, life's realities began to permeate and muscle away their passion. A career-ending injury during the final minutes of the championship football game had dealt a death knell to Sean's scholarship opportunities with Division 1 universities. As a result, he found himself working for the railroad—a job his grandfather helped secure. Becky could not accept the long hours and unpredictability of his job. Adding to the tensions, Sean resisted her pressure to marry. Two years after they graduated, she played a trump card by breaking up. She overplayed her hand in thinking Sean would capitulate. A few weeks later, he was at the Marines boot camp.

Becky's eyes widened when she opened the door to find Sean standing there, "Oh, my God! Has something happened to Kinsey?"

He quickly grabbed her arm to steady and reassure her. "No, it's nothing like that. This has to do with Skylar Montgomery. Is there somewhere we can talk?"

"Skylar?" Confusion showed in her eyes. She was still leaning into him. Sean's attention was pulled to Harvey Bennett walking through the foyer.

He eyed Sean as he took him in steadying Becky. "Has something happened?"

Sean slowly extricated his hold on Becky. "No, but I need to talk to Becky." He looked at her, "Is there somewhere we can talk in private?"

"Becky, do you want me with you?" Harvey asked, his eyes hard as he looked at Sean.

"This is official business, Bennett."

Becky grasped the tension between the two men. She also relished the idea of spending time with Sean. When he had returned to Bekbourg, he made clear that their relationship was ancient history, but she had never purged him from her desires. "It's okay, Honey. Sean and I can step into the office." She returned her attention to Sean, "This won't take too long?"

Harvey didn't know the history between the two. His hostility toward Sean emanated from his recent legal problems with prosecutors and taxing authorities brought on by one of Sean's investigations. "Okay, but if you need me, I'll be in the den."

As they were sitting, Becky said, "I'm sorry about overreacting. Kinsey is out with some friends, and when I saw you, I panicked thinking something had happened to her."

"That's understandable, Becky, but like I said, this pertains to Skylar Montgomery."

"You said that, but I don't see how I can help. I barely know her."

"Simon thought you might know something. She is missing."

"I'm sorry, Sean, but none of this makes sense to me. She's missing? Simon told you to talk to me?"

"I understand that Simon and Harvey were on a business trip?"

"That's right. They've been in Columbus. Harvey returned this afternoon. I assume that Simon did?"

"He did. Skylar's not home. Simon told me that there was a possibility that you and she had taken a trip, maybe to Columbus, to shop or something."

Becky paused, "No. Harvey and I dined with them last weekend. He thought Skylar and I might want to tag along and shop. We both had plans and weren't able to go. I haven't talked to her since then."

"How did she seem to you?"

Becky pondered the question. "I guess fine. She was quiet, but then, the men did most of the talking about a business deal."

"Usually when people are out to dinner, they are having a good time. Did it seem like she was enjoying herself?"

Becky pursed her lips. "Not really. I mean she was polite, but she seemed to have something on her mind. One thing, she said she was fighting off a migraine, and that can be painful."

"You said you hardly knew her. Had you been around her before the other night?"

"I met her when they came to the dealership shortly after they moved to Bekbourg. Simon bought a large SUV for himself and a new Cadillac for her. She had a small older-model sports car. I remember thinking at the time that she didn't really seem all that excited about getting a new car. Maybe she didn't want a large car since she was used to a small one, but anyway, they traded both of their cars and bought the new ones. I've seen her around, like at the grocery store or places like that."

"Okay, Becky. If you think of anything, give me a call," he said as he handed her a card.

"How're your parents and Linda?" Becky asked as he stood to leave.

"They're fine. Dad keeps talking about retiring, but I don't know when he's going to get around to it. Mom is doing fine—staying busy with the church and her volunteer work. Linda is busy with work and keeping up with her two children. You probably know that she and her husband are both lawyers in Cincinnati."

"Yes, I knew that. What about you, Sean? How do you like being back in Bekbourg?"

Sean's business was finished, and he didn't want to linger, "I like being back. It's worked out for me. Now, I'll let you get back to your guest," he opened the door into the foyer. "Call me if anything comes to mind. Take care, Becky."

"You, too, Sean."

Chapter 24

Despite the late hour, Sean pulled into the driveway where Skylar's sister lived. The interior lights burned bright. His arrival must have alerted Skylar's sister, because as he approached the house, she opened the door and walked onto the porch. When she saw Sean, she crushed her hands to her heart. The dim overhead porch light failed to douse the alarm Sean saw in her eyes as he neared her.

"Mrs. Ramirez, I'm Sheriff Neumann. I'm sorry to bother you at this hour."

"Has something happened?" she asked as she reached for the porch rail for support.

"I just came from talking with Simon Montgomery. He hasn't seen Skylar since he returned earlier today from Columbus. I was wondering if we could talk."

Her shoulders sagged as her arms dropped to her sides. "Come in."

As she directed him to a chair, Sean heard a man's voice, "Nat, who's in there?"

Natalia excused herself and walked back the hall. He could hear muffled voices as he looked around the modest living room. It was clean but lived in. Throw pillows were eschewed, and an embroidered throw was partly hanging off the sofa. The floral design on the upholstery was worn, and pathways and patches were worn in the blue carpet. An open bible lay face down on a side table under a lit lamp. Sean wondered if he had interrupted her reading.

Sean was drawn back to the shriveled woman as she walked back into the room. She looked nothing like Skylar. Her haggard face and long drab hair streaked with gray aged her well beyond Skylar's beauty and sleek athletic body. "I'm sorry, Sheriff. My husband was asleep and heard us talking. I told him you had come to talk about Skylar."

A man suddenly appeared from the hallway to stand behind Natalia. From his appearance, he had hurriedly dressed in jeans and a T-shirt that hung lopsided over his left shoulder. His feet were bare. He stepped around Natalia as she moved to the closest chair. "What's going on?" the man scowled.

"I'm Sheriff Neumann, Sir. Mr. Montgomery is concerned about his wife. She wasn't home when he returned from a trip to Columbus. Her car is still there and so is her purse. He thought Mrs. Ramirez might know something about her. What is your name?"

"Luca Ramirez, Natalia's husband. Have a seat, Sheriff."

Sean turned toward Natalia, "Mr. Montgomery said he tried to call you about her."

"He called and left a message. I didn't call him back." Natalia was looking at her hands clinched together in her lap.

"Was there a reason why you didn't return his call?"

Luca spoke up. "You might as well tell him, Natalia. Montgomery's going to find out anyway."

Natalia fingered away a strand of hair that had fallen in her face. "I didn't know what I would say to him. My sister left him."

"Your sister left Mr. Montgomery?"

"Yes. While he was on his business trip, she packed up everything on Friday afternoon and then left before he got back."

"Where was she going?"

"To D.C.—where she lived before they met. She has a job and has already rented an apartment."

"Do you know the name of the apartment complex?"

"No, but she is going back to work at the Pentagon. She worked there before they got married."

"Her husband didn't know about all of this?"

"No. She wasn't going to tell him until she got to D.C. Then, she was going to call and tell him."

"Why the secrecy?"

Natalia shook her head. "She knew he would try to talk her out of it. He is a very domineering man. My sister does not like conflict."

"Did he ever abuse her?"

"No, I don't think so. She never told me that, and I really don't think she would have stayed with him if he did."

"You said she packed her things. Did anyone help her?"

"Yes. Danny Chambers. She rented a truck from Danny. He was going to help her pack Friday evening. She didn't have much. She had a few pieces of furniture that she had before she got married and her personal things, so it wasn't going to take long."

"She left Friday evening?" Sean wondered if she had all of this planned, why he didn't see any indication of her having packed when he was in her house. Also, why was her purse still in her car?

Natalia nodded.

"Have you tried to call her?"

"Why would she try to call her?" interrupted Luca. "She knew Skylar's plans."

Sean turned his attention back toward Natalia. "Do you mind trying now?"

"Of course." She tried calling, but Skylar did not answer.

"What about friends? Is there someone who might know something about her?"

"She volunteers at Mary's foundation twice a week. She worked there Friday morning. Usually, she works until around two o'clock."

"What about any other friends?"

Natalia had pulled out her rosary beads and was nervously thumbing the cross. Her voice had a slight tremble. Luca spoke up, "Sheriff, all these questions are scaring my wife. Skylar should be in D.C. by now. She'll call Montgomery when she's ready. We don't want to be involved."

Luca's reference to his brother-in-law by his last name did not go unnoticed. "I have to follow up. Anything that Mrs. Ramirez can tell me will be helpful."

"It's okay, Luca." Natalia murmured and looked back at Sean. "She never made any close friends in Bekbourg. She played tennis with some women. I don't know their names. Liz and Tanya are her close friends in D.C. I don't know their last names. I know she still talks to them. When she was in D.C. recently, she stayed with Liz."

"How long have Simon and Skylar been married?"

"Over three years."

"Was there another man?"

Natalia's head slightly shook, "I think she would have told me if there was someone."

"Did Skylar have migraines?"

Natalia's eyebrows arched in surprise. "Migraines? No. My sister is healthy. She doesn't have colds or anything like that."

"Mrs. Ramirez, what can you tell me about the relationship between Skylar and Simon Montgomery?"

She sighed. "At first, she was happy, but then things changed. He was very bossy and made decisions without telling her. I think when my sister started to think she had made a mistake by marrying him was when he decided they were moving to Bekbourg. He grew up here. She grew up here, too, but she never wanted to move back. He bought the house where they live without telling her."

"Was she afraid of him?"

"No—not exactly. I think she sometimes found him intimidating."

"When you see them together, what are they like?"

"Oh, we rarely see him. He feels he is too good for us. Skylar and I get together sometimes for lunch or coffee, but we've only been to their house a handful of times for the holidays. He's never been here to our home."

Sean looked at Luca. "Is there anything else you can think of?"

"No. Natalia talks to her sister. Not me."

Sean stood to leave. "Okay. I'm sorry to stop by this late. If you hear from her, please let me know, but also, tell her I would like to talk to her."

Chapter 25

The next morning, Sean called Simon and got the names of Skylar's tennis partners and other people she knew and asked Alex and Syd to talk to them and see if they had heard anything. Sean also called Danny Chambers and ran by his house. Danny owned a successful service station and an antique car restoration business.

Whenever he saw Danny, it took him back to their high school days because Danny's features had not aged. During high school, boys were envious of his good looks, while girls teased the shy boy who was indifferent to his handsome appearance. Even today, Danny could hold his own against any leading-role movie star.

Sean sat back in the wide wooden rocking chair and took in the glistening dew on the colorful display of spring flowers. When Danny appeared with two cups of freshly brewed coffee, Sean ribbed, "You are a man of many talents, Danny."

"How's that?" Danny asked as he sipped his coffee.

"I see you're a landscape extraordinaire."

"Shit. You know better than that." Sean was grinning. Danny chuckled, "I'm just good for hauling things." Danny was married to Sally, his high school sweetheart. Their son, Drew, was a CPA in Bekbourg.

After they talked for a few minutes, Sean said, "Skylar Montgomery's husband called me last night and said that she wasn't home when he got there yesterday, and no one has heard from her. When I talked to her sister last night, she said that Skylar was supposed to rent a truck from you to move some things on Friday afternoon. Did she get the truck?"

Danny scratched the back of his neck as he looked downward. Danny was as loyal as a puppy and would honor her wish. "It's okay, Danny. Her sister told me she needed the truck to move her personal things out of the house. I know about her plans to leave Simon and her desire for secrecy."

Danny was relieved. "Whew. For a minute, I felt like I was between a rock and a hard place. You know I'd never hold out on you, Sean, but I sure don't want to talk about my customers."

"I understand, Danny. That's why everyone in Bekbourg trusts you. That, and of course, no one knows cars better than you."

Despite his success, Danny was the same humble person he had been all his life. "I don't know 'bout that, Sean. Anyway, here's what happened. She came by a couple of weeks ago to rent a truck. She told me she was moving to D.C. so she wouldn't be returning it. She only had a few pieces of furniture, like a couple of small tables and chairs, a chest and her clothes. So, I thought a small cargo van was all she needed. She wanted to make sure the Brigadier didn't find out. I told her I wouldn't tell anyone. I offered to help her load her things, Then, early this week, she stopped by and said that her plans had changed, and she was hoping to get the van on Friday afternoon rather than on Saturday. The van I was going to rent her wasn't scheduled to be back until Friday after six. She was going to call me, and I was going to drive over and help her load everything. She was going to drop me off at the station and leave from there. When I didn't hear from her, I called a couple of times, but she never answered. I thought maybe her plans had changed. I left a message with my personal cell phone number, because I could help out this weekend if she needed me. She never called back."

"How did she seem when you talked to her?"

"She was polite like she always is, but she seemed distracted or stressed, but heck, she was leaving her husband and planning to drive by herself to Washington. I'd say she had a lot on her mind. Wish I had more information, Sean, but that's all I know."

"Okay, Danny. Thanks. Sorry for dropping in on you like this."

"Say, it's no problem. When you called this morning and said you needed to talk to me, it gave me a good reason to play hooky from church."

Sean chuckled, "Does that mean I'm in the doghouse with Sally?"

Danny grinned. "She'd never put you there, Sean. I'm the only one that gets that privilege."

Sean laughed and slapped Danny on his shoulder as he started down the stairs. "Give her my love, and thanks for the coffee."

Chapter 26

Later that afternoon, Sean received a call that a body had been found floating in the lake at the Lake Shore development. The scene near the lake was filled with flashing lights and on-lookers. After checking things out, Sean called in the state's medical examiner and forensics team.

The Brigadier was not in the crowd, so Sean drove to his house. Simon still had on his golf clothes from having played an earlier round. "Come in, Sean. I was getting ready to have a beer. Would you like one?"

"No. I'm sorry, Simon, but I have some bad news."

Simon looked up from pouring the beer, "Oh?"

"A body has been pulled from the lake here. I'd like you to come with me before they take the body."

Simon remained stoic as he set the bottle on the bar and sat down on the bar stool. "You think it's Skylar?" he asked.

Sean said, "I need a confirmation."

Simon closed his eyes for a moment and then looked at Sean, "I wasn't expecting this."

"There will be an autopsy—given the circumstances."

Simon kept his emotions in check as he looked around the room. "I guess an autopsy is necessary," he said as a foregone conclusion. Sean gave him time. Simon's attention finally returned to Sean, "Does her sister know?"

"I came here first. If you want, I can tell her after we finish up at the scene."

"That would be best, I think. I was never that close to her family."

Simon rose, and Sean followed suit.

When the crowd saw Sean and the Brigadier walking toward the ambulance, a solemn silence followed gasps from the curious onlookers. The retired military man's courage was on display as Simon held his head tall and walked to the waiting van. After he confirmed her identity, Sean told him that they would need the forensics team to inspect his property. "Do what you must, Sheriff."

"They will be coming from Columbus, so it may take them a couple of hours to arrive. In the meantime, my assistant, Alex Ogle, will accompany you away from your home until they are finished with their investigation."

Simon trained his eyes on Sean, "Is that necessary, Sheriff?"

"Under the circumstances, yes." Sean's words booked resolve, but then with more compassion, "Until we know more about the circumstances leading to her death, we have to be thorough in our investigation."

"Will I be able to get back in there tonight? What about clothes?"

"I'm sorry, Simon."

"So be it. I'm ready to leave."

Simon turned to walk away, and Sean noticed Harvey Bennett pushing through the crowd to approach Simon. Sean asked Alex to keep Simon company until the forensics team could wrap up. Simon must have told Harvey, because they walked up and told Sean that Simon would be at Harvey's until he was allowed back in his house.

Sean could hear the TV blaring as he approached the door. A man's voice yelled for Natalia to "get the door." When Natalia appeared and saw Sean, her eyes widened in alarm. "Mrs. Ramirez, can I come in?"

"My sister?" she whispered.

"We need to talk, Ma'am."

Luca, slouched in the chair, stiffened and looked at Natalia. "Is this about her sister?"

"Mr. Ramirez, I'd appreciate it if you would turn off the TV. I need to talk to you and Mrs. Ramirez."

Luca complied. Natalia sat on the sofa, and Sean took a seat nearby. Her face had paled, and her hands were trembling as she rubbed the rosary's beads and cross. Initially, Sean thought she might be going into shock—her breathing was shallow and her eyes wide with distress. There was never an easy way to break news about the death of a family member. "I'm sorry to have to tell you this, Mrs. Ramirez. We found Skylar's body in the lake a good ways from their house."

Luca cut in, "What do you mean, Sheriff? We thought she was in D.C."

Natalia looked upward and did the sign of the cross. She gasped and clutched her mid-section and leaned forward. Tears were coming down her cheeks. "Oh, dear Lord, Skylar," she murmured. "Skylar. Skylar."

"Calm down, Nat! Let the sheriff talk. What happened, Sheriff?"

Sean did not appreciate Luca's harshness, especially given how upset Natalia was. "I'm sorry, Mrs. Ramirez."

He explained that Skylar's body would be taken to Columbus where an autopsy would be performed.

She was slowly rocking back and forth, still gripping her stomach. Her face was awash with tears.

Luca straightened in his chair. "Nat, shit happens. The sheriff knows what he is doing."

"Mrs. Ramirez, when was the last time you talked to your sister?"

She continued the rocking motion, unresponsive to Sean's question. Luca spoke up, breaking her spell, "Nat. The Sheriff asked when was the last time you talked to Skylar."

She jerked to face Luca and stopped moving. "When I got off from work the other day, she had come by to see me," she managed to tell Sean.

Luca spoke out. "She came to your work? You didn't tell me she did that. Why didn't she just call you?"

Natalia's eyes widened, and her breathing became more labored, "That's when she told me she was leaving on Friday instead of Saturday. I told you about that."

Slapping her hands across her mouth, she jumped up and ran down the hall to the bathroom. Luca stood and yelled after her, "Nat, it doesn't matter."

Sean wondered why Luca cared that Skylar had visited Natalia at her job but did not think now was the time to ask.

"Mr. Ramirez, when did you last talk to Mrs. Montgomery?"

Luca blew some hair that had fallen in his face. "Hell, I don't remember." He flopped into his chair. "It's been a long time."

"Okay, maybe you should go check on your wife. If either of you can think of anything I should know, call me."

Chapter 27

Rylee's diaries coincided with each school year. In her freshman diary, she began by recording an entry daily, but as the school year proceeded, she did not write every day. The diary entries revealed that Paige was her closest friend with whom she shared her secrets, but she and Paige frequently hung out with other girls. As the diary's words came alive, Cheryl could envision the girls over milkshakes or during sleepovers swapping views on boys, girls, styles, makeup, classes, and school activities.

It wasn't until she started into the sophomore year's diary that the journal entries became germane.

October 7. *Hi, Diary. EXCITING NEWS! I was running to beat the bell so Cranky Gilbert wouldn't give me detention. Maybe I should take her an apple! Haha! I ran right into a senior football player. So embarrassing! He and another boy started laughing. The best part is he put his arms around me so I didn't fall. I'm still tingling! Oh my gosh! He's such a man! He didn't even move when I ran into him. Wish I'd been wearing a varsity cheerleading banner rather than JV! He might have talked to me. So glad Cranky Gilbert didn't call on me. The kids would have laughed cause no way was I paying attention. I messed up on a cheer during practice cause I couldn't get my mind off him. Paige teased me and kept bugging me about my dreamy smile. I didn't tell her—yet!*

October 8. *Bummer!!! I saw dream man talking to some football players. He didn't even notice me. Sigh! Who is he taking to the Homecoming dance? Wish I was the lucky girl! But no way Big Sis would let that happen. Can't date til I'm 16—that stinks! During the pep rally, I only had eyes for him. I cheered extra loud when they called his name. Paige and the other girls looked at me like I was silly—who cares.*

Sherrie Rutherford

October 19. *Oh, my gosh, Diary. I have such a crush! I look for him all the time in the hall. My heart sank when I saw him walking with Jen. Don't know if they're going steady. Sure hope not! He doesn't know I'm alive. Wish I wasn't too chicken to say something to him. I'd feel like dropping through a hole if he ignored me or laughed at me.*

January 4. *Back to school blues! Boring! Cranky Gilbert— yuck! Dream man doesn't know I exist!*

January 15. *Dear Diary. Slept over at Paige's last night. I hinted I was crushing on a senior football player. I didn't dare tell his name, but we spent all night giggling. I so wanted to tell his name but can't risk it. I'd have to drop out of school if she let it slip. I'd be a laughing stock. Paige will be the first to know if I get enough courage!*

February 14. *Valentine's Dance and guess who didn't get invited by her dream man? I'm desperate. Maybe I should run into him again. Maybe a second time would be a charm. He might think I'm an air head. He's so mature. He shaves, his voice is like a man. He is strong. He is PERFECT! This stinks so bad. If only . . .*

March 16. *Oh Diary. My heart is broken wide open. I heard him tell his friends he got into the college he wanted. He'll be leaving Bekbourg. It's hopeless.*

Paige's recollections were confirmed that Rylee wanted a boyfriend.

April 2. *Spring break was awesome! Paige and I had a blast at the beach. Cute boys! Especially Jonathon and Stan! Too bad her parents wouldn't let us go out with them, but we had fun swimming and playing Frisbee and volley ball. I need to find a real boyfriend. Like they say there's a lot of fish in the sea. Found that out at the beach. Haha! I can't be the only girl next year without a boyfriend! No more mother may I after Robyn leaves for college. Look out boys! Here I come! Wish me luck Diary!*

Sherrie Rutherford

May 8. *I found the one!!! At the church high school picnic. Hogan Slater was playing catcher and stopped the game to show me how to bat during the softball game. We started laughing so hard, the pitcher yelled at Hogan to hurry up. When I hit the ball, I screamed with excitement and forgot to run. He told me to run to first base. He was laughing. He pretended to be in slow motion as he went to get my ball— which only went about three feet! I made it to first base before he threw. His team was yelling for him to throw and get with it. I went up to him after the game and told him thanks. He stopped talking to the other boys and started talking to me. He's a junior! I'm in love Diary!!! The girls will be so jealous! I've got to dress cute tomorrow! Makeup and hair peeerrrfect! I'm jittery about talking to him tomorrow at school, but I got to try. He's perfect!*

May 10. *I did it, Diary! I said hi to him, and he knew my name!!! We were still talking when the bell rang and had to rush to class. This is it! I know it is—fingers crossed!*

May 21. *I'm floating on cloud 9! At the school picnic today, Hogan came up and started talking. We stayed with each other the rest of the picnic. He said he looked forward to seeing me at church tomorrow. I can't wait! I felt like we were a couple. Everyone was looking at us. Oh, Diary. My heart is fluttering. My dream may be coming true!*

July 2. *It's official Diary! We're going steady! He gave me his class ring. I put tape around the back to hold it in place. I can't wait to show it off at church tomorrow. I'm his girl!!! Robyn has let me double date with Paige and her boyfriend. Hogan seems okay with my big sister's rules, but I told him she was leaving for college soon. I called Paige as soon as he left. She and I were screaming on the phone! She and Ralph haven't gone all the way yet. Hogan's kissed me, but that's all. When we start dating by ourselves, we can do more. The other girls are. I don't want to be left out.*

Sherrie Rutherford

I'm going steady! Repeat the refrain!!!

Cheryl was now to the part of Rylee's diary where her junior year began.

September 2. *I am so happy. I cheered extra loud when Hogan went into the game tonight. The other cheerleaders were laughing. After the game, we went to Frau's with Paige and Ralph. It's like we're married, just not living together. We've been talking a little about what it would be like to be married. I can't wait. He's hoping his dad can get him a job with the utility company when he graduates. I told him I wanted lots of babies. He laughed and liked the idea. I can tell he's a little worried about the draft, but that's why we need to get married and start a family fast! When he drove me home tonight, we sat in his car and French kissed for the first time. The other girls had talked about it. Now, I can talk about it, too! I pushed my chest into his when he kissed me. He didn't touch me, but I wouldn't mind if he did. Paige and Ralph went all the way this summer. Since we're going steady, if Hogan wants to, count me in!*

September 25. *Sorry I've been ignoring you, Diary, but it's been crazy. Hogan's the one! Everyone knows I belong to him. When I walk up to him at school and he's talking to friends, he stops and pays attention to me. I cheer for him when he goes in the game. When I go to his parents' house for lunch after church, it's like we're already married. I help his mom in the kitchen, and he and his dad are somewhere talking. His little sister Joy is so cute. I showed her a cheer. Even their dog Bingo likes me! Now for the juicy part. We went to a drive-in last night and kissed the whole time. He didn't try anything, so maybe he thinks I'll get mad. I may hint at it soon. I've been practicing writing Mrs. Hogan Slater.*

November 12. *WE'RE ENGAGED! Oh, Diary, he asked me to marry him! It was soooo romantic. He took me to the GilHaus for dinner and then we went to the park and he got down on his knee and proposed. It's hard writing because I can't keep my eyes off my ring! I started squealing. He was laughing and asked if that was a yes. I jumped on him kissing him and laughing. He finally got to put the ring ON my finger. It was chilly but who cared. We sat in the gazebo and decided everything. The wedding is the first weekend after I graduate from high school. I already know my bridesmaids. We want four kids! I told him I wanted two girls and two boys. He was laughing and kissing me. We talked about baby names! I AM SO EXCITED! I told him that since we're engaged, I would be okay if he wanted to do it. He wants to wait for our wedding night for it to be extra special. I told him okay, but I won't lie. I was disappointed. Paige and some other friends have already done it. Maybe he'll change his mind. But, I'M ENGAGED!!! I called Paige about being a bridesmaid, we kept screaming! I want to remember this day FOREVER!*

Chapter 28

Ronnie Vin, with the state's forensics' department, and Dennis Douglass, DD as he preferred to be called, from the state coroner's office, were on a conference call with Sean. The three had worked together on some complex cases since Sean had joined the sheriff's department. Alex, Sean's assistant, sat in on the call.

DD continued, "Sean, it looks like the body was in the water about thirty-six to forty-eight hours. The cause of death was drowning. When the victim hit the water, she was still alive, but I can't say if she was conscious. There was a mixture of alcohol and anti-anxiety medication in her system, which could have impaired her judgment or physical abilities." Sean remembered seeing the bottle in her purse and asking that forensics examine its contents. "Given that she was dressed in a skirt, pullover cotton sweater and leather shoes, I think we can rule out swimming. We found something else. There was a bump on the back of her head. I'll send you a drawing of the exact location. It wasn't hard enough to break the skin, but it could have rendered her unconscious. Based

147

on our exam, I think it was fairly recent. It was the size that it would be if you raised up and hit your head hard on a cabinet door."

"Did it appear she had eaten recently?"

"She had eaten a small amount of chocolate shortly before she died."

Ronnie picked up the conversation, "Sean, we don't know how she got in the lake. It had not rained in the three days leading up to her death, so there were no slippery surfaces on the deck from precipitation. The canoe was moored to the side post when we arrived. We brought it to the lab. No water marks were found, but given the temperatures, if she had been in the canoe, it would have had time to dry. We found fingerprints from both Mr. and Mrs. Montgomery, but no indication of blood or tissue or anything to lead us to believe that an accident or struggle occurred in the canoe. The edges of the boards making up the deck of the pier are angular, so I think if she fell and hit her head there, it would have left a gash. The pier posts are rounded, so if she slipped and hit her head, it's possible it would not have lacerated the skin. But she may have hit her head earlier."

"What if there was a struggle, and she hit her head?" asked Sean.

"That could have happened, either on the pier or somewhere else," replied DD.

"Another thing, Sean. We found a cell phone in the skirt's pocket."

"Her husband said she kept her phone with her, so when we found the body, I contacted the service provider. I should be hearing from them soon with her phone's activity."

"Good to know," said Ronnie. "Maybe that will shed light on what happened. Getting to DD's point about the chocolate, we found an opened box of chocolates in a cabinet. We tested it, but nothing unusual showed up. The box held sixteen chocolates, and ten were missing. Fingerprints belonged to the victim and her husband. There was also a bottle of wine in the refrigerator which was two-thirds empty. Nothing unusual about the contents, and again, the fingerprints belonged to the victim and Mr. Montgomery."

"So, that could have been the chocolate she ate soon before her death."

"The timing would work. Also, we found dirty dishes in the dishwasher which we tested. There was a coffee cup with only the victim's fingerprints. There was a small bowl that had contained some premixed yogurt and fruit, which only had her prints as well as a spoon. There was also a wine glass, which had residue of the wine we found in the refrigerator. That glass had both the victim's and her husband's fingerprints. The rest of the dishes had both of their fingerprints. My guess is that she put the clean dishes in the cabinets, and that her husband fixed something for dinner Saturday evening and breakfast Sunday morning. Those dishes had both of their fingerprints. This is purely speculation, but based on the dishwasher's contents, I think she started a new load with breakfast Friday morning. The dishwasher was about three-quarters full."

"What about the wine glass? She could have had wine the night before?"

DD weighed in, "Yes, but the wine glass also had her husband's fingerprints."

"Mmm. I need to follow up with her husband to see if he remembers seeing the glass or the chocolates since they both have his fingerprints."

"Were you able to find out if something was going on in the lake that could have caused a current to transport the body that far away from their house?" asked Ronnie.

"Yes, I talked to Harvey Bennett, the developer, and he said they had the spillway open from the heavy rains earlier in the week. He showed me on a map, and the current is consistent with where we found the body."

"We figured it had to be something like that if the body went into the water there at the house."

"Yeah, I had the county engineer with me when we talked to Bennett. I think we can assume she went in at the pier behind their house." Sean asked, "She went to college on a swimming scholarship, so she was a strong swimmer. How likely is it that she could have drowned even if she had the combination of medication and alcohol in her system?"

"It's possible, Sean. It's hard given the condition of the body and the length of time in the lake to know the exact levels in her system at the time. The question is why was she in the lake fully dressed? If she accidently fell off the pier, it's possible that she was impaired to the extent she couldn't make it back in, but that is not a far distance. Of course, if she was unconscious, then we know the answer to that. If she accidently fell and hit her head on the post, it might have stunned her, or knocked her unconscious. If she was merely stunned, given the substances in her system, that might have impeded her from getting back to shore or the pier. Certainly, her clothing could have affected her ability to swim out. What we can confirm is that the cause of death was drowning."

"What can you tell me about the bottle of anti-anxiety mediation?"

"It was a thirty-day supply. The bottle in her purse was a second refill on a three-refill limit filled twenty-seven days ago. There were twelve pills missing from the bottle, so it doesn't appear she took it on a regular basis. The prescription was first prescribed and filled nearly four months ago." Ronnie gave Sean the doctor's name.

"You mentioned the wine bottle. Was there evidence of other alcohol at the house?" asked Sean.

"There were some beer and wine bottles in the trash, both in the kitchen, in the game room downstairs, and in the outside trash bin. The only prints we've found belong to Mr. and Mrs. Montgomery. We went through all the trash. The trash in the house had not been emptied in about three days—our best guess."

After they completed the call, Sean and Alex went to see the doctor who prescribed the medication for Skylar. He told them that he couldn't go into details, but that he had prescribed the medication, a thirty-day supply, to be refilled three times. When she came in almost four months ago, it was her first visit. She explained to him her marital relationship and said that she was having a difficult time. A friend of hers had suggested she get a medication that could get her through the rough personal time. The physician told them that, based on his judgment, giving her the medication was justified. Sean described the number of pills she had taken since it was first prescribed, and the doctor was not alarmed. He told Sean that it sounded to him that she was judicious in taking the medication even though it appeared she was taking it more frequently since the second refill.

After they left the doctor's office, Alex asked Sean if he thought she had committed suicide. Sean said that he couldn't rule out anything. He told Alex about his conversation with Mary Zimmstein. Because they were extra busy at the foundation that day, Skylar did not leave until almost four o'clock. Skylar did not take time for lunch.

"So she must have taken the pill and drunk the wine on an empty stomach?" Alex asked.

"It appears that way."

"How did she seem to Ms. Zimmstein?" asked Alex.

"Good question. She said Skylar seemed different—edgy and even irritable or impatient. She had never seen that in Skylar. She chalked it up to the unusual flurry of activity. Skylar insisted though in staying and helping Mary get everything finished. Mary had no idea of her plans to leave Bekbourg."

"Chief, it just doesn't seem like someone who committed suicide."

"We have to keep an open mind. It's possible that when she got home, the weight of her decision to leave her husband overwhelmed her."

They also discussed that another possibility was she walked to the pier out of a sense of nostalgia since she was planning to leave that night and would likely not return. She had obviously taken some anti-anxiety medication to take the edge off the stress she was feeling. Because of the mixture with alcohol, she lost her balance and struck her head and fell in. "Even if she wasn't unconscious, with the drugs and alcohol and the heavy clothes, she couldn't make it out."

"But, if she was struggling with someone and fell and hit her head, that person could have panicked and pushed her in the water, or it could have been intentional," offered Alex.

"Yes, or she fell, and the person didn't know how to get her out," Sean reasoned.

"That too," agreed Alex. "But, we don't know if she already had the bump on her head."

"No, that's right. There is a lot we still don't know. We need to find out if anyone was up there. Let's drive by and talk to the guards at the gate leading into the Lake Shore development and see what they can tell us."

"Sheriff, her sister said that she was planning to load her things that evening and leave. It seems odd that you didn't see anything packed, like her clothes or her personal things, when you got there Saturday evening."

"I've been thinking about that, too. Danny was going to come over and help her pack. Maybe she was waiting for him to get there and have him help her. She didn't appear to have all that many clothes. It's also possible she was going to start packing after she went to the dock *if* she walked down to it. If she was concerned that her husband might come home early from his trip, she wouldn't want her things packed up for him to see. That tells me she was waiting until Friday to pack, but she ran late getting home from Mary's foundation, so maybe she did just need some time to unwind and walked to the pier and lost her balance."

Alex was silent until he asked, "Do you think the Brigadier knew she was planning to leave?"

"He had to have heard from someone at the Pentagon. I can't imagine he didn't, but I plan to ask him when we see him."

Chapter 29

Sean and Alex parked off to the side and walked up to the guard gate. Sean introduced Alex and got the guard's name. "That was sure terrible about Mrs. Montgomery. Hate it, just hate it. Can't think what the Brigadier must be goin' through."

"It must have shaken up people around here?" Sean probed.

"Oh, sure did. Ever'one that comes through here is talkin' 'bout it."

"Do you know of any conflicts Mrs. Montgomery had with anyone who lives up here?" asked Sean.

The guard's eye rounded, "You thinkin' someone did somethin' to her?"

Not wanting the rumor mill to start churning, Sean answered, "You know how these things go. We have to ask all the questions and cover all the bases."

"Oh, sure. No, I can't think of anyone who might be at loggerheads with Mrs. Montgomery. She was a nice person."

"Which hours is the guard booth staffed?"

155

"From eight o'clock in the mornin' 'til midnight. There're three of us who rotate shifts. Eight hours per shift, and we rotate days off since there are three of us."

"Who was working on Friday, the day she died?"

"I worked from two on that day. The other guard had a dentist appointment. We cover for each other like that." He gave them the name of the other guard who had worked earlier that day.

"Do you keep a log of everyone entering and leaving?"

"Ever'one enterin'. The residents have a remote to the gate here and can drive through that lane there if cars are waiting in this lane, but we have a video of every car comin' in. For everybody else, they stop here just like you did, and we write their names." The guard hesitated, "I didn't mean you, Sheriff. I ain't goin' to write your name."

Sean smiled, "It's okay. Wouldn't bother me if you did. After you log their names, do you let them through?"

"Depends. If our residents give us their names ahead of time, we let them through without calling the resident. But, if we don't have approval to let 'em through, we call the home to make sure the resident okays it."

"What about the Montgomerys? Did anyone visit them that day, or were there any people on a preapproved list that went in to see them?"

The guard opened a binder. "Let's see here. I don't see anyone that came in that day to visit them. Now, let me look at the preapproval list."

He pulled out another binder. "Yep. Their landscape company is preapproved, but they only come on Thursdays."

"What about housekeeping?"

"No, none of that for them. Oh, yeah. Mrs. Montgomery's sister and her husband—Mr. and Mrs. Ramirez. They were preapproved."

"Did they come often?"

"I can't say how often since I ain't here all the time, but she came a few times around lunch time when I was here."

"What about Mr. Ramirez—did he come often?"

"I hardly ever saw him. I think maybe he came to help with somethin' 'round the place. They have a big lot with lots of trees. Also, he's handy with fixin' things."

The guard paused. "Let me check somethin'." He paused and turned to another page. "That's what I thought. Mr. Ramirez was here on that Friday."

This surprised Sean. "Was his wife with him?"

"Nope, just him."

"What time?"

"It was in the afternoon, kinda late." He told Sean the time.

"You happen to know why he was coming to see Mrs. Montgomery?"

"No. It was hectic that evenin'. Someone was having a lot of company for dinner, so I was busy checkin' them in."

"Is their place near where the Montgomerys live?"

"No. They live on the other side of the lake."

"Any idea when Mr. Ramirez left?"

"Nope. We don't have a video camera that records cars leaving."

"I'd like a copy of the list of everyone who came through that day, including anyone preapproved."

"Sure thang, Sheriff. You need for me to git it right now?"

"We're going to drive up to see the Brigadier. Can you have it for me when I get back?"

"Sure. Not a problem. I got a small machine here I can make copies."

"That's good. One other thing—I am going to need the video of everyone entering that day."

He told Sean he'd call him as soon as he had it.

Chapter 30

As he drove toward the Montgomery place, Sean wondered what business Luca Ramirez had coming into Lake Shore that evening. It was odd that he had not mentioned it when Sean went by to tell them of Skylar's death, but maybe he forgot, or maybe he intentionally did not tell Sean. Was it to see Skylar, and if so, why? Or, was he coming to do work for someone who lived there? He was doing odd jobs, so it was possible that he had a business reason. They needed to find out.

"Sean, Deputy, come in. Have a seat. You said there was something you needed to ask me?" Simon said.

"How are you doing?" Sean asked.

"Well, it is a shock. Skylar was a beautiful young woman. It's tragic. Of course, she was my wife, so I also have those feelings to work through."

"These things are never easy, despite the circumstances."

Simon cocked his head, "Is there a hidden meaning there, Sheriff?"

"Were you aware that Skylar was planning to leave you?"

Simon's eyebrow arched. "Huh, I guess her sister told you that. Look, Sean, there is a significant age difference between me and Skylar. I knew that when I proposed. Like most couples, we had our ups and downs. We went through a rough patch a couple of months ago, but we were working through things. Skylar is." Simon shook his head. "I find it difficult to think of her in the past tense. Skylar was an independent woman. That was one of the things that drew me to her."

"It was more than that, Simon. She was planning to move out while you were in Columbus and drive to D.C. She had taken a job with the Pentagon."

Simon paused. "Are you sure about that?"

"Yes."

"You've surprised me with that one."

He offered them something to drink. They both declined, but he poured himself a beer. "If she was planning to leave me, maybe she just needed some breathing room. I would certainly have tried to talk her out of it, but if she needed time, I would have worked with that too. In the end, we would have worked things out."

"You know a lot of people at the Pentagon. I'm surprised you didn't know."

"Not what you are telling me. I told you we went through a rough patch a while back. It started because I did get a call from someone who I knew there and who knew Skylar. He thought we were planning to move back when he called to ask me about her interviewing there. It came as a surprise to me. I raised it with her, and she confirmed that she was talking to them. But I thought part of our understanding was that we were going to work on fixing our marriage. I didn't know she was continuing to pursue that."

"Who was it that called you?"

Simon hesitated. "I hope you understand, Sean, but I don't want to give out his name. I don't want to involve him in this. You know how funny the Pentagon can be about talking outside the campus."

"We'll leave it like that for now, Simon, but I may need his name at some point."

"Understood."

"My information is that she planned to leave that evening. That she was renting a truck and was going to load her things Friday evening. You didn't see anything packed when you got here on Saturday?"

"No, nothing. The house looked just like you saw it."

"The medical examiner said she had eaten chocolate soon before her death."

Simon's left eyebrow slightly arched. "Huh. Now that you mention it, when I got home, her box of chocolates was sitting on the countertop. There was also a wine bottle and glass sitting there. I put the glass in the dishwasher and the wine in the refrigerator and the chocolate box in the cabinet where she keeps it."

"You didn't think to mention that to us?"

"No. Every afternoon, Skylar had this thing. She would eat two pieces of chocolate and drink wine. When the weather was nice, she'd go down to the pier and sit and enjoy her ritual. The rest of the time, she sat over there." Simon pointed to a chair and drink table tucked in the corner next to a large window overlooking the lake. Distinct from the rest of the décor, the chair and table were smaller in stature and feminine in flair. "Skylar wasn't one to always pick up after herself, at least not immediately. So when I saw it there, I just automatically put everything away and didn't think about it until you mentioned it."

"The autopsy results came back. There was a combination of alcohol and drugs in her system."

Simon's nonchalance gave way to protest, "Drugs? No way in hell would Skylar be taking drugs. There's a mistake somewhere."

Sean observed Simon. "The drugs were a prescribed anti-anxiety medication. The bottle was in her purse the first day I came by. You didn't see the bottle in her purse?"

"I didn't look in her purse. I respected her privacy, just like she respected mine."

"You didn't know she was taking an anti-anxiety medication?"

"No. She never told me. I find this hard to believe. Skylar is, was, just short of being a health fanatic."

"How did she seem to you? You were around her more than anyone I've talked to."

Simon leaned back and took some time to answer. "If you had not just told me about the medication, I would have said she was fine. But, thinking back, I did notice that she was not her usual self. She still exercised on the equipment downstairs nearly every day and swam and canoed some now that the weather is warmer, but she seemed distracted. Maybe depressed is a better word. She was drinking more than usual, but certainly not to excess or to the point she was impaired."

"What alcoholic drinks did she usually drink?"

"Mostly beer or wine around here. When we went out to dinner, she might have a scotch or martini."

Simon's eyes sharpened. "You're not suggesting that Skylar committed suicide?"

"I'm not suggesting anything, Simon."

Simon nodded.

"Okay, Simon. The coroner will be in touch about returning the body to you."

"Thanks, Sean. I don't mean to take my frustrations out on you, but it's rougher than I like to admit."

"I understand, Simon. Call me if you think of anything."

Chapter 31

Sean and Alex's next stop was to talk with Natalia. Sitting across from her, he pondered what life's burdens had bowed her shoulders and stymied joy from her heart. It was hard to envision her smiling since an inverted frown marked her face.

She fingered the rosary beads. Sean asked if she was aware of Skylar taking anti-anxiety medication. Sean leaned forward to better hear her. "She told me she got something from the doctor. I didn't know what it was. I knew she was unhappy, but I thought it was temporary until she got settled in Washington."

"Did she confide in you about their relationship?"

She shook her head. "Skylar never told me a lot. She knew I didn't care for him. Skylar didn't like confrontation, so I doubt they argued much. She silently carried her emotions. She could be mad at someone, and they would never know. Once she reached a boiling point, then she would take action." Sean noticed tears trickling down her cheeks. "She finally decided she could no longer take living with him and made arrangements to leave him. She didn't spend a lot of time talking to me about the details."

"Did she tell you that they went through a difficult time a couple of months ago and were working to save their marriage?"

"No. All I knew was she wanted out and she had a plan to leave over the weekend."

"Do you think it's possible she changed her mind?" Sean was thinking about nothing being packed.

"No."

"Did you see her often?"

"Sometimes when Simon was gone, like out of town, or golfing, I'd go to their house for lunch. In the summer, we'd sit out on the pier. Other times, we'd meet somewhere for lunch. We tried to see each other about once a month—maybe more if Simon was gone."

"What about your husband—did he go there often?"

Natalia looked confused by the question. "There were a few times that Skylar would need something done when Simon was gone. One time, a large branch broke off during a bad storm, and Luca went out and cut it up and hauled it away. One time when Simon was gone deep-sea fishing for a week, Skylar decided she wanted to plant flowerbeds and needed some help. Things like that. But, he didn't go there often."

"What about Friday?"

"Friday? The day she disappeared?"

"Yes."

Sean saw her confusion morph into alarm. She stammered, "I, he. He wouldn't have gone there. There was no reason."

"Was it possible that he went there and didn't tell you?"

"There must be some mistake if you think he was there Friday."

"Where was he Friday?"

She thought about the question. "He had a job that morning. I also worked that morning and got off at noon. We had lunch here. I don't know what he did that afternoon. He might have been looking for a job."

"So, you had lunch together here?"

She nodded.

"When was the next time you saw him?"

After thinking, she shook her head. "He came home around ten that night. Sometimes he goes to Knucklepin's. That's where I think he probably was."

"What was their relationship?"

Her eyes pleaded to end the questioning. "He helped her out sometimes, like I said. She always paid him. It's not that they didn't get along so much as they didn't have anything in common. They didn't have much to say to each other."

"Where is Luca?"

"I don't know. He didn't have a job today."

Sean changed the topic's direction, "Mrs. Ramirez, do you think Skylar would have done something to herself?"

Her mouth formed an "O" as her head shook. Her words faltered, "No. No. She would never do that."

Her knuckles were white from her grip on her rosary beads.

"Mrs. Ramirez, I know these questions are difficult, but I have to ask them. I know you want answers to what happened to Skylar. If you think of anything, let me know."

Luca's vehicle was spotted at Knucklepin's by one of the deputies. Sean decided that was as good a place as any to talk. Percy, the long-time bartender, was wiping the bar when Sean entered. "Hey, Sheriff, how are things?"

While walking toward the bar, Sean replied, "Just fine. Looks like you're busy tonight." Sean glanced around the dimly lit room. Customers were sitting around scarred and scratched round oak tables in battered dark oak chairs. Plastic salt and pepper shakers, napkin holders and condiment containers provided tabletop decor. The bartender greeted his patrons from behind a long, plain oak bar. Some of the customers opted to sit at the bar on the round bar stools bolted to the dark hard wood floor.

"Yep, can't complain. I see you're in uniform. Don't suppose you want anything?"

"Not tonight. I see someone over there I need to talk to. You take care."

"You, too, Sheriff."

As Sean moved toward the table, the noise level dropped as the patrons watched with curiosity. Once he came to stand at the table where Luca sat, most people went back to their business. Sean spoke, "Evening, men."

Murmurs around the table greeted him in return. Sean eyed Luca, "I need to talk to you."

Knowing they weren't invited, the three other men did not wait around.

Sean sat opposite Luca, "You didn't mention you were at the Montgomerys the evening Skylar died. Why not?"

He shrugged, "Didn't see a need to. I drove up there, and no one was there, so I left."

"What time was that?"

"I don't know what time, but it was getting dark." He looked pointedly at Sean. "The guard there probably has a record."

He did not know if Luca was fishing, but Sean was not going to tell him he had talked to the guard. "Why were you there?"

Luca wiped his forehead with his hand. "The night before, Nat asked me if her sister could spend the night on that Friday night. I didn't want us to get involved and told her 'no.' During the day on Friday, I got to thinkin'. She was movin', and Nat might not see her for a long time. Once she graduated from college, she never came back here. I decided to go up there and tell her to come by and stay the night."

"You didn't see her?"

"No. I didn't see the moving truck, so I thought she might have already left. Nat told me she might do that. I walked around back just to make sure no one was there. I left."

"How long were you there?"

"I don't know, man. Just long enough to see that she wasn't there."

"Did anything look strange?"

"No."

"Were there any lights on in the house?"

Luca considered the question. "I don't remember. I rang that fancy doorbell twice and then walked around back. No one was there, so I left."

"Where did you go after that?"

"I came here."

"Did you come straight here?"

"Hell, I don't remember. I may have driven around some. I just know I was here."

"The other day when I talked to you and your wife, you seemed angry that she didn't tell you Skylar came to see her about the change in plans. Why's that?"

"I just felt she should have told me. I thought Skylar had called. That's all."

When Sean continued to look with inquiring eyes, Luca blurted, "You're not accusin' me of havin' somethin' to do with her drowning?"

"No, Mr. Ramirez, I'm not accusing you of anything, but I do need to check things out. If you think of anything, here's my card."

Chapter 32

"I'm sorry, Ann. I should have made that bid."

"It could have happened to anyone, Lucia. The distribution of the trumps worked against you."

Kye, Lucia, Ann and Milly, all retired teachers, were enjoying their weekly bridge game. Lucia smiled, "You're being generous. My mind is not where it should be."

Kye suggested, "Let's take a break and have cookies and coffee. Lucia, you and I are partners next. It'll be our time to win."

Milly spoke up, "Are we changing partners?" Milly was hard of hearing.

"Yes, dear," said Ann, "but we're going to have some coffee and eat Kye's homemade cookies."

Milly stopped shuffling. "Kye makes the best cookies. These are shuffled," she laid down the deck.

Once Kye had served everyone, Ann asked Lucia, "Dear, did you have Skylar Montgomery in your class?"

Lucia smiled ruefully, "How did you know she was on my mind?"

Ann sipped her coffee, "Oh, let me see. She was a student, and as teachers, we always carry a memory about each one. It's never easy to hear these things, no matter how long ago they were our students."

"That is so true," said Lucia. "I never had Skylar, but I am close to her sister, actually half-sister."

"That's Natalia?" asked Kye.

"Yes. Those girls had such a difficult time growing up."

"What was their situation?" asked Ann.

"Their mother grew up very poor. She was a waitress at Frau's, and when she was fifteen, she met a man who worked harvesting crops. She got pregnant with Natalia. Unfortunately, her parents were put off by him being Hispanic and turned their backs on her. He married her, and they moved into an old mobile home. I don't know anything about him, but when Natalia was about four, he was killed in a car crash. Natalia's mother wasn't stable. Natalia's memories of her mother drinking were there from the beginning. Skylar was born when Natalia was almost eight. Natalia didn't think her mother even knew who Skylar's father was. Natalia took care of Skylar best she could.

"When Natalia was a high school junior, she met her husband, Luca, who was a few years older. He worked as a maintenance man for Randall

Thompson, keeping up all those mobile homes in Acorn Knoll. Natalia told him that she would only marry him if Skylar could live with them.

"I think because I am Hispanic, Natalia gravitated to me in high school, and we have stayed in touch. Natalia is intelligent. She loved reading. Still does. When she was taking care of their mother, I took her books from the library and returned them for her. Anyway, she had two miscarriages. The last one left her unable to have children. Luca worked hard and provided for them the best he could, but he is overbearing. He didn't want Natalia working, but as soon as Skylar was fourteen, he wanted Skylar working. Natalia felt he resented Skylar and having to support her. Natalia refused to let Skylar work. She wanted her to make good grades and stay on the swim team. Skylar was a star swimmer.

"Well, Skylar left for college on the swimming scholarship and never came back. She and Natalia stayed in touch, but Skylar was busy, so it wasn't all that frequent. Natalia and Skylar's mother was diagnosed with the early-onset of Alzheimer's, and Natalia brought her into her home to care for her. I went over to help her when I could. She not only had the stress of caring for her mother, but Luca was resentful. By then, Skylar was married and working. Luca thought Skylar should have been helping out financially so they could put their mother in a care facility or at least bring in a caregiver. Natalia wouldn't dream of asking Skylar. I doubt Skylar even realized how bad it was. Natalia cared for her for about five years until she passed away."

"Bless her heart," Ann murmured.

"I know," said Lucia. "She has been through so much."

Kye poured everyone more coffee. "Natalia must have been very happy when Skylar moved back here."

"Oh, she was, but from what she told me, Skylar wasn't pleased about it. She loved D.C., but her husband wanted to get involved in some business deal, and so they moved here."

"I wonder what happened with Skylar? Do you think it an accident?" asked Ann.

"Mmm." Lucia took a sip of coffee. "That's why I am distracted. I saw Natalia yesterday. I'm afraid she is close to a nervous breakdown. She said the sheriff asked her if Skylar might have committed suicide. That's out of the question in her mind."

"What about an accident? Could she have slipped and injured herself and accidently drowned?"

"I asked Natalia if she thought it could have been an accident. She didn't know."

"Well, if it wasn't a suicide and it wasn't an accident, doesn't that mean someone caused it?" Kye frowned. Ann pursed her lips, and Milly, who had been following the conversation by partial hearing and reading lips, looked expectantly at Lucia's lips.

Lucia shrugged her shoulders.

"If someone was involved, does Natalia have any ideas who?" inquired Kye.

"And why?" followed Ann.

"If she does, she didn't say. I assume if she does, she told the sheriff. She was so upset. She told me she couldn't talk about it anymore. I really am worried about her. She's always been frail, but she is wasting away. She is religious, and the thought of Skylar dying alone, drowning, is talking a toll on her."

The women had finished their refreshments, and they helped Kye take things to the kitchen.

Ann asked Lucia if she felt like playing the final round. "Of course. I need to redeem myself."

"Alright," Kye chuckled. "Let's see who deals."

Cheryl and Sean set up a small table out back of the duplex and invited Kye to join them for Sean's special grilled BBQ chicken. Cheryl made a salad and cornbread, and Kye insisted on bringing brownies. Buddy lay on the ground waiting his turn for leftovers. The warmth from the small firepit kept the coolness of the evening at bay as the sun set once again. The crisp spring night would soon give way to summer's pasty heat and pesky insects.

Kye was halfway through her meal when she said, "I have a name for your diner, Sean, when you retire as sheriff."

Sean's lips shifted in a left-sided grin, "Yeah?"

"Sheriff Sean's BBQ Chicken."

Cheryl and Sean broke out in laugher. "I'll write that down, Kye, so I don't forget."

"Be sure you do, Sean," Kye grinned. "It's a guaranteed winner—both the chicken and the name."

Another round of laugher rang out.

"If you don't want to talk about it, Sean, just tell me, but Skylar Montgomery's death has been on my mind. She was one of my students—a smart and talented girl. I was happy when she got that scholarship to go to college. I knew she could make something of herself."

"Did you have her sister?"

"No, but a friend of mine did who is a retired teacher—Lucia Delgado. She was talking about the family situation during our bridge game."

"What did she have to say?"

Hearing what Kye told him filled in some blanks. He now understood why the two sisters did not resemble each other.

Chapter 33

Reading the diary made Cheryl sad. Rylee filled almost every page with plans for her wedding and her dreams of their future. The writings described the house she wanted and plans for decorating it. She and Hogan even had planned names for their first child. Although she shared in her diary her occasional frustration that Hogan was delaying intimacy until their wedding night, they were a happy couple and shared their exuberance with those around them.

However, Rylee's life turned upside down in December.

December 14. *Oh, Diary. I saw HIM at Frau's when I was with Mom and Robyn. My heart started fluttering. I didn't want Mom and Robyn to notice, but I couldn't stop looking at him. He is such a man! He must be home for Christmas break. He told his friends he'd see them at the Christmas parade. I'm engaged to Hogan. Why am I feeling like this about him?*

December 17. *I hope I didn't make a mistake. I was at the parade and needed to go to the bathroom in the drug store. He saw me and started talking. I don't think he remembered me. He told me he was on break from college. He asked if I'd like to go out sometime. I told him yes and gave him my phone number. Maybe he won't call. What if he does? I can't believe I would two-time Hogan. If the phone rings, I'll have to answer. Robyn and Mom can't find out. I'm so confused.*

December 21. *I can't think, so I'm just going to write. I met him tonight. I parked in the Shopper's Pavilion lot to meet him. I got there early so I could put on makeup and make myself look older. I left my ring at home. While we were eating, he did most of the talking about what college was like. I tried not to think about Hogan. He asked me if I wanted to go somewhere and have a beer. I didn't want him to think I was a kid, so I said sure. Oh, God. He*

177

took me to a motel. I was so nervous, but I didn't want him to know. Anyway, Diary, I guess you can guess what happened. He was surprised when he saw it was my first time. After that, he treated me like I was special. I finally told him I needed to get home. He drove me to my car. Mom and Robyn were in bed, thank goodness. If Robyn asks in the morning, I'll just tell her that Paige started feeling sick, so I didn't stay the night.

December 22. *Diary, I don't dare tell anyone about everything but you. All day, I've felt different. Robyn asked me if I was okay. I told her I might have the same stomach virus Paige had, so I stayed in my room all day thinking about last night. I feel so different today. I'm a woman now. I keep thinking about him. I guess since he and I did it, I should tell you who he is. I'll call him B since it's the first letter in his name. I don't think Mom or Robyn will ever read you. God, I've never been so confused in my life, and alone. I can't tell anyone about this. Not now. What if I never hear from him? I don't want Hogan to find out.*

He'd break up with me for sure. I can't even think what the girls might say. Even Paige might turn on me. I've got to find a way to act normal. He knows it was my first time. Maybe he'll decide he likes me. He told me he'd call. I can't date two guys, can I? What to do?

December 27. *You won't believe this, Diary, but B called me yesterday, and we met again. I think he likes me. He was gentle with me this time. We talked afterwards. He told me he wanted to see me again before he left for school. He has to get back early. We're meeting again tomorrow. Robyn left yesterday to go on a short trip with her friends, so I don't have to worry about her getting suspicious. Mom doesn't need the car at night. I haven't seen Hogan since Christmas. We've talked on the phone. I told him I was with Paige. I want so bad to tell Paige, but I just can't. Not yet.*

December 29. *We went to the motel again. He gave me a phone number for his dorm room when I asked if I could call him sometimes.*

He told me he had a roommate so try not to call much. He told me he might come home for spring break, and he'd like to see me. I told him I'd like that too. B is so grown up. He didn't mention going steady, but maybe he will soon. What if B decides he wants us to get married? Oh, God, what will Hogan do when I tell him? I know I want B.

Cheryl was surprised Rylee never told Paige more about B, because the diary entries bore evidence of her distress.

January 4. *Hi, Diary. School is a real drag. I don't want to cheer at Friday's basketball game. I'm trying to act normal, but Paige wants to know what's going on. She thought something is wrong between me and Hogan or with my mother. I can't stop thinking about B and what we did. It's so hard to act normal around Hogan cause I don't want to break up with him, because I want to get married, but if B asks me to marry him, I'll marry him. Life is mixed up right now. I wish I could tell someone, but I can't. I'm afraid*

Mindset of Murder

Paige might be mad at me for doing Hogan this way.

February 1. *I haven't heard from B since he left to go back to college. I hope that doesn't mean he forgot about me. He said we would see each other over spring break. He's probably just busy at school. I miss him, but I'm busy doing things with my friends and Hogan. Paige and I bought our dresses at the Shopper's Pavilion for the Valentine's dance. She was surprised I wasn't more choosey. Guess why.*

February 26. *I'm scared Diary. Real scared. I just realized today I've missed two cycles! What if I'm P??? What am I going to do??? I have to tell B. I've got to call him cause what if he doesn't come home for spring break? I've not talked to him since December. If I am P, then he'll marry me. No way will Hogan want to marry me. God, I can't think about telling Hogan! What will Mom and Robyn think? What will Hogan's parents think of me? Paige? The kids at school? Oh, Diary.*

March 6. *I tried calling him, and his roommate kept telling me he wasn't there. I finally told him it was urgent. Oh, God. I know B didn't want to talk to me cause the roommate covered the phone and then B answered. I asked him if he was coming in for spring break. He was mad and told me he had other plans. He was getting ready to hang up, and I couldn't help it. I yelled I was pregnant. I was crying so hard. He didn't say anything. He finally asked why I was calling him when it was Hogan's. I don't know how he knew about Hogan. It was terrible. He was so mad at me. I told him that it wasn't Hogan's, he should remember our first time together. He accused me of lying and trying to trap him. I started crying again and told him that it wasn't Hogan's. He told me he couldn't talk, but he'd change his plans and come in over spring break and we'd work it out. I could tell he wasn't happy, but maybe, before he gets here, he'll realize we need to get married. His parents are important people here. We could elope. Oh, Diary. I won't care what people say as long as he marries me. He'll marry me. I know he will. It's his baby.*

March 17. *B finally called me back today and asked if I still thought I was pregnant. I told him yes. He wanted to know if I'd told anyone. I told him I hadn't, that I wanted to talk to him first. He said that he was coming in for spring break. I'm going to meet him tomorrow at the park after dinner. He said we'd talk it out. He wasn't mad like before, but he was in a hurry. Hope this means that we're going to get married soon. Maybe I'll be Mrs. B before this time next week. Cross my fingers!*

That was Rylee's last diary entry. *What happened the next night?* Cheryl wondered. Rylee had borrowed her mother's car to meet B—the police found the car at the park. Did she call Hogan before that meeting, but why would she do that? In any event, Hogan was home watching TV with his parents. If B told her he was willing to marry her, would she have called Hogan to tell him, and they met at the park where Hogan struck her and then committed suicide by train? But why call Hogan that night to tell him? And, why would B have left her alone? Did B leave Rylee thinking she was going home? Did she drive somewhere and call Hogan and they met back at the park—where she told him that she was marrying B? What if B didn't agree to marry her? Was it possible that B killed her, but why would Hogan have killed himself?

That night during dinner, Cheryl told Sean about Rylee's diary and what she had learned from conversations with others. He was intrigued with her research. "You seem pretty sure that it wasn't Hogan who struck her, but maybe the police's conclusion was correct."

"Why do you say that?" she asked.

"Well, the first thing is you don't know who called him at home that night. From what Milly said, whoever called, it didn't seem to rattle him. He told his parents he would be back soon. What if it was Rylee who called him? What if she told him to meet her in the park? I could see at least two scenarios there. One is that after she told B she was pregnant, he agreed to marry her, and Rylee wanted to tell Hogan and get it over with. The second is that B refused to marry her, and she panicked and called Hogan to meet her at the park to tell him and plead for forgiveness. In either case, think about this from Hogan's standpoint. She tells him that, one, she's breaking up with him, or two, she's pregnant, when he would know the baby was not his. Even a mild-mannered guy like Hogan is going to be shattered by the news. Maybe he did impulsively hit her like the police said?"

They ate in silence while Cheryl gathered her thoughts. "I thought about that, and it could be what happened. But why would she have decided to tell him that night? Wouldn't she have at least told her mother and sister first?"

Sean tilted his head, "Possibly, but not necessarily. Perhaps she just wanted to get the hard part over—which would be telling Hogan."

"There is that, but from what I could tell about Rylee from her writings, she was in over her head, and under either of those two possibilities, I'm not sure she would have thought to tell Hogan that quickly."

"Another question: What if B suggested she go ahead and tell Hogan, if B had decided to marry her?"

"If that was the case, wouldn't B have hung around to be there when she told him?" Cheryl asked. "Wouldn't B have been prepared for Hogan's reaction?"

"Good point," admitted Sean.

"Something Jules told me is what makes me think Hogan didn't commit suicide, and if he didn't, then that makes me think that someone other than Hogan hit Rylee," said Cheryl.

"What's that?"

"Jules said that when they came around the curve as they were coming into town at the crossing, Cecil had already blown the horn, which is very loud, but when they saw the body lying there, he laid on the horn until he was past the body. You know how loud that can be."

Sean shook his head. "Those horns can even make windows vibrate in nearby buildings."

"Right. Sean, Jules said the body never flinched, and they could see it clearly by the train's bright headlight. In his opinion, to never even flinch, Hogan was either passed out from alcohol, unconscious, or dead. According to the coroner's report, no drugs or alcohol were in his system."

Sean took a sip of coffee. "So, your point is that he was either unconscious or dead. Rylee, by herself, could not have put him across the track."

Cheryl nodded, "That's my thinking."

"So, what is your next step?" Sean asked.

"To find out who B is."

Chapter 34

The starting point was to identify B. From what Cheryl knew, he was in the grade ahead of Hogan—two grades ahead of Rylee. He was on the football team, and his name started with B.

Cheryl went to the county library and found yearbooks for the years that Rylee was a sophomore and junior. She was transfixed by Rylee's class picture, a girl frozen in youth by her untimely death. A dimple accented her infectious smile and hinted at her spunkiness. Cheryl willed the photo to disclose secrets, but of course, none were revealed. Cheryl scrutinized each page before moving to the next. Her breath hitched when she came to the varsity cheerleading team photo. The photographer captured Rylee laughing as she stood surrounded by the others. Standing taller than most with long blonde hair bouncing at her shoulders, Rylee's beauty demanded attention. Next to her stood Paige—their arms intertwined. On the adjoining page, impromptu photos caught Rylee looking out to the field and an action shot of her jumping as the team led the cheering fans.

Cheryl then turned to the section featuring senior class photos. Hogan was a handsome, wholesome young man. Could rage erupt from the innocence that peered back at her, Cheryl wondered. Unlike most of his unsmiling teammates, Hogan grinned with ease. He was spotlighted on two other pages, one of him escorting a homecoming princess and on the senior class officer page. Cheryl also found class pictures of Hogan's best friends, Chad Earnst and Austin Towman.

Turning to the preceding year book, she searched for names in the senior class that started with a B for members of the football team. Billy Abbott and Baxter Colbert were the only two who fit the criteria. While there were other senior boys whose first or last names started with a B, she didn't focus on them since they were not football players. Cheryl looked for other pictures of Billy and Baxter. Billy had been voted Most Likely to Succeed, while Baxter had been selected Most Athletic. When Cheryl returned to her office, she learned both men still resided in Bekbourg.

She decided it was time to publish the story and see if anyone came forward with additional information. Her next step would then be to interview Billy and Baxter.

Photos of Hogan and Rylee appeared at the top of the front page article in the *Tribune*.

Mindset of Murder

*What really happened to
Hogan and Rylee? New Questions
Emerge Nearly Forty Years Later
by Cheryl Seton*

*It was spring of
1967. Hogan Slater was
a senior in high school, a
member of the Schriever
High football team and
an active member in his
church. Right after his
graduation, he had a job
waiting with the local
utility as a lineman. I've
spoken to several people
who remember Hogan
and describe him as a
young man popular with
his classmates and eager
to volunteer with youth
groups at his church. He
had an engaging
personality and a kind
heart. He was in love
and looking forward to
marrying his high school
sweetheart when she
graduated from high*

school the following year.

Rylee Flowers, his fiancé, was a junior in the high school and a member of the varsity cheerleading squad. She was a stunning young woman with long blond hair and a dimple that was ever present, because there was always a smile on her face. According to those close to her, students and adults alike were drawn to both her magnetic personality and her vivacious energy.

Even with the Vietnam War shadow looming over the country, Hogan and Rylee were making wedding plans and discussing names for the children they planned to have. Their time together was brief but filled with young love and enthusiasm for their future together.

Mindset of Murder

Something very terrible happened, though, the night of March 18, 1967, that ended their dreams and shattered the lives of those who knew them. According to the police reports, conclusions were reached that Hogan and Rylee were together in the county park, and for reasons unknown to this day, Hogan hit Rylee hard enough to make her fall and hit her head, causing her death. The police then theorized that Hogan laid down on the railroad track and waited for the nightly train to take his life as it passed on through Bekbourg on its way to Cincinnati.

New evidence has come to light which casts doubt on the police findings. What now appears likely is that Rylee was planning to meet a man that evening at the park, but it was not Hogan. Whoever hit her did so with such force that she fell and hit her head on a rock, killing her. That evening, Hogan received a phone call while watching TV with his parents. They never knew who called him that night or why, only that he abruptly left after assuring them he would return home soon. Only, he never did.

Jules Leroux, a railroad employee who was on the train's engine that night, said that the engineer frantically blew the horn when they saw something laying in the track, but there was no movement. The train could not stop in time to avoid running over the body. He has questions about the suicide conclusion, though, because "generally if someone wants to commit suicide, they just step out in front of an oncoming train. They don't lie down on the track and wait." Why was Hogan's body lying on the track? Was he unconscious, or already dead?

Those familiar with the case have recently come forward and raised questions about the police investigation. Through a preliminary review, it appears that further investigation into this tragedy is warranted. If anyone has any knowledge they think might help, please contact the writer at the Bekbourg Tribune.

Chapter 35

The nickname, "Dusty," stuck early on in Dusty's time with the railroad because his nervous energy kept the dust stirred up on surfaces from the tapping of his fingers or things he held and from his foot's pumping when he was sitting. Not only that, but his rapid speech, and lots of it, sometimes ruffled the feathers of the other railroaders. Sitting at the table with Dusty were Mule Head and Chaw. Railroaders were forever giving each other nicknames. Chaw got his from always having a chaw of tobacco resting in his jaw, and Mule Head because he was about as stubborn as they come. Chaw, a conductor, had recently retired from the railroad, and Mule Head had retired years earlier on disability from injuries received during a train wreck. They were regulars at Frau's for breakfast and sometimes at dinner. Dusty joined them most mornings after he'd worked the night shift or before heading out on a day run. Jules was another frequent member, and occasionally others would wander in.

Anita had just filled their coffee cups and headed to turn in their orders, when Dusty popped the question that had been on his mind since reading the morning's *Tribune*, "Did you all see that article in the paper this morning about those kids that died several years ago?"

Before the other men could answer, Jules walked in and headed toward the table. Chaw piped up, "Look who it is. We didn't think you would be here being such a celebrity. We thought you'd be taking kudos down at the courthouse."

As Jules approached the table, he took a bow, "At your service as usual, gentlemen."

Jules tucked his napkin in at his collar and looked at the menu. Anita hurried up. "Same as usual, Jules?" she asked.

"Yes, fair Anita. Thank you."

She poured him some coffee and headed toward the kitchen.

Dusty's leg was bouncing—as he had a fork in one hand and a knife in the other ready to attack his food, which had yet to be delivered, "Well, are you going to tell us about it?"

"Tell you about what?" asked Jules as he wiped his silverware off with his napkin. Jules cleaned the engine cab every time he got on the train to make a run. The men were accustomed to seeing him wipe off the eating utensils.

"Why didn't you tell us you had been interviewed about this story about that boy being hit by the train?" asked Dusty.

"There are a lot of things I like to talk about, and I would like to be in the spotlight for a lot of other things, but this is not one of them. I take no joy in this notoriety." Jules responded as he sipped his coffee. "I wasn't sure when it was going to show up in the paper. There are things we don't really like talking about that much."

"Tell us about what happened that night in your own words. The paper doesn't really say that much," urged Dusty.

"Well, we were heading into town. We had a new brakeman with us. Bart Fedders was the brakeman."

Chaw piped up, "Bart the Fart Fedders? That old stinker? I remember him. About as clueless a man I ever knew."

Mule Head hooted. "Ain't that the truth? Remember when one of the men buried a knuckle pin in the bottom of Bart the Fart's grip. Those damn things weigh about twenty-five pounds. He carried that knuckle pin around for a month before he found it."

Dusty said to Mule Head, "I can't believe he didn't notice *that*. Even you would notice something like that."

Chaw and Jules laughed as Mule Head shook his head.

"What I remember about Bart the Fart," said Chaw, "was that his wife was always there at the station when the pay checks were handed out to get his. I bet that poor SOB never saw a dime from his checks."

Dusty wanted to get back to the newspaper story, "So anyway, Jules. What happened?"

"Well, like I said, we were heading into town that night, and I was telling Bart about the railroad and how we were making up time coming through Bekbourg and explaining how Cecil was getting ready to slow down, and the next thing we know, Cecil is yelling that something's on the track. He's blowing the horn and putting the train in emergency. I think he instinctively knew it was a person, but there was no way he could stop the train in time." Jules took a sip of coffee, "I had just told Bart about the hog story."

"Oh, no, not the hog story," groaned Chaw.

Jules stayed on track, "Bart was pretty freaked out about that, and then this happened. What was really strange about this whole incident was the young man didn't flinch or anything— never moved a muscle. Even when we got right up to him, he still never moved a muscle. We tried to tell the police that, but they decided it was suicide, even though we never thought it was."

"What do you mean he didn't move? You thought he was passed out?" asked Dusty.

"Just what I said. He didn't look alive."

"I know what you mean," said Chaw. "We've come up on dead animals on the track, and they don't even flinch."

Everybody at the table stared in silence at Chaw. Dusty cocked an eyebrow and deadpanned, "Really?"

Chaw looked around the table, "Whuuut? You know what I mean."

They all shook the heads.

"Chaw, you've been retired too long," quipped Dusty.

Mule Head decided to move on, "Well, why did they say it was suicide?"

"Well, the body was so mangled that they didn't have evidence of anything else. They could have named it anything. As it turned out, it fit perfectly about that young lady. Anyway, Cecil was beside himself. I took the train on into Cincinnati for him, and he didn't work for two weeks. He took two weeks' vacation. He was really shook up. It shook me up too, but not like Cecil."

Chaw nodded, "Yeah, I remember that. Everybody was talking about that, thought he was going to retire early. They had an inquest. Only took one day. They decided it was suicide."

Jules said, "I don't like talking about this, but to this day, I don't believe it was suicide."

Chapter 36

Sean received a print-out of incoming and out-going phone calls from Skylar's cell phone and their house phone. Skylar and Simon rarely used the house phone. The phone calls to and from the house phone were inconsequential as related to the investigation. From her cell phone, Sean saw that Skylar and Simon had not spoken by phone since he left for Columbus on Thursday afternoon. Sean saw where Skylar had talked with Danny. No recent phone calls were recorded between Skylar and her sister. Two calls she recently placed to D.C. were made to a rental truck company and the other to an apartment complex. Skylar had called a phone number in Arlington, Virginia, several times over the last ten days, and Sean learned that the phone number belonged to a woman named Liz Kruse. Sean recognized "Liz" as a name of one of Skylar's good friends mentioned by Natalia.

He was planning on calling her, but she called him first. "Sheriff Neumann, my name is Liz Kruse. I just read on the internet that Skylar

Montgomery drowned. Oh my God. I can't believe it. Skylar was one of my best friends."

She told Sean that they had worked together for years at the Pentagon and that they had stayed in close contact after the Montgomerys moved to Bekbourg. She was expecting Skylar to arrive in D.C. When she couldn't get in touch with her, and the apartment complex told her that she had not arrived, she checked on-line on the local newspaper and saw the story.

"Sheriff Neumann, this doesn't make any sense. Skylar was an excellent swimmer. Reading between the lines of the story when it talked about a mixture of drugs and alcohol being in her system, it looks like someone is thinking she either died accidently or by suicide. In my opinion, that's barking up the wrong tree."

Sean smiled. The soft luring cadence of her thick southern accent leisurely recast a two-syllable word into three—and turned a three-syllable word into a mouth-full. A reminder flashed of his friend, Clint, who spoke of climbing a "te-ree" hoping to wait out his momma's wrath for busting his brother's nose when they were kids.

"Let me assure you, Ms. Kruse," he said to allay her concerns, "that I haven't reached any conclusions. I'm trying to get to the bottom of what happened. You seem certain that it wasn't accidental or intentional. Why do you say that?"

"I know Skylar."

"She was going through a rough time, leaving her husband."

"Of course it was a rough time, but so was it when her first husband was killed."

Sean thought she had a good point there. He admired her spunkiness despite her grief—delivered with a determination to assuage him of any notion that Skylar took her own life. "Her sister told me you and Tanya were very good friends with Skylar. Maybe you can answer some questions."

"Ask away."

"What can you tell me about Skylar's relationship with her husband?"

"I assume you don't want to know their intimate details?"

Sean laughed, "No, you can skip that."

"Your call." Even though Sean was alone, he shook his head. "I'll start from the beginning, if that'll help."

Sean leaned back in his chair with a large notepad and pen. "Okay."

"Skylar left Bekbourg after graduating from high school and moved to Columbus to attend college on a swimming scholarship. There, she met a boy who was in the R.O.T.C. program. After college, they married and moved around for a few years. She was able to pick up jobs on the various bases as a civilian assistant. Her husband was on assignment in Bosnia. He and three men were on patrol, and he stepped on a land mine and was killed. Skylar enjoyed working for the military and applied for a position at the Pentagon. With her experience and being the widow of a fallen soldier, she got the job.

"That was about eight years ago. I was assigned to show her around the first day she was here, and we had drinks that night after work and have been friends ever since. At first, despite me and Tanya encouraging her, she wasn't interested in dating. T and I were worried that she wasn't able to move past her deceased husband, and all her beauty and personality would go to waste. *Finally*, she started going out with some guys, but nothing serious.

"Then, one day, a new prince charming walked into the Pentagon, or so we all thought. At first, she wasn't sure she wanted to get involved with Simon since he was a lot older, but he didn't look his age. 'Throw your hat in the ring' I said to her, 'and see what happens.' She finally went out with him, and of course, it was to the nicest French eatery in D.C. He didn't spare anything in his courtship of her.

"Fast forward. They got married, and at first, everything was hunky-dory. He took her on a big fancy honeymoon overseas, and they moved into his spacious condo here in D.C. He didn't want her to work, so she gave up her job." Sean heard her sigh. "In retrospect, I should have thought more about that, but I figured they would be traveling and living the good life. Little by little, T and I noticed when we all got together that something wasn't right. She wasn't her peppy self. I guess Simon had lived by himself so long that he just took for granted he didn't need to talk to her before he made decisions. He'd plan weekend trips or make dinner plans for them without telling her and expect her to go along. What really got to her was that he couldn't stand for things to be messy. Skylar wasn't a slob, but things lying around or hanging haphazard in her closet didn't bother her, if you get the picture. She told us she finally insisted that he quit harping on her about the way she kept her clothes hanging or folded.

"Where things really started to go south in the relationship was when he up and decided they were moving to your town there. He just dropped it on her. She cried that night at dinner when she told us. Apparently, he assumed since she grew up there, she would like to move back. That's the last thing she wanted. Sure, her sister lives there and she loves her sister, but it held bad memories from her childhood. He even had bought a house without her getting a chance to see it. He told her he wanted to surprise her, but Tanya and I thought he maybe just wanted things his way.

"After they moved, she felt isolated. She didn't want to reach out to people there, because she didn't want to be there. She called me a few months ago and told me she just couldn't take it anymore. The final straw was that he was putting pressure on her for money. She had a nice nest egg from her first marriage. She came to realize that Simon was all about putting on airs. Acting like he had more money than he did. Acting like he hobnobbed with big shots. Well, there was some guy in Bekbourg who Simon wanted to do a deal with, Harvey someone. She didn't want any part of that, and she wasn't about to let go of her money. She came from poverty so she knew the importance of a safety net. That's when she contacted someone here at the Pentagon and asked for a job."

"I don't understand. Why didn't she just tell Simon that she wasn't going to loan or give him the money?" Sean asked.

"Well, that's where it gets interesting. That house there is in Simon's name. Simon has a second mortgage on it. She didn't know this when they got married, but he had invested a lot of money in something in South America with some of his buddies. Turned out to be a *really bad* investment. As Skylar told me, he was over-extended, and he wanted to do the deal with Harvey because it was a sure thing and he saw a fast return. Skylar thought he was about to lose everything, and she wanted no part of that. She had finally had enough."

"Did they have a pre-nuptial agreement?"

"Yes. She told me that they kept their financial affairs separate, and what belonged to her before the marriage was hers and vice-versa. He didn't have any claim on her money except through the will, but since that was changed, he didn't have any rights to it even if she died."

"So, she was leaving him and planning to file for divorce?" asked Sean.

"Yes, once she got up here. She already had retained a lawyer to handle the divorce. The lawyer had already written a new will for Skylar."

"She had already changed her will?" Sean asked.

"Yes, she had, and Skylar signed it. Here's what happened. When Skylar and Simon got married, they had an attorney draw up wills where if one died, the other one got the estate. Skylar kind of felt guilty doing that because she had her will made for her sister to get everything, but she went along with it. If she didn't already have a life insurance policy made out to her sister, I don't think she would have, but it's a nice chunk of change, so she did. I know how much she cares about her sister, so I told her to get the will changed right away."

"Do you know if her sister knows about any of this?"

"I know she knows about the life insurance policy. I don't know if she knew about Skylar's will. One more thing since I'm on a roll. Skylar never cared for Nat's husband. She thought Nat could have done better for herself. He had this macho thing. He didn't want her to work outside the home, and he controlled all the money, only giving her enough to run the house. She was dependent on him. Then, he lost his job about two years ago, and finally, when they were about to lose their home, she went to work. Skylar gives her some money on the side, but he'd blow a gasket if he knew. She even told Nat to leave him and move in with her in D.C."

"Was Natalia thinking about it?"

"I don't think so. Skylar was not sure how long they could keep their house, and he was climbing higher and higher on the jerk scale."

"You said Skylar never wanted to return to Bekbourg because of bad memories. Do you know what those were?"

"It was a rough childhood. Her mother couldn't care for her, and then being raised by Natalia where Skylar felt resentment from Luca. Natalia tried hard to do the best she could, and Skylar knew that. She told me getting that swimming scholarship gave her the break she needed. Once she left, she never wanted to go back. She didn't even go back for her mother's funeral. So, you can see why she would be unhappy with Simon for moving them back there."

"Did you know that she was taking anti-anxiety medication?"

Sean heard Liz blow out a puff of air before answering, "Yes. When I said she had been through a rough time when her first husband died, that was true, and no one will ever convince me she committed suicide. But Skylar was under a lot of stress. We talked about it the last time she was in D.C. Just making the decision to leave Simon and then trying to get back on with the Pentagon and then finding an apartment and working out the move—it was a lot. Then, of course, she was dreading Simon's reaction. She thought he would hound her to hell and back. She told me about getting the prescription. She thought it would help her until she got past everything. She never intended to take it on a regular basis—just to get over a rough spell. When I talked to her about three weeks before she died, she was down in the dumps. We talked about everything she had to do. She told me that she had been taking more of the pills. I told her that once she was settled in her new apartment and on her job, she wouldn't need them anymore, and she agreed."

"Did Skylar mention anything to you about her and Simon trying in the last couple of months to patch up their marriage?"

"No. She *never* mentioned that, and I'd find that hard to believe."

"Did she tell you that someone at the Pentagon told Simon about her trying to get a job there?"

"No. I guess I wouldn't be surprised if that happened, although people should not be talking outside the walls about employment matters, but a lot of people knew him and her."

"What do you think his reaction would have been?"

"Gosh, I don't think he would be happy, but once Skylar made up her mind, I don't think he could have talked her out of it."

"One other question. Do you know if Skylar suffered from migraines?"

"I never heard her say anything about that. I don't think so."

"Okay. I'm glad you called. If you think of anything else, call me."

"I will, and I'll talk to Tanya and see if there is anything else, but Sheriff Neumann, Skylar would not have taken her own life. She was going through a rough time, but she had a plan, and she was excited about returning to D.C."

Before they hung up, Sean got Tanya's contact information. No one that Sean talked to knew of Skylar having migraines. He had even circled back to her doctor to see if he knew about that being an issue, and he didn't. Sean was beginning to think she wasn't enjoying being at the dinner with Harvey and Becky and used that as an excuse for not being overly social.

Chapter 37

Each time Sean saw Natalia, she seemed more drawn and forlorn. She had a skeletal quality with her weight loss, and crevices had replaced the wrinkles in her face.

"Come in, Sheriff. Let me get you some coffee."

"Only if you're having some."

Her hands trembled as she set the coffee in front of him.

"Mrs. Ramirez, did Luca know of the life insurance policy that your sister had in your name?"

"Yes, Skylar did that a long time ago. He knew, but Sheriff Neumann, he would not kill her," she pleaded.

"What do you know about her will?"

"I never thought about it. She took out the life insurance policy when she went to work at the Pentagon. I don't know anything about a will."

"Did you know that Skylar had a will that left everything to you?"

Natalia eyes widened. "No, I did not know that."

"Who did you think was named in her will?"

"I have no idea. We never discussed it." That could be, thought Sean. Before Skylar married, Natalia would have been her closest heir. After she married, Simon would have been—absent a will saying otherwise.

"There were hard feelings between Skylar and your husband."

She looked at her hands but remained silent.

"I need for you to tell me about that."

She slowly raised her head. Sean saw the strain in her eyes. "They never argued, if that's what you mean. When they were together, they mostly ignored each other. Luca complained to me about her; he thought she looked down on him. Skylar never said much about him to me."

Sean watched her, "But, she wanted you to leave him."

Natalia looked at Sean with surprise. She wanted to ask how Sean knew, but instead said, "Yes. She wanted me to move to D.C. with her."

"Were you planning to?"

She looked out the window, "No."

"Did Luca know she wanted you to move to D.C.?"

She was startled by the thought. "You haven't told him, have you?"

"No."

"Do you know if anyone has?" she asked.

"Not that I know, but you don't think he knew?"

"Nooo. We never talked about it around him." She looked into Sean's eyes. "I know what you are thinking, but Luca did not kill my sister."

"Would Luca have told Simon that your sister was leaving and moving to D.C.?"

Natalia considered the question, "I don't think so. The only time they ever talked was when we all four were together, and that was rare. Even then, they hardly spoke to each other. Luca mostly stayed quiet. He sometimes went outside to walk around, but her husband never went with him."

"Did Luca tell you why he went there that evening?"

"That night after you asked me about it, I asked him. He told me he went there to tell her she could spend the night at our place. She asked me about spending the night. At first, I didn't want to ask Luca. But then, I got worried because I didn't think she should be driving late. That's why I asked him."

"Do you think he went there to ask her to spend the night?"

"Luca can be selfish, but he also has a good side. He knows I love my sister, and he is not heartless. I never saw her after she left Bekbourg. With her going to Washington, I knew I might never see her again. I said that to Luca the night I asked him if she could stay with us. I believe what he told me, Sheriff."

Chapter 38

"Hey, Jules, has the newspaper lady asked you anymore about that boy being killed by the train?" Dusty asked as Jules walked up to join the railroad gang for breakfast.

"No." Jules sat and tucked his napkin in at his neck. The three men looked at Jules as he picked up the menu and began his studious review.

Mule Head shook his head, "It's the same menu every morning, Jules."

Jules ignored them. Anita came up and refreshed everyone's coffee, "Your usual this morning, Jules?"

"Yes, fair Anita. I think I will have the two eggs over easy, bacon, hash browns, and the toast light."

"You men want a refill?" she asked as she moved to pour more coffee.

After she walked away, Mule Head looked at Jules, "Something I never understood, Jules, is why you call her 'fair Anita.' Isn't 'lass' what they call women over there?"

Jules pulled back his shoulders, which were already ramrod straight, "'Lass' is not French."

"Even I knew that, Mule Head," said Dusty. "It's English, isn't it?"

Chaw added his two cents, "I thought it was Scottish."

About that time Sean walked in, and Dusty yelled over for him to join them. "Sit down, Sean. We got this large table. There's plenty of room."

Anita came and poured Sean coffee and took his order. "How are things with all of you?" asked Sean.

Chaw spoke up, "This retirement thing is getting old."

Sean grinned, "Already? It's not been four months. How come?"

"My old lady has this list of things she wants done around the house, and now that it's getting warm, she's got my nose to the grindstone."

Jules asked with a glint in his eye, "How many lists does she have?"

"Too damn many," grunted Chaw.

Dusty hooted, "You might start to wonder how you ever had time to work on the railroad by the time she gets through with you."

Except for Chaw, who was scowling, the men were laughing.

Mule Head spoke up, "Well, if you need something to do, you can help me get everything set up for the big car show at the fairgrounds."

"Oh, it's about that time of year," said Jules. "I enjoy looking at all the cars that Danny Chambers brings. He has some real beauties."

Mule Head swiped a napkin across his mouth, "He sure does, but nothing tops that 1969 Dodge Charger Daytona that the Brigadier brought to the show last year."

Sean perked up, but before he could ask about it, Jules said, "Now, that is some car."

"That's because there were only a few hundred made," Mule Head was a car enthusiast. "That is the ultimate muscle car. Slick as can be. Had that tall tail on the back. The Brigadier's was the first one I had ever seen. Took my breath away to see a machine like that. Those babies could flat scream."

Jules spoke up, "I had never seen one either. It was certainly in mint condition. He told me his father gave him that for a birthday present when he was in college, and he's had it all these years. We were talking about how rare it is. He had offers from people wanting to buy it but said he wouldn't ever part with it. I can see why."

"Hell, I sure wouldn't if I had it," said Mule Head.

"Does he drive it?" asked Dusty.

"Well, he drove it to the show. He told me he drives it some," Jules said as he took a sip of coffee.

"I'll be sure to look for it this year," Dusty said. "I had to work last year and didn't make it."

"Well, I hate to bust your bubble, but he's not bringing it this year," said Mule Head.

"Huh? Why not?" Dusty was disappointed.

"I don't know. I just heard that he wasn't bringing it. We were going to make a special place for it like we did last year, because everyone wanted to look it over."

Jules said, "It could be that he's not in the mood with that beautiful wife of his dying."

"That could be the reason," said Mule Head. "I was sure looking forward to seeing it again."

Sean remembered seeing the empty garage space at Simon's house. He wondered where Simon's collector car was.

Chapter 39

The Brigadier slammed down the phone. "Damnit! I've had it with those damn accountants. I'll find somebody else." He walked to the bar and poured a double. The day had gone from bad to worse. First, he received a call from an attorney in D.C. who got his name from Natalia. She informed him that Skylar had changed her will before she died, and at the request of Natalia, she was giving him a "courtesy call" that Skylar was leaving all of her belongings to her sister. That included all of her personal things, which were in his house. He wasn't going to take that sitting down, he had told the lawyer. They had a will drawn up when they married. As far as he was concerned, that was still valid. She told him that he was free to contest the new will, but everything about it was legal. He'd assured her that he would "see her in court."

Now, his accountants were refusing to play ball and fudge financial reports just enough to gloss over that bad Venezuelan investment that had drained him. The private investors who he met in Columbus were insisting that his accountants provide financial reports. Part of their "due diligence" they said. He had just gotten off an hour's-long phone call with his accounting team. He needed them to remove from the report the records about that damn investment in Venezuela. Once the projected returns started rolling in from Harvey's "Lake Meadows" investment, he'd be solvent again. His financial woes were temporary.

Interrupting his brooding was the sound of an approaching vehicle. He walked to the front door and looked out the side panel. "Shit! Neumann is the last person I want to see." He moved back to the bar and poured another splash, waiting for the doorbell to sound.

He took his time in answering the door.

"Simon, I have some questions I need to ask you," Sean announced.

While Simon was stoic as usual, Sean noticed something was different. His face was tight and flush, and it seemed early in the afternoon to be nursing a scotch.

"Let's have a seat. What's this about now?" asked Simon— pointing Sean toward a chair.

"I understand that Skylar recently changed her will leaving everything to her sister."

Simon shrugged, "I just learned that myself from an attorney in Washington."

"That must have been a disappointment. From what I understand, she had a nice nest egg."

Simon lifted his glass to take a drink, "She had money when we got married. She could do with

217

it what she wanted. Nothing to me one way or the other."

"You couldn't have used the money?"

Simon took his time as he savored another sip. "Sheriff, what is it with you? Last time you were here, you were asking about my marriage. Now, you're asking about Skylar's money."

"I understand that you asked Skylar to use her money in the investment that Harvey is planning. That you didn't have the funds."

Sean waited him out. Finally, Simon replied, "I don't know what you've heard, but whatever it is, you're misinformed."

"You didn't try to get Skylar to loan you some money?"

"She was my wife. But, I never expected her to do anything she wasn't comfortable with." He shrugged, "So, I moved to plan B, and it's all in the process of working out."

"What is plan B?"

"Now, Sheriff, I'm not about to talk about confidential matters."

Simon picked up his glass, "I need to get another drink." He stood and turned his back to Sean, "I think you'd be better off doing what the county pays you to do, and that is catching the bad guys. That's not me."

Chapter 40

"Hey, Sean, I understand from Cheryl that Skylar Montgomery drowned. That's too bad."

"Yes, it is, Milton. Say, what are you doing calling in to your boss on your honeymoon?"

Milton chuckled. "You would too if you worked for her," he teased about Cheryl.

Sean could not help but grin thinking about Cheryl as a boss.

Milton continued, "Martha and I are here in Surf City for a day or two. Then we're going to Charleston. She has a sister there. After that, we'll start heading back."

"That's great to hear."

"Yeah. I don't want to leave Martha too long sitting by the pool. One of those men might make a move."

Sean laughed. "I don't think you have anything to worry about Milton. She only has eyes for you."

Sean heard Milton huff, "Want to keep it that way. You remember me telling you that I had an old newspaper buddy who might know something about the Flynn Taggart case?"

"Yeah."

"Well, as it turns out, Devin Petru and his wife still live in Jacksonville, North Carolina. He's semi-retired, but he's keeping his fingers in the business like me. He covered the reporting of Montgomery's wife's murder. He made me copies of all the articles. I'll put those in the priority mail to you tomorrow. He covered the murder investigation and the court martial. But, Sean, he told me some interesting things. One of Devin's buddies, Nate Kamisky, is a former cop who got injured and retired from the force on disability. A few years after Caroline's murder, Devin and Nate were having drinks and trading stories and they got to talking about that case. Nate became a private investigator, and he had a friend who was a former cop. They started a two-man private investigator business. This is what is crazy. Nate's partner, who is now dead, was on a retainer by Simon Montgomery when he was stationed at Lejeune."

"Why did Montgomery need a private investigator?"

"To keep tabs on his wife, Caroline. Montgomery knew she slept around."

"Huh. How long did this go on?"

"Well, a couple of years. Nate said Caroline was a fox. Montgomery traveled a lot. Sometimes he was gone for long periods. The PI didn't follow her all the time. It was kind of like Montgomery just wanted to know who she was sleeping with. A couple of the men were civilians, but most were from the Base—two or three officers and a couple of enlisted men. She'd have her kicks and that'd be that until the next one. Get this—one of the officers was the lead investigator in the case against Flynn."

"Wait. What's this?" Sean interrupted.

"Here, let me check." Sean could hear Milton turning pages. "Yeah, here it is. Keaton. Donald Keaton was one of her lovers. Nate and his partner couldn't believe he wasn't conflicted out of the case, and hell, Simon Montgomery knew he had slept with his wife."

"You mean the PI had proof Caroline slept with Keaton and reported that to Montgomery?"

"Yep. That's right, and all that was *before* she got involved with Flynn."

"Damn. Now that's news," said Sean.

"Well, there's more. My buddy said that Nate told him her fling with Flynn Taggart went on longer than with any of the others. When it first got started, he'd follow her to a small motel up the coast and she'd get the room. Flynn would soon show up. After a few times, he didn't have to follow her. Montgomery knew when they were meeting and would tell him when to show up at the motel and watch for the rendezvous. He'd take his pictures and leave."

"How did Montgomery know when she was meeting Flynn?"

"Hell, he had the house phones bugged."

Sean was silent as he digested the information.

"It's too bad that Nate's partner had not been asked to survey the motel the night she was murdered. A lot more might have been known about what happened."

Too bad, indeed, thought Sean. "Was that unusual—that the PI wasn't asked to follow her that night?"

"Not according to Nate. I guess Montgomery didn't want to pay for every time they met."

"Mmmm."

"Well, I better get to my bride."

"I appreciate this, Milton. I hope Martha doesn't mind you spending your honeymoon working on this."

"Not at all. Gives her a chance to shop or sit under an umbrella sipping drinks with little umbrellas."

Sean laughed. "Enjoy the rest of your trip."

After they hung up, the smile quickly faded from Sean's lips. Had Keaton killed Caroline? Was that why he sped the court martial along? That would explain why he framed Flynn—he wanted an open-and-shut case, but why would he want to kill her? Equally intriguing was if Simon knew Keaton had been sleeping with his wife, Simon would know that was a conflict of interest. Hell, as a former lover, Keaton could have been her killer. So, why didn't Simon object to Keaton as the lead investigator? Better yet, why didn't Simon report

Keaton? If Simon didn't consider Keaton a suspect, why not? Maybe since Flynn was her current lover, he assumed Flynn was guilty when the scarf was discovered in his car. Did all these twists mean that Flynn wasn't guilty, or were they just useless intellectual exercises to a murder case that had been rightfully decided?

Chapter 41

Jorge and Gabe were waiting in the hall as school let out for the day. "Hey man," Gabe gestured to Jake.

Jake walked over, "What's up?"

"Thought we'd go over to Frau's and get a burger. Don't tell us you can't go because of the pip-squeaks."

"Who?"

"You know. The nerds." When Jake didn't react, "Your video group." Gabe and Jorge were snickering.

Jake wasn't one for much reaction, so his only response was, "Let's go."

"Say, did we see this right, that you're an assistant director for your group's project?" needled Jorge.

Gabe teased, "Hell, they must be desperate, Jorgie. With Sir Jake as director, you know what that means?"

"What?"

"We're going to kick their tails in the competition."

Jake continued to ignore them as they walked to their vehicles. Gabe hooted, "Jake, my man, did they give you one of those director chairs?"

Jake reached his truck, which was parked beside Gabe's, "You all still doing a video about football?"

"Yeah," Gabe grinned. "It's about a football hero, Jorgie, who gets injured during a championship game but keeps playing anyway. Makes miraculous catches. Guess who wins the game?"

Jake's eyes twinkled, "The other team. Let's go. I'm hungry."

"Shit no, man." Jorge and Gabe were laughing as they went to follow Jake to Frau's.

Chapter 42

Billy Abbott had graduated two years ahead of Rylee in school, was a football player, and his first name started with a B—the type of boy Rylee described in her diary. When Cheryl walked into the hardware store, a young man who was stocking supplies looked up and asked if he could assist her. He smiled when she asked to speak with Billy Abbott. As he walked toward her, he answered, "I'm Billy. What can I do for you?" Seeing Cheryl's surprised look, he laughed, "You must be looking for my dad. He's Billy too. He's in the office. I'll take you back."

Billy Senior explained that the hardware store was a family business that went back to his grandfather. His son, Billy Junior, was a senior in high school and worked there during his spare time learning the business. "Both my kids are going to take over for me some day. My daughter is a sophomore at OSU in the business college majoring in finance. Billy J. is going into marketing. Between the both of them, my wife and I should be able to travel during our golden years."

Before Cheryl could comment, he continued. "Ms. Seton, I like those business segments your newspaper has been running. If you're here to talk about our family business, now is as good a time as any," he grinned.

Cheryl smiled and assured him that he was on her list of businesses to feature, "But there's something else I would like to ask you about."

"Shoot. I'll try to help if I can."

She learned that, like his children, he worked during high school as time allowed. He explained that during football season, he wasn't able to work much. Billy had also attended OSU and came home during every break to help out with the hardware. He met his wife during college. She never worked in the store, but Cheryl knew that she was active in the church and the Bekbourg Garden Club, which supported community charities.

Cheryl smiled, "Do you remember if you attended the Christmas parade when you were home your freshman year?"

"They all blur together, but I would have been there. I came home every Christmas break, so I would have been there. We sold a lot of materials for those floats. I wanted to see them for myself." He chuckled, "Heck, I still enjoy going. It's a family tradition for us."

"Do you remember a girl named Rylee Flowers?" Cheryl asked as she carefully gauged his reaction.

"Ha. I read your article about Rylee and Hogan. You really think there is more to the story?"

"I think there could be. More important, others do."

"I don't know much about the case, but based on what I knew of Hogan, I'd probably fall into that same camp. I didn't know the girl. I knew who she was, but she was two years younger. I did know Hogan, though. He was a year behind me and was on the football team."

"Were you in Bekbourg when it happened?"

"Sure was. I was on break. I'll never forget. The train hit Hogan on a Saturday night. Our family went to church the next morning—that's where we heard the news. Everyone was torn up by it. We didn't know about Rylee then. They didn't find her body until later that day."

"What can you tell me about Hogan?"

"He was friendly and did a lot around church. We both did." Billy shook his head, "One of the reasons Hogan wasn't a starter on the team was that he just didn't have the passion it took. He never seemed to mind that he wasn't a starter. Heck, even if he just barely played, he celebrated like the rest of us when we won. I'm not saying he didn't try. He worked hard in the weight room and during practice."

Cheryl asked, "Schriever is known for its winning football teams. How did you all do your senior year?"

Billy grinned, "It wasn't one of the finer seasons. We only made it to the regionals that year."

Cheryl smiled. "There was a player on your team, Baxter Colbert. He was a running back."

"Oh, sure. He was one of our stars that year. Several of us were surprised that he didn't get a scholarship, but his parents had money, at least they did. Come to think of it, by the time Bax was a senior, there may not have been much left."

"Oh?"

"Yeah. His dad inherited it when his parents died. Mr. Colbert was on the county commission, so he was up there when it came to influence. This was a long time ago. Anyway, he had a gambling problem that finally caught up with him when Baxter was in high school. Baxter went to college up north, maybe in Akron or Toledo. I don't remember. I lost track of him. I know he lives here. Comes in occasionally."

"Did he date many girls during high school?"

"Oh, look. He was popular with the guys *and* the girls: the 'star running back.' I don't remember him dating anyone specific, but I know he took girls out. He and I didn't run in the same circles, but being on the team, I heard things." Billy hesitated. "His dad knew people. I don't know how to say this. Baxter knew some older women, if you know what I mean."

The conversation wound down, and Cheryl committed to contacting Billy for a column in the business section of the *Tribune*.

Chapter 43

Baxter Colbert was the other senior football player whose name started with a B. Cheryl studied the hardened man who stood before her. Through her research, she learned that after graduating high school, Baxter Colbert had attended a college in Akron, Ohio, but dropped out toward the end of his freshman year and joined the army. After serving four years, he returned to a family in financial ruins. His father had died in a single car crash, and his mother and sister lived with her parents on a small farm. Nothing remained of the land his dad had inherited, and the bank accounts had long been depleted. Baxter pulled a trailer onto his mother's family farm and began working the crops, and over time, made a fair living. He married a woman with two young children, who were now grown, and she and he lived in what had been his maternal grandparents' house.

His weathered face was lined with age, making him appear older than he was, but he was muscular and sturdy. He met her as she got out of her car.

"Thank you, Mr. Colbert, for meeting me."

"What is it you want to talk to me about?"

Cheryl suspected he was not one for niceties, so she jumped in with her questions, "Do you remember a student from your time in high school named Rylee Flowers?"

His dark eyes did not flicker, "Yeah, I remember her. She was a sophomore when I was a senior. She was a cheerleader. I also remember her sister, Robyn, who was ahead of me. Night and day."

"What do you mean?"

"Robyn was all work, no play. I always thought she should loosen up. Kind of an ice queen when it came to anything but studying. Her younger sister was just the opposite. She was about having fun."

"Were you friends with them?"

"Naw. I just made it my business to grade the girls." He looked at Cheryl, "That's how I was back then. I guess some high school boys are like that. Can't say I don't still look at women, but from a distance. I'm married."

"Did you date either of them?"

"No. Robyn wasn't my type, and while her little sister was a looker, she was too innocent for my taste."

"Were you surprised when the incident involving Rylee and Hogan Slater happened?"

"So, is that why you're here? I was curious. I don't know if I was or not. I never knew him that well. Probably wouldn't have even noticed him if he hadn't played football. I guess anyone's buttons can get pushed."

He must not have read my story on Rylee and Hogan, or he wants me to believe that, thought Cheryl. "So, you were here in Bekbourg when the incident happened?"

"Yeah. You don't strike me as a slacker, Ms. Seton. You probably know that my old man was in the process of running through with the family's money. I came back from college during breaks to help however I could. After I joined the army, I sent some money to my grandparents to give my mom. I didn't want Dad to get his hands on it. It wasn't a problem after he died."

"Did you go to the Christmas parade when you were in? That's a major event during the holidays here."

He looked at her, trying to read her mind, "I went a couple of times during high school, but that wasn't why I was here over break, to go to parades."

Having satisfied his curiosity as to the purpose of Cheryl wanting to talk with him, he was through talking. "I've got things to do," he said as he turned to leave.

"Thank you, Mr. Colbert, for your time," she raised her voice hoping he would hear as he walked away.

Kye and Buddy were on the front porch of the duplex when Cheryl arrived home. Buddy went charging off the porch to greet Cheryl. He was running circles so fast she found it difficult to pet his head. After she got him settled and rubbed his head and neck, he went galloping back to the porch and plopped down between the chair where Kye was sitting and the chair he planned for Cheryl to occupy. Cheryl and Kye were laughing as she sat. They talked for a while about various things until Cheryl turned the topic to Baxter Colbert.

"Of course I remember Baxter," Kye said. "I taught him junior year English. He didn't really apply himself and was tardy a lot, but I had lots of boys like that," she grinned.

Cheryl smiled with understanding.

Kye explained that he was a good football player and the boys looked up to him. "He was more mature and worldly than the other boys. Not that he traveled, but he knew more about how the world worked. His father was a county commissioner. At one point, the family was wealthy. Baxter's mother had some money, and his father came from money. Unfortunately, it was no secret that Baxter's dad gambled away his family's fortune."

"Was Baxter a bully or violent?"

"No, he wasn't a bully. He didn't go picking on the other kids, but I can't say he wasn't violent. Back then, boys around here went into Koot's before they were twenty-one. Baxter wasn't even eighteen when he started going there. I'd pick up bits and pieces from overhearing the students' conversations. I heard that he would get in fights there at Koot's, but apparently he could handle himself."

"What about with girls?"

"I know girls flocked around him at school, but I don't know who he dated or anything like that."

"So, he joined the army and then came back and helped out on his mother's family's farm," Cheryl said.

"Yes. I was concerned about him during school—that he might take off on the wrong side of the law or go down the path his dad had followed. He was an unsettled young man. If he had not been such a good football player and stayed in school for that, I don't know if he would have graduated. The wreck he had was terrible, but maybe it was a blessing in disguise. It was after that when he joined the army, which appeared to make a man out of him."

"What wreck?" asked Cheryl.

"It was a miracle that he survived. I think it was the same weekend that Hogan and Rylee died. I remember thinking at the time we could have lost three students in one weekend."

Hearing this put Cheryl's curiosity in high gear. "Oh my gosh, Kye. What happened?"

"Well, with his father being a commissioner there wasn't much written about it in the paper. Rumors were that he had been drinking and was speeding. He was driving on the highway heading toward Columbus and lost control and crossed into the other lane where Mr. and Mrs. Dodson were driving home from Columbus. Mr. Dodson swerved and ran into a ditch. They weren't really hurt, but their car ended up with some scraps and scratches. Baxter went off the side of the road and clipped a phone pole, breaking it in two. I never saw the car, but I heard he was lucky to be alive. Thank goodness, he survived. He was banged up with bruises and cuts, but no broken bones. It was hushed up around here. I never heard anything else about it, but soon after, Mr. and Mrs. Dodson were seen driving around in a brand-new Cadillac."

"Do you know which night this happened during that weekend?"

"No, dear. I don't know if it was Friday or Saturday night. I just remember clearly that it was the same weekend as Hogan and Rylee's deaths."

Chapter 44

Sean had not wanted to get pulled into Caroline Montgomery's murder case. However, after hearing from Milton that Simon had hired a private investigator and knew Keaton had an affair with Caroline, Sean wanted to know why Simon had allowed him to head up the investigation. So, he drove to his house.

"Sheriff," Simon said when he saw Sean standing there.

"Hi, Simon. Mind if I come in?"

"No, but I don't have much time. I have lunch plans."

After they were seated, Sean told him about Flynn coming to Bekbourg and claiming his innocence. He was hoping that Sean might be able to help.

Simon huffed, "Don't they all claim they didn't do it. Sounds like he's after notoriety or his pension. Hell, who knows what drives a man like that."

"Well, you may be right, but if he was guilty, he's served his time. Why not move on with his life?"

"Sean, I don't know what to tell you. That's up to you if you want to believe that lying scum. I must cut this off. I need to leave." He started to rise from his chair.

"Just a couple of questions. What did you know about Donald Keaton?"

He lowered himself to the chair's edge. "I knew he was MP, and he was the lead investigator in Caroline's murder case."

"Did you or your wife know him well?"

When it fit his purpose, Simon was a pro at masking his emotions. He gave *nothing* away about knowing Keaton had slept with Caroline. "I didn't. Caroline did a lot socially. So, she could have known him better than I did. I traveled a lot, so I wasn't always there to attend the social events."

"Did you talk to him during the investigation?"

"There wasn't much to talk about. I received a call when I was at the conference in D.C. that I needed to immediately return to Base, which I did. He met me at the airport and took me into a private room and told me that Caroline had been murdered. It wasn't long after that when they found her scarf in Flynn's car. After he informed me about that, I don't remember talking to him much about the case."

"At the time, it seemed to me that Keaton fast-tracked Flynn's case. Do you know why he would have done that?"

Simon shook his head, "I never thought about it being fast-tracked. Hell, he had the evidence. Seemed like an open-and-shut case, so why delay?"

"Did you know about Caroline and Flynn being involved?"

Simon stood. "It came out during the investigation. Sean, don't let that lying scum drag you into a rabbit hole. I don't have any intention of thinking about the past. Now, I need to leave or I'll be late." Simon paused before he continued, "I can't tell you how to do your job, but if I were you, I wouldn't let Flynn pull you into whatever game he's playing. He killed my wife, and as far as I'm concerned, they should have thrown away the key."

As far as being pulled into the rabbit hole on this twenty-year-old case, Sean felt he might already be there.

That damn sheriff is becoming a nuisance, thought Simon as he drove to his lunch meeting with Harvey. *Hell, I've got enough on my mind without his constant badgering. Why in the hell is he asking all these questions about our marriage and my finances? Now he's asking about Caroline's death. What the hell is going on? Why all the questions about that ass, Keaton? How could he have been drawn in by that SOB Taggart? I don't have time for this shit. Hell, he works for the county. Maybe they need to rein him in.*

As Harvey was driving to the GilHaus to meet Simon for lunch, he was trying to decide how best to approach Simon. Harvey did not want to dip into his personal investments if he could avoid it. With the amount of funding he was expecting from Simon's investment, he would be able to finalize the purchase of the Steinsen and Kye's properties and cover some other outlays. But, he needed Simon's commitment soon. The other investors were getting impatient with how long the project was taking to come together and had conveyed to him they were considering pulling out if things were not soon finalized. Fortunately, they were impressed with Simon and approved of his participation in the project and recognized that him being a retired brigadier general would add gravitas to the development. His influence and connections would carry a lot of sway, and Harvey could already envision how partnering with Simon might be an asset for future developments.

Harvey had talked to Simon over the phone a couple of times since Skylar's death—during which Simon had not brought up the project. For his part, although he was hankering for Simon's participation, Harvey thought it would be poor taste to broach the subject so soon after her death. But, business was business, and he needed to gently push Simon to get refocused on the project. During their breakfast that Saturday morning before they had left Columbus, he thought Simon was ready to move forward. He even gave the other investors Simon's phone number so they could address any final details.

Harvey arrived early at the GilHaus and asked to be seated along a wall where they could talk in private. He looked at his watch for the third time and began to wonder if something had come up when he saw the hostess directing Simon his way. "Sorry I'm late, Harvey. Something came up."

Because Simon was habitually punctual, Harvey was concerned, "Is everything okay?"

"I see you've got a drink. I'll join you on that."

Harvey called over the waitress. After he and Simon had ordered drinks and placed their orders, Harvey said, "I got a call from the other investors, and they are ready to move forward. Not surprisingly, you impressed the hell out of them. I know you have a lot on your plate right now. If there is anything I can do to help move things along, Simon, just tell me. My attorney will be glad to handle any paperwork, or work with yours. Whatever we need to do, we will."

Simon didn't want to lose this opportunity, but until he could figure out a way to avoid showing the other investors his financial reports, he needed to navigate for more time. "Thanks, Harvey. There has been a lot of paperwork involved with Skylar's death. I've had to make filings and reports, and it's still not over. I sure as hell want to be part of your project. It's impressive and a nice investment opportunity."

Simon decided on the drive to the lunch to see if there was some wiggle room in getting Sean off his back. So, he put his toe in the water. "What do you know about Sean?" He watched Harvey as he sipped his scotch.

Harvey's eyes widened, "You mean as sheriff?"

"Yes. I've only lived here a little over a year. Granted, he has been instrumental in solving some big cases, but it strikes me that he gravitates toward the spotlight, if you get my meaning."

"Yeah, I know what you mean. Why do you ask?"

Simon set down his glass. "That's the reason I was late today. He was up there asking about something where our paths crossed twenty years ago."

Harvey set down his glass. "Twenty years ago?"

"Yeah. Look, it's not something I like to think about, but you remember that day when you, Noel and I walked out of here, and that man was standing there?"

"Yes."

"Well, he had recently been released from prison for a murder conviction. He's a con man, and I'm concerned that he's somehow conned Sean into believing he was innocent."

"How would Sean fit into this?"

"He was on the investigation team that helped convict him. They found the evidence in his car. Anyway, I don't see any reason for Sean to be involved in that case and wasting my time like this. But, it's not just that, he's been up to my place several times asking questions about Skylar. It's getting tiresome. I don't know what happened. I was in Columbus. You know that. The best I can figure, she was walking along the pier and must have fallen in. She was fully dressed, and for whatever reason, she couldn't make it out. Unfortunately, she likes to have wine in the afternoon. Anyway, I've got a lot on my plate right now, and Sean is not making it any easier."

"Mmm," Harvey murmured, thinking about the timing of his development and how Simon was not focused on it.

Simon took another drink. "That's why I was asking about Sean. Hell, I don't even see how something that happened twenty years ago while he was in the Marines could be in his jurisdiction here. I don't understand his motivation unless he thinks he can make a name for himself by casting doubt into that case. It's a damn power play as far as I'm concerned."

"I can't see any other reason," said Harvey. "The man was convicted. You said they found the evidence that tied him to it?"

"Yes. It was an open-and-shut case. Then, with all this bullshit around Skylar's death, why keep trying to find shit that's not there? I'm beginning to think he must be seeking publicity and grandstanding because he has aspirations for higher offices. That's the only thing I can figure. But, you ask about what you can do to help. I can't think of anything. As long as Sean is chewing up my time with all this nonsense, I can't focus on what I really want to do, and that is to invest in your new development."

Chapter 45

It was after hours, and everyone had left for the day except for Harvey. He heard the door chime when the front door to his office building opened and knew that Noel Fischner had arrived. Harvey walked out in the hall and motioned for Noel to follow him into his office.

"Care for a drink?" asked Harvey.

"Sure."

Once they were seated, Harvey said, "I had lunch with the Brigadier today, and I am concerned that Sean's recent glories in solving the murders has gone to his head."

Noel took a sip, "What do you mean?"

"I think you would agree with me that there is no way the Brigadier had anything to do with his wife's death."

"Of course not. From what I've heard, they think it was an accident."

"That's my point. I don't know why Sean would be harassing one of Bekbourg's finest citizens."

"Sean's bugging the Brigadier?"

"Yeah. From what he told me, Sean's been to his house several times wasting his time with irrelevant bullshit. Anyone who doesn't have his head up his ass knows the Brigadier didn't have anything to do with Skylar's death. Hell, he was in Columbus with me on a business trip when she died."

"Why would he be harassing the Brigadier? That doesn't make sense."

Harvey agreed. "It gets more bizarre. You remember that day outside Gil's when that man wanted to talk to the Brigadier?"

"Yes."

"Well, that man was convicted of murder twenty years ago. Simon didn't tell me the details, but somehow, Simon was involved. Sean was one of the military police who investigated the guy, and they found the evidence on him. Now, that man is trying to clear his name and is trying to get Sean to help."

"What?" Noel asked.

"I don't see how a sheriff of Bekbourg can use taxpayer dollars like that, but he is. Sean's turning into a publicity hound. He may even be thinking about running for county commissioner. Just think about that, Noel. Whoever he runs against, would lose, and once he is on the commission, he'd call all the shots. Maybe he wants to be governor. Hell, I don't know, but what I do know is that he's running around the county

245

unchecked. We're talking about a retired brigadier general for God's sake."

Noel took a drink, "I know what you mean. Ever since he came back, he's acted like he's the king."

Harvey leaned forward. "I figured we were on the same page about Sean. Now, what can be done about it?"

Noel thumbed the condensation on his glass. "Well, I need to give it some thought. He's popular around here—football hero and all."

Harvey needed action. "Hell, isn't this about wasting county resources?"

Noel cleared his throat, "Yeah, seems like that. I can't promise there is a lot I can do. You know Sean, he's like a bulldog."

Harvey's patience evaporated, "I don't give a damn, Noel. I bankrolled your campaign. Now, I expect results. I don't care how you do it—just get that damn sheriff off the Brigadier's back."

Chapter 46

"Where's Jake?" asked Claire.

"I told him that he didn't need to be here for this part," explained Lilly. "He's not in this scene."

"Oh, right." Claire seemed disappointed. "He's had some good ideas."

"Yes, but this is pretty straight forward," assured Lilly.

Lilly and Claire looked up as they heard a vehicle pulling up. Jake saw the surprise on Claire's face when he stepped out. "What?" he asked.

"I thought you weren't coming since Anton isn't in the filming today."

"Yeah. So? I'm the assistant director," he said as he looked over the front porch where the set was.

"That's good. I mean, you do have good ideas," Claire murmured.

Lilly stifled a chuckle.

Jake asked Lilly, "So this is where you are playing the ghost of her," he nodded toward Claire, "great-great grandmother?"

"Yes. Do you have some ideas?"

"I might. Let's go look at the porch. Where are the other two?"

"They should be here soon."

"Have you looked at any of the film yet?" asked Jake.

"Not real close, but I'm not worried. Reid knows what he's doing. He and I worked on a project last semester. We'll capture the film to an editing computer and then start editing." Lilly thought from Jake's questions, he might be interested in helping. "We can always use another person if you want to help."

"Naw. I was just curious."

Reid and Brian pulled up, and the teenagers started work on their movie.

Chapter 47

Sean received the newspaper articles from Milton about Caroline Montgomery's murder. Most of what he read, he remembered. One thing that he did not realize, however, was that Caroline's sister, Carrie Reiter, had attended the trial. Sean decided to call her and see what he might learn. She still lived in Atlanta, her hometown.

"Sheriff Neumann, your voicemail said you wanted to talk to me about Caroline."

"Yes. I apologize if my phone call raises memories about your sister's death. I was a junior investigator on the case at the time. Actually, I didn't get brought into the case until toward the very end. The reason for my call is that Flynn Taggart, the man convicted of your sister's murder, was recently released from prison. He came to see me. He claims he didn't kill Caroline."

"I see." She paused before continuing, "Do you believe him?"

"Did Caroline ever talk to you about him?"

He heard her sigh. "Yes."

"What can you tell me about your sister?"

"Well, for starters, she was unhappy in her marriage. Our dad retired from the army. Growing up, Caroline had a thing for military men. 'Something about a man in uniform,' she'd coo. My sister met Simon when she was in college and he was attending the Citadel. They married after college. Caroline was happy for the first few of years with all the glitz of being an officer's wife, but as time went on, she realized that Simon singularly aspired to out-achieve his father, who was blanketed with awards and ribbons from his service in the Marines. She was beautiful and charming, so she was an asset in his career pursuits, but she found her life lonely and empty. He was gone for long periods, and she started looking elsewhere, if you understand what I'm saying."

"Do you think he knew?"

"I don't know. I worried about that, but Caroline assured me that he wouldn't find out. She said she was discrete, and everything was casual. I didn't approve of what she was doing, but I also understood to some extent. What was she going to do if she got out of the marriage? She had never worked. Not even during college. Also, despite being unhappy with Simon, she enjoyed the attention of being an officer's wife as he moved up the ranks.

"She met Flynn at a holiday party. Simon left sometime in January on a trip, and she called him. At first, he refused to meet her. Maybe that was a hook. Men fell at her feet. She found out where he went for drinks and showed up there. My sister could be persuasive. Anyway, she ended up flipping over him. She told me he wasn't a phony. He didn't care what others thought of him—didn't kiss up to people. He was respected for his accomplishments. She fell in love—I think for the first time in her life. Caroline also thought Flynn cared for her, but he told her he wasn't ready for a commitment."

"What about him being an officer and having an affair with an officer's wife?" asked Sean.

Carrie laughed, "I asked her about that. That was one of the things she admired about him. He thrived on danger. Lived on the wild side. He just didn't think about it."

"So, she didn't believe he was concerned about being found out?"

"Not from what she told me."

"If Caroline had fallen for him but he wasn't equally committed, did that cause a friction between them?"

"I don't think so. Caroline didn't give up on them, but what she did give up on was her marriage. She told me that she was making plans to divorce Simon. With Flynn, she saw there was more to life than what she had with Simon. If Flynn moved on, she was moving on."

"Did she ever talk about Flynn being harsh with her?"

"No, never. I have to say that my sister had good fortune there. She never had a man abuse her.

Even with her lovers, she stayed friendly with some. There was only one who I was concerned about."

"Who was that?" asked Sean.

"It was the man she was seeing before she met Flynn. Had an unusual first name."

Sean frowned, "Would that be Hutch McAlistair?"

Sean heard her recognition, "That's him."

"What happened there?"

"They had been seeing each other a short time when Caroline decided she was ready to move on. Despite her efforts to end things, he kept calling her. One time when she was at a store, he came up to her and was pushy about her seeing him again. It unnerved her. She kept driving around, making sure he wasn't following her before she went home. He wouldn't take no for an answer. She finally started hanging up on him. I got concerned, because I didn't know if he was one of those crazies who might do something. One night when she and Flynn were at a bar, he was there and made a scene in the parking lot. Flynn told her to go back inside. Caroline never knew what transpired after she got inside, but whatever happened, that man never bothered her again."

"Was there anyone else you can think of who might have had a reason to harm Caroline?"

"Well, Simon, since he was her husband. He was tone deaf to my sister's emotional needs. I wondered how he would take it if she left him. He was so focused on his career, I don't know how he would have responded if something might derail his ambitions."

"When you talked to Caroline, was she at home?"

"Yes, of course. She didn't work, and unlike now, there weren't cell phones."

"I appreciate your time. This had been helpful."

"Good. Since you are looking into this, there's something I want to say. I sat through the trial. I never met or talked to Flynn, but I watched him. I knew what my sister had told me about him. I know he was convicted, but I remember wondering at the time if he was guilty."

"I'll give you my phone number. If you think of anything else, give me a call," Sean said.

Sean wanted to kick himself for letting Flynn's case get to him. The more he learned, the more questions he had, but to what end? He did not see this leading to anything that could help Flynn prove his innocence, and he still was not convinced that Flynn was innocent. He called the motel where Flynn was staying but the clerk said he had checked out. Just as well, thought Sean. If Flynn ever contacted him again, he would tell him what he knew and let Flynn and his attorney handle things. Sean decided it was time to move on.

There were several moving parts in Skylar Montgomery's death that he needed to stay on top of. Something did not feel right. Her friend Liz was absolutely convinced that she did not kill herself or die by accidental drowning. But, if someone was responsible, who? The only two people who came to mind were Luca and Simon. Luca's motive could be money, and so could Simon's. The irony there was that she had changed her will. Another motive for Simon was that she was planning to leave him.

He decided to talk to Harvey and see if there was any time on Friday that Simon was not accounted for. For now, Sean was going to treat the case as unsolved until he was convinced otherwise.

He also wanted to find out more about Luca and Natalia's financial situation as well as Simon's. Sydney had recently joined his department right out of the academy. She had an understanding about financial matters that none of his other deputies had, and he trusted her to turn over every stone. He asked her to see what she could find out about Ramirez's financial situation. Since Liz, Skylar's friend from D.C., mentioned that Simon had investments in South America, he called Lucky, a long-term friend who worked for the FBI out of their Columbus office, to see what he could find about Simon's financial standing.

Chapter 48

Framed pictures of ribbon-cutting ceremonies and various hard-hat construction sites lined the light gray walls of the conference room. Sean sat at the black, acrylic oval table waiting for Harvey Bennett. Out of courtesy, he stood and shook hands with Harvey, but neither man was inclined to exchange pleasantries. Sean opened up with, "I understand that Simon Montgomery is considering investing in the Lake Meadows planned development."

"That's right."

"It's my understanding that you invited Simon to Columbus to talk about the project the weekend his wife died."

"What a tragedy. I'd just had dinner with them a few nights before that happened. I invited Simon to Columbus to meet the other investors and talk in detail about the development. We all met there on Thursday evening for drinks and dinner. Friday was filled with meetings and golf, and then we had dinner. Some of us stayed around for breakfast Saturday morning. I offered up another round of golf on Saturday afternoon since Simon had missed the golf game on Friday, but everyone had other plans." Sean saw the second when Harvey realized his blunder.

"Why did Simon miss the golf game?"

"He had to beg off because of a stomach bug. Nothing major. He went to his room but was feeling better by dinner. I was concerned it was something he had eaten, but he assured me it wasn't."

"Did anyone else have that problem?"

Shit, now Sean will be bugging Simon about missing a damn golf game. Harvey did not like that he had stepped into this quagmire, but he did not see how he could avoid answering. "Not that I know of. Everyone else played golf."

"When did you last see him on Friday during the day?" asked Sean.

"Ah, I can't be all that sure. You know how these things are—people coming and going."

"Harvey, if I have to, I'll have everyone who attended hauled in to the station to answer my questions. Now, try again."

Harvey narrowed his eyes but answered, "We wrapped up our meeting and then had box lunches brought in. I'd say sometime after twelve-thirty. After we ate, the rest of us headed back to our rooms to get ready for our tee times starting at two o'clock."

"When was the next time you saw him?"

"It was that evening when we had drinks. I don't remember exactly. Six-thirty. Seven o'clock—maybe. Dinner was at seven-thirty."

Sean was thinking that it took about an hour-and-a-half, two hours at most, to drive one way, so Simon had plenty of time to make a round-trip from Columbus to Bekbourg before the dinner.

"Did you notice anything unusual about Simon over the weekend? Was he anxious to leave Saturday morning?"

"No, I can't say I noticed anything unusual."

"Before I leave, I need a list of everyone who was with you that weekend and their contact information, the itinerary, and the name of the hotel."

Harvey picked up the phone to tell his secretary. "My assistant is getting that for you. I'll walk you out."

When Sean returned to the station, he asked Alex and Syd to contact the invitees to Harvey's weekend business meeting and to go to Columbus and talk to the hotel management about Simon's whereabouts during the weekend.

Chapter 49

While Sean was jogging the next morning, he found his thoughts drifting back to Caroline, Hutch, and Flynn. Had Hutch been following her and discovered their love nest? He could have killed her and framed Flynn. Maybe Flynn had fallen for her, and she tried to end it, and he killed her. The other side of that coin was the possibility that Flynn wanted to end the relationship and she threatened to expose the affair. That would have destroyed his career with the military, which was a motive for killing her. But, why would she disclose the affair since her infidelity would become front and center in her own marriage?

Then, there was the whole crazy thing about Keaton being her former lover and Simon tapping their house phone. Sean could understand why Simon would not want it to become common knowledge that his wife was sleeping around, but why let Keaton handle Flynn's prosecution? Was Simon using Keaton to railroad Flynn? Why target Flynn? Maybe through the bugged phones, he heard Caroline telling her sister that Flynn meant something more to her than the others? Maybe

Simon didn't want her to leave him, because he viewed it as a career killer? But, he was out of town. Flynn theorized that Simon hired someone to kill her, but Sean found that hard to believe. Letting someone in gave them knowledge about his involvement, making him vulnerable if that person ever decided to talk. Even if he wanted her killed, why frame Flynn when there had been so many others? Was it because he was the most recent, and she had fallen for him?

Sean came back to the question that had continued to nag him since Flynn walked into his office—if he was guilty, why would he be trying to prove his innocence, particularly since he had paid the price? Of course there was his pension and his reputation, but again, after twenty years, that was a long-shot. Simon called Flynn a con man—was he? Caroline's sister did not make him out to be a con man, but she admitted she did not know him. Sean needed to know more, and if he could locate him, Hutch McAlistair might fill in a piece of the puzzle.

It took some doing, but Kim was able to locate Hutch McAlistair. He was a manager at a food distributor in Wilmington, North Carolina. "Sheriff Neumann, I'm surprised to get a call from a sheriff in Ohio. Is this about one of my employees?"

"No, nothing like that. This has to do with a murder investigation twenty years ago out of Camp Lejeune."

"Oh."

"You remember Caroline Montgomery?"

Hutch hesitated, but then replied, "Yes."

"There's been some new things arise, and at the time, I was a junior criminal investigator on the case. I'm following up on some loose ends."

"Okay. Well, what do you want to know?"

"First, were you ever in the military?"

"No."

"Did you know anyone from the Base?"

"Casually, there were some guys I'd see around Jacksonville at the nightlife scene, but I didn't really know them."

"You lived in Jacksonville at the time?"

"Yeah. I delivered food items for a local distributor there."

"How did you know Mrs. Montgomery?"

"I met her at a bar. She was looking for a fun time, and we hit it off."

"Did you know she was married?"

"No. She never mentioned it or I might have had second thoughts. I never knew until I heard about her death in the news. Heard she was married to a big shot on the Base."

"What did the investigators ask you?"

"Who?"

"The MP's who were sent to investigate her murder?"

"No one ever talked to me."

Sean was not expecting that reply. Fritz had told him that Keaton was going to talk with Hutch. "No one ever interviewed you in the case?"

"No. Why would they?"

"Tell me about your relationship with Mrs. Montgomery."

"What's there to tell? We had a fling. Nothing to it."

"Mr. McAlistair, I understand that Mrs. Montgomery ended the relationship and that you didn't like that. That you kept calling her and even confronted her."

"Whoa. I see where you're going with this. I didn't kill her. No way. Look, I was young and stupid back then. Yeah, I didn't like it when she dropped me like a hot potato. One day we're going at it hot and heavy, and the next thing I knew, she wouldn't talk to me. I admit that I was a jerk about it, but I finally got the message and moved on."

"Why did you stop pursing her?"

"Look, I'm not proud of this, but one night I saw her with another man at a bar. I was a few sheets to the wind and made an ass of myself in the parking lot. That guy laid me out before I knew what hit me. He could have really messed me up but didn't. Once he had my attention, he told me I better not bother her again. I didn't want that kind of trouble. She wasn't worth it. I never called her again or ever saw her."

"Do you remember where you were when she was killed?"

"You're kidding? No, I don't remember where I was that long ago, but what I can tell you is that I did not kill her."

As Sean hung up, Kim buzzed him that Fritz Marlow was on the other line. Before he picked up, he thought, *for something I didn't want to get involved with, I'm up to my neck.*

"He, Fritz, how are things in California?"

"Can't complain. Say, after you called me about the Montgomery murder case, I got to thinking. Like a dog with a bone, I just couldn't let go, so I called the commanding officer who I worked under when I was transferred to California to handle the domestic violence case. He remembered, because he told me he thought it was weird. The bottom line is that it was Keaton who got the wheels in motion for me to be transferred. Through the chain-of-command, he sent out the word that he was overstaffed at Lejeune. My commanding officer jumped at the chance to get my level of experience. Keaton was ready to move with the transfer, and my CO wanted to jump on getting me onboard before he lost the chance. Sean, I don't know if this means anything, but it seems odd."

"Yeah, it might. Did you and Keaton have a history?" Sean was thinking about their prior conversation when Fritz spoke of his disdain for Keaton.

"Look. As much as I thought Keaton was an ass and back stabber, I knew not to get on the man's bad side. I kept my head down and did my job. He'd take credit for our successes even though he was too busy schmoozing with the top dogs to have any involvement in the investigations themselves. Frankly, I was glad—kept him out of our hair. I must have been good at hiding my contempt, because he was fair in the evaluations."

"Yeah. From my little experience with him, I can't imagine him giving you a good evaluation if he'd had something against you."

"That's for certain. Say, I guess the police chief's report turned out to be a dead end."

Sean's brow arched, "What police chief's report?"

"You didn't see it in the file?"

"No. I never got a chance to review the file. Keaton had the file, and I just ran his errands and carried his bags."

"Huh, that's just like that SOB. It was damn near impossible to work for that idiot. He controlled every iota and took credit for whatever he could and sure as hell broke the sound barrier in blaming others if he thought his ass was in a sling. He was the biggest butt-kisser of the officer corps I ever met."

"What about this chief's report?" Sean pressed.

"Oh, yeah. Thinking of Keaton boils my blood. Anyway, you know how the civilians like to keep up with what's happening in and around the military bases. That's a big part of their lives and economy. So, they follow things through the local TV and newspaper as well as the rumor mill. I got a call one day shortly after Flynn had been arrested from a police chief in a small municipality around Jacksonville, North Carolina near the Base." He gave Sean the name. "He told me he had some information that we should know about. That they might have some information on Flynn's whereabouts on the night of the murder."

"What was the information?" Sean quizzed.

"I never got a chance to find out. I told Keaton about the call and that I was going to follow up, but he told me he would handle it, that he needed me to do something else. I don't remember what it was, but I remember thinking it was a bullshit errand. I never got to talk to Hutch either."

Sean said, "Well, I talked to McAlistair, and he told me that no one ever interviewed him about Mrs. Montgomery's death."

"Huh? I don't know what to say about that, Sean. I was planning to interview him, but Keaton told me he would. I don't know if Keaton thought we had the killer so he didn't see the need, or he just didn't follow up." Sean heard Fritz exhale. "Flynn was emphatic that he was innocent. If I'd known Keaton wasn't going to interview McAlister, I sure as hell would have. You say you talked to Hutch. What's your take about his possible involvement?"

"He denied having anything to do with it, but you know what that's worth."

"Yep. Well, if I think of anything else, I'll let you know."

"Sounds good. Thanks."

Chapter 50

During dinner, Cheryl told Sean about Baxter's wreck on the same weekend that Hogan and Rylee died. "He was speeding north out of Bekbourg toward Columbus. He must have been heading back to Akron."

"So you're thinking he might have been involved in their deaths and then was trying to get out of town?" asked Sean.

"It's definitely a possibility. The problem is that I can't find anything in the police reports about the wreck or in the *Tribune's* archives."

"That's interesting—especially given the severity of the accident and the fact that two other people were involved."

"Rylee's diary said that whoever the boy was, his parents were important people in Bekbourg. His dad being a commissioner would fit that bill," said Cheryl.

"Honey, there is someone who might be able to give you some information." Sean suggested Cheryl contact Jack Rhodes. Jack had been with the sheriff's department for years before retiring nearly fifteen years ago as sheriff. Jack had helped fill in the blanks for Sean on some cases.

"The last time I visited him, he was recovering from hip replacement surgeries and doing much better. He must really be doing well, because when I called him a few weeks ago to catch up, he told me one of his fishing buddies in Sebring had introduced him to his sister when she was visiting from Venice, Florida. Jack said things moved fast. He rented out his place; they got married; and they are living in Venice at her place."

"Oh, wow! Well, good for him."

"Yep. I'll give him a call and see what I can set up. You'll like meeting him."

Chapter 51

The county commissioners had worked their way through the meeting agenda when they came to an item that Noel had asked to be included. The Chairman, Lance Pruitt, turned to Noel. "You wanted to discuss the sheriff's request to fill this deputy position?" Normally, Sean's request for commission approval to fill a deputy position recently vacated would be on the consent agenda.

Noel leaned forward. "Yes, before we approve this request, I think we need to take a look at how the sheriff is managing his department. We all want crimes solved and criminals put away; but we are a small county, and we don't have unlimited funds. It has come to my attention that he has been using a lot of state resources, and I just don't see the need. We have a county coroner and a lab that can do forensics. Heck, we have the sheriff's department, so I don't understand why he's always running off to the state police. I suggest before we grant this request, we have a complete audit done of the sheriff's department. He could be running our county into the ground. We may have to raise taxes to pay for all these state services."

Noel's suggestion of some possible mismanagement in the sheriff's department perked up the few citizens who were in attendance. Rhonda Winger, a *Tribune* reporter was furiously writing. The Chair glanced at the third commissioner for guidance, but he shrank into his chair and pretended to be reviewing a paper in front of him. Lance was a portly man with thinning white hair. A white undershirt peeped out around his neck under his plaid shirt pulled tight against his girth. He removed his black rim glasses and rubbed his eyes. Once his replaced the glasses, he rotated his chair toward Noel. "Sean's been doing a fine job since he became sheriff. No one from our treasurer's office has said anything about him being outside his budget. Are you suggesting he's been spending money that hasn't been appropriated?"

"I don't know what he's been doing. That's why I think we need a full-blown audit done—to see. I mean, he's been using all these state resources, and that can't be cheap. The county sure doesn't want to be hit with a surprise like that. None of us want to have to tell our citizens that we're going to have to increase their taxes."

"Do you have any numbers from the state?" asked the Chair. "I'm not inclined to order an audit without something behind it. Heck, those audits cost money, and they take a lot of time. The sheriff is busy and so are his officers. He's short a deputy. That's why he wants to fill the position."

Noel saw the reporter taking notes. The people in the hearing room were listening. He did not know how, or even if, the *Tribune* would report on his actions, but if it didn't report, he'd use that as an opportunity to claim that Sean was mismanaging his department and the local newspaper was helping in the cover up by not reporting. *See how Sean would defend that one with his girlfriend being the owner of the paper.* He figured Harvey would be pleased with his efforts today, especially if he could finagle a time-consuming audit that would keep Sean out of everyone's hair. "I don't have any numbers from the state. That's why we need to hear from Sean on this. To make sure everything is transparent, an audit is in order."

Lance unfolded some gum and put it in his mouth. "I tell you what. My suggestion is that we do what you suggest and talk to Sean about all this. I don't want to jump the gun and order an audit without knowing more. We'll have Sean come and tell us about all this and then decide." He swirled to face the third commissioner, "Riley, what do you think?"

Riley nodded, "I like that idea. Let's hear from Sean first."

It was not what Noel had hoped for, but at least it was a step in the right direction. He would have his assistant pull together everything she could find so when they met with Sean, he could raise enough questions that would leave the other two commissioners with no choice but to order a full audit. In any event, he likely could not sway the two commissioners today, so best to play along. When Lance asked Noel, Noel nodded, "I look forward to hearing what the sheriff has to say. That's a good first step, but I think the sooner we meet with him the better. We've got to get a handle on what's happening with the sheriff's budget before it gets more out of hand than it already is."

The following evening, Sean had some papers spread out on the kitchen table when Cheryl returned from visiting with Bri. "Hi Sweetie," she said as she kissed him on the cheek and patted Buddy. Courtesy of Bri, she laid a box of freshly-baked scones on the counter. "What's that all about?"

"Reports and budget matters I'm reviewing for a meeting with the commissioners."

"Huh," she leaned up against the counter and hid a grin. "Is this a follow up to their public meeting yesterday?"

Sean eased back and drily replied, "Yeah, that's the one."

Gosh, he is so sexy, thought Cheryl as she appreciated his tall, fit body leaning back in the chair. His piercing eyes always captivated her. She loved to watch his lips, which went from thin to thinner the more intense he got. Only those closest to him ever benefitted from seeing his handsome face don a smile.

Cheryl pretended to be serious but couldn't hide the mischievous glint in her eyes. "The commission meeting that was fairly and objectively reported on in the *Tribune*?"

"Yeah, that's the ticket," he easily repeated. "I believe you're referring to the story with the heading, 'Sheriff in hot seat at County Commission meeting.'" Cheryl saw the humor in his eyes despite the serious expression he attempted.

It took all her control not to crack a smile, "I know that reporter. Rhonda Winger covers the county government."

Sean's brow arched as his lips stifled a grin. "Yeah, I believe that's her. She's the one who reports with a dogged determination that the public is entitled to the unvarnished truth?"

Cheryl's grin grew. "That's the one."

Sean's bright eyes held humor. "The one who loves roasting the sheriff and all other county officials? Let me see if I can remember some of her quotes in this morning's paper." He snapped his fingers, "Yeah, I remember now, 'possible mismanagement in the sheriff's department,' and here's my favorite, 'we've got to get a handle on what's happening with the sheriff's budget before it gets more out of hand than it already is.'"

Cheryl's laughter rang out around the kitchen. As her laugh dwindled to giggles, she pushed away from the counter. "Unhuh. Well, seeing that you're busy trying to salvage your reputation, Sweetie, I'll take Buddy for a walk and let you work."

Buddy heard "walk" and pranced to the door. Sean's eyes shone with devilment as he stood and took Cheryl in his arms. "I love you even though your newspaper takes my name in vain." Cheryl's laugh was smothered by his passionate kiss.

Chapter 52

Cheryl walked out of the Sarasota airport and immediately noticed the warmer temperature and bright sun. Sean had arranged for her to meet Jack Rhodes. She rented a car and drove to Venice, Florida.

"Hi, Cheryl. Come in."

"Thank you, Sheriff Rhodes."

Jack Rhodes was Bekbourg's sheriff for several years until he had retired almost fifteen years ago and moved to Florida. He was a fountain of information about investigations and many who lived in Bekbourg during his tenure.

"Now, you've got to call me Jack. Let me introduce you to my young bride, Darla."

Darla tended toward the stout side with short grayish wavy hair springing about her face. Her smile widened, "Listen to him. Come in and make yourself comfortable. You must be tired and hungry after flying down here. I've got sandwiches and lemonade, and coffee to start with."

Jack rubbed his stomach, "And, because we've got a guest, she made her special egg custard."

Cheryl enjoyed getting to know them both. Darla was a retired teacher and had moved to Venice, Florida, about ten years ago from Illinois. They were learning to golf and played Bingo two nights a week. Cheryl looked forward to reporting back to Sean on how well things had worked out for Jack.

After lunch, Darla poured coffee and excused herself to the back porch where she resumed knitting a baby blanket for a new grandchild expected in four months.

"Okay, Cheryl. Sean didn't tell me what you wanted to talk about other than an investigation from nearly forty years ago."

"That's right." Cheryl pulled out copies of the police report and the newspaper articles and handed them to Jack.

After glancing over them, he frowned. "That was a damn tragedy, pardon my language. I was the assistant sheriff when that happened. The dispatcher put out the call when the train officials contacted him. I showed up along with another deputy. Cecil Davis was the engineer. He was pretty shaken as were the other two men in the cab with him that night. Just outside of town, they came round the curve and saw something lying in the middle of the tracks. They tried to stop, but hell, there was no way it could stop in time. They saw it was a body before they hit it. There was an investigation, and the train was in compliance with the speed limit, so they weren't at fault. The body was found under a box car about ten cars back. If you've seen the report, you know there was no way to get any reports about marks or evidence on the boy. Since we didn't have anything else to go on, we marked it down as a suicide. His car was parked off to the side of the road near the crossing. His family, especially his mother, was overwrought with grief.

"Then, the next day, Rylee's mother's car was spotted at the park, and after searching, we found her body back in the woods. The coroner determined that she had been struck hard in the face, causing her to fall and strike her head on a rock. She died instantly according to him."

"The report didn't show evidence of sexual activity," noted Cheryl.

Jack looked inquiringly at Cheryl, "No, and you probably saw in the report there was no evidence of her struggling. Her clothes weren't torn; no skin under her nails."

"Her sister told me she was pregnant."

Jack shook his head. "Yes, that was in the coroner's report. She was about three months along. Both families were good people. The sheriff didn't want people gossiping. He came out quickly with his conclusions, and the reporters never looked at the coroner's report. There was enough heartache to go around."

"You were conducting the investigation. Rylee's sister said you told her and her mother about the pregnancy."

"Yeah. When I heard from the coroner, I went to Rylee's mother's home, and her sister was there. I needed to tell them in case that might cause them to think about something else I should know. They had no idea she was pregnant. I never got the chance to ask Hogan's parents about it or any of the kids' friends to see what they knew. The sheriff closed down the investigation."

"He closed it down? Why?"

"All he said was that it seemed open and shut and that people were suffering enough."

"Did that seem odd to you that he would do that?"

Jack took a drink of coffee while he considered Cheryl's question. "The sheriff called me into his office and told me the matter was closed. I remember walking out and standing near the receptionist's desk, and I could tell that Viv was out of sorts. She was our receptionist at the time and happened to also be Hogan's mother's first cousin. Of course, she had been upset anyway, but the scandal that Hogan had killed Rylee and all really burnt her. She never let on in front of the sheriff, but she and I were buds around the department. Anyway, I could tell she was fuming. She told me that Randall Thompson had called earlier and talked to the sheriff. It wasn't long after that when Viv said she heard the sheriff tell someone on the phone that the investigation hadn't turned up anything suspicious and that the investigation was over. She then said, 'Money talks around this town. He,' meaning the sheriff, 'won't do anything if it means ruffling feathers. I don't believe for one minute Hogan did what they say, but we'll never know, now, will we?'"

"What do you think she meant by that?"

"Well, I asked her who she meant, but she didn't say, and frankly, if she knew, Viv was smart enough to not to say. It was different back then, Cheryl. Randall Thompson ran the county, and people didn't want to get on the bad side of him or his cronies."

"Do you have any idea who may have wanted the investigation shut down?"

"I thought about it some back then. Randall was certainly known to sleep with young girls, but I don't think he was personally involved in this. Both families were well known and members of the church there. I couldn't imagine either of those kids being mixed up with Randall. For all I knew, a family member of one of the kids had called Randall and asked him to intervene to get the community past the situation. Rylee was engaged to Hogan, so I just assumed the baby was his and the tragedy unfolded like we thought."

"What if the baby wasn't Hogan's? What then?" asked Cheryl.

Jack frowned. "Well, that would change everything. For Randall to have been involved, it was either because he was personally involved. But, like I said, I don't believe that. So then my next guess is that whoever the father was of Rylee's baby got Randall involved. Or, the father of the boy who got her pregnant called Randall. That seems more likely to me. If a boy was the father and he killed Rylee, his father could have asked Randall to call off the sheriff's investigation." Jack paused, "Yeah, if that boy's father was a crony of Randall's, I could see him asking Randall to intercede and stop the investigation."

"Jack, what about some boys a couple of years older than Rylee. I understand that Baxter Colbert's father was a county commissioner. Was he a crony of Randall's?"

"Oh, yeah. They were thick as thieves. Trust me. He wouldn't have been on the county commission if Randall wasn't behind it. Randall hand-picked both the county commissioners and the officers. Colbert had a gambling problem. Lost it all. If his wife's family hadn't had some money, I don't know what would have happened to the family. His wife moved in with them with the daughter when he died in a car crash. Baxter was in the military by then."

"Do you know if Baxter dated Rylee?"

"No, I don't know anything about that. He was a damn good football player, but what I also remember about him was that he was a scrapper. He'd hang out at that biker's bar, Koot's, that Randall owned. He did his fair share of fighting."

"What can you tell me about the car crash involving Baxter?"

Jack considered the topic while he drank some coffee. "Well, I don't know much about that, because that was the same night as Hogan's death."

Cheryl interrupted, "The same night?"

"Yep, it was late, and not too long before the train incident. The sheriff didn't show up at the train site that night, which surprised me at the time. However, I later heard that he had been called out to where Baxter's crash happened, so I guess he was handling that mishap."

"I couldn't find a police report on that."

Jack smirked. "I can't say I'm surprised. The sheriff handled it, and it was a commissioner's boy."

"Do you know if anyone was in the car with Baxter when it happened?"

"I never heard that. I just heard that it was the Dodsons in the other car and they weren't hurt, at least not much." Jack drank another sip of coffee. "Old man Dodson was seen driving a shiny new car after that."

"What about Billy Abbott's father?"

"You mean the owner of the hardware store?"

"Yes."

"Well, if you're wondering if he might have had a reason to ask Randall to shut down the investigation into Hogan's or the girl's deaths, that seems unlikely. The Abbott family was successful in their hardware business and pillars in the community when it came to the church and charity events. Abbott was a deacon in the church. I'm sure he knew the Thompsons, but they didn't circulate with each other. I just can't see him ever falling into Randall Thompson's web. I never heard anyone speak badly about his business or business practices."

"I see, but if he thought his son was in serious trouble, he could have asked Randall for help."

Jack rolled his neck to loosen the kinks. "You make a good point that you never know what you might do in those circumstances. Abbott was smart enough to know that if he asked Randall to step in, he and his business would have been forever in Randall's debt. Like selling his soul to the devil. I sure can't guarantee it didn't happen, but as between the two boys you're asking about, Baxter seems the more likely one."

"Mmm." Cheryl sipped her coffee considering Jack's observations.

Jack interrupted her thoughts, "Now, if what you're looking for is someone who could have gotten Randall to stop the investigation, there was another boy who was in Baxter's class whose dad had a lot of influence with Randall. The boy's dad wasn't a commissioner, but he was an important man around town and wielded a lot of influence. He wasn't the type to bow to Randall, that's for sure, but he and Randall did a couple of business deals together."

"Who was that?"

"Ford Montgomery. He was from the area and went off to a military academy for college and came back wearing so many ribbons and medals I don't know how he walked. He was a general when he retired. He married a younger woman, and their son, Simon, was about ten or twelve when they moved back to Bekbourg. Everybody called him 'the general,' and he and his wife were *always* on a pedestal. Ford was a power-player around town until his death. He was the grand marshal in several of the parades and the guest of honor for many events. She was active in all the social circles until her health started failing. Once when the governor came to town, they were the official welcoming committee."

"You said that Baxter got in fights. Did he get in other troubles?"

"Well, drinking and drag racing and stuff like that, but I never heard of him stealing or vandalizing—that sort of thing."

"What about Billy Abbott or Simon Montgomery?" Cheryl wasn't sure what Simon's middle name was, but she would check when she returned to Bekbourg. "Did they get into trouble?"

"Neither one really. Certainly not Abbott. I don't remember ever pulling him over for speeding or drinking. I caught Simon speeding some, but back then, we just would warn the boys. If it got to be a problem, we'd have to do something."

"Do you know if any of these three boys hung out together?"

"I doubt any of the three hung out with the other two. Simon didn't walk as straight a line as the Abbott boy, but he was too self-disciplined to put up with someone like Baxter. That's probably because that was how Ford Montgomery was. He walked with his back straight and head up, and he was a no-nonsense man."

As they wrapped up their conversation, Jack said, "It's too bad you're flying back tonight. Darla and I would like to have showed you around our downtown. We could give you a tour. Also, you'd like the jetty, and we could show you the pier and get some delicious seafood to eat.

"I wish I had more time, too. What little I saw driving here, I loved the Mediterranean architecture in the quaint downtown."

"Well, you and Sean will have to find time to come back." Jack draped his arm around Darla's shoulders, which caused her smile to widen. "We love Venice. It's our city-paradise by the ocean."

"Sean and I will make a point to visit real soon."

Chapter 53

Sean met with the three commissioners and the county treasurer, Jason Worley. The chairman thanked him for being able to meet so soon and explained, "Sean, everyone here, and hell, everyone in the county except the criminals appreciate the job you've been doing. As you know, Noel is new to the commission and is learning his way around. We all want to make sure that everyone around the county knows we're taking our jobs seriously. Not that we think you're doing anything wrong. But when Noel raised his concerns about the budget, we wanted to meet with you so we would be able to assure people that there's not going to be a tax increase because of the expenditures by any of the county departments."

Sean had some files in front of him. "Sure, I understand. What is it you would like to discuss?"

The chairman looked over at Noel, "Why don't you tell Sean about your concerns?"

Noel straightened his shoulders and waved some paper, "I have a letter from the state's accounting office that summarizes the expenses for work you have called on from the state police, medical examiner and forensics, since you first joined the sheriff's department. These expenses are *three times* more than your budget for these services," Noel stressed as he looked at the other two commissioners. The chairman coughed. The other commissioner scratched his head, and the treasurer watched with interest. Any intention by Noel to embarrass or provoke Sean fell flat—not even an awkward blink from Sean's stoic face.

Noel felt emboldened that he was scoring points in his take-down of Sean. "As I said at the public meeting earlier this week, I don't see why the county should be paying for the state police *and* a sheriff's department. Sure seems redundant. It's the same with the other two services. Doc Emerson can handle the coroner duties just fine, and we have a lab at the hospital that can handle forensics. These are hard-working people, competent people. They deserve the confidence of everyone in the county. We don't want them, or people around the county, feeling they're incompetent or undervalued. Aside from the budget questions, we don't want a morale problem." Looking at the other two commissioners, he continued, "Like I told them the other day, we need an audit of the entire sheriff's department to get to the bottom of this potential mismanagement."

Sean looked at the chairman, "It would be helpful to see what the commissioner is referencing. Can someone get me a copy of the letter?"

Lance nodded, "I'll get us all copies." He pressed a button, and a clerk appeared to make copies. While they waited, the chairman and the other commissioner talked to Sean about the upcoming football season. They were disappointed with the team's record. Jason Worley, the treasurer, wondered out loud if the school board had made the right decision in the head football coach they had selected. Noel fumed they were less focused on the budget and more concerned about the football program. He ignored the conversation and fumbled through papers while they waited for the clerk's return with the copies.

After the clerk distributed the copies, the Chair said, "We'll give Sean time to take a look at this." He turned toward Noel, "I know you're new to the commission, but in the future, we need to have copies of things like this so we can be prepared."

Noel's face tightened, but he remained silent.

After everyone had read the letter, the Chair asked Sean if he needed more time to look into its contents. "No." Sean looked at the treasurer, "Jason, I notice this letter says that Commissioner Fischner asked for it to be prepared. Have you received any notification that the state plans to charge any of these costs to the county?"

"No." He looked at the commissioners. "And, it would surprise me if the state allocated these costs back to us."

Noel stiffened. "What's that supposed to mean?"

"Well, we're a small county, Noel, and the state resources are there to help out, especially the sheriff's department. If you notice, these were serious law enforcement investigations that required manpower and expertise beyond what Bekbourg can provide. A small-town sheriff's department is not staffed to do justice to cartel drug operations and major murder investigations. Doc Emerson is good, but he does not have the equipment or labs to perform forensic medical exams like the state. Same with the forensic crime services needed for these complex cases."

Noel bristled. "Well, even if we're lucky this time and the state doesn't allocate these costs back to us, we may not be so lucky next time. It seems to me that we need to have a procedure in place that Sean needs our approval before he brings in the state. We don't need them looking into everything around here. We can take care of our own things," he glanced at the treasurer, "unless something extraordinary happens. But, he should still get our approval."

Sean spoke up. "Let me address your concerns about the budget, Noel. I knew when I brought the state in on these matters outlined in this letter that these costs would not be allocated back to us, for all the reasons Jason laid out. Now, this idea of getting prior approval to bring in the experts is not the way things work. Part of being the sheriff means that I have the autonomy to bring in professionals and experts in criminal cases." Pointing to the letter, Sean continued, "No one at the state level ever questioned my judgment on these cases. I have been in law enforcement for twenty-five years. I know how to run a criminal investigation."

The Chair jumped in, "And the people around Bekbourg know you do, Sean. Hell, that's why they voted you in as sheriff. I think what Jason and Sean said is right. Doc Emerson will be the first to tell you that the state expertise was needed on these murder investigations, and the same is true with our hospital lab. They do not have the staff or equipment needed for these types of investigations."

Noel felt his push to audit Sean slipping away. "Well, it goes beyond the budget. I heard that Sean is investigating a murder that happened twenty years ago that didn't even involve Bekbourg. Not only that. The case was solved." Noel glanced toward the two commissioners. "I'm glad he's locked up the criminals, but it's his cavalier way of doing business that needs a check. We need to audit what he's working on *and* his budget. Maybe it's just me, but isn't it a conflict for our sheriff to moonlight on other investigations while we're still paying his salary?"

The Chair looked at Sean, "Sean, what's this all about?"

As much as Noel was a jerk, even this was out of character for Noel. He wasn't one to pick a fight unless he felt slighted or threatened. Since Sean had returned to Bekbourg, nothing happened that Sean was aware of that would put him in Noel's crosshairs. Someone must have put Noel up to this. He was referring to Caroline Montgomery's death, but why? Sean didn't want Noel's effort to poison him with the other commissioners. He had to get control before they launched a frivolous and time-wasting review. "I came here today prepared to discuss my year-to-date expenses against the budget, which I am glad to do. Just so you know, we are under budget in our expenditures. Everyone in my department works hard. We've been able to manage so far, but I need approval to fill the vacant deputy position. Otherwise, the overtime will start hitting my budget, which I can't avoid, unless I start to lean on the state police for routine matters, which we don't want to do."

Sean looked at Noel, "Now, on the other matter that Noel has raised, I assume he does not mean to interfere with an ongoing investigation." Both commissioners jerked around to look at Noel. Sean continued, "I have always taken my oath of office seriously, and my department is dedicated to upholding the law and serving the residents of Bekbourg. So, I know you understand when I say that I cannot discuss the merits of any ongoing investigations."

The chairman looked at Noel. "I haven't heard anything today that suggests there are any concerns with Sean's budget. You say that you heard a rumor that he is moonlighting, but unless you have some facts, I'm not going to insert this commission in an ongoing investigation. What do you think, Riley?"

The other commissioner voiced support for the chairman's decision. Noel was in a box. Harvey would be furious if he mentioned the case involved the Brigadier, but without doing so, the commissioners were unwilling to order any further review, and even then they might not be inclined. He made one final attempt, "Something started a rumor. Seems to me we should look at the sheriff's department closer and review its expenditures before we approve a new hire."

"We can't investigate every rumor out there about our county officials. We'd bust our own budget. Sean, I'll see to it that your request to fill that vacant deputy position will be put on our next meeting's agenda. I'll also make mention at that meeting that we had this follow-up as we discussed at the public meeting and that it was determined that nothing merits an audit into the sheriff's department. I appreciate everyone's time today."

When Noel saw Sean walk into his outfitter's shop, his eyes rounded, and he leaned back against the counter. Sean looked around and saw the shop was empty.

"Noel, I want to talk to you about that meeting with the other two commissioners where you accused me of moonlighting. You have no business interfering with the sheriff's department. I am a duly elected official just like you are, and I have my responsibilities just like you do. You seem to have the attitude that you can tell everyone in the county what to do, but I'm going on record right now that you are not going to tell me or the sheriff's department what to do. Maybe in the old days the commission told the sheriff what to do, but you don't tell me what to do—just so you know. If you think I'm doing something improper, bring in the state police. I'll be more than happy to talk to them, but if you do, you're the one who is going to have to answer a lot of questions, especially, who put you up to this."

Chapter 54

In Syd's research into the finances of Luca and Natalia Ramirez, she discovered that Luca and Natalia were behind in payments on their house, and it seemed unlikely the bank would grant them a second mortgage given the house's assessed value and their lack of income. Their credit card had reached its limit. Prior to Skylar's death, it looked as though they were going to lose their house. However, the life insurance policy would be enough to cover what was owed with a little left over.

Syd learned from the attorney in D.C. who Skylar had retained that the couple had entered into a prenuptial agreement, which kept Skylar's assets from before their marriage separate from Simon's. Given the change in the will, Natalia would inherit a nice sum from her sister's estate.

If money was a motive for Skylar's death, Natalia and Luca were big beneficiaries.

Soon after Syd reported back to Sean on the Ramirez's financial difficulties, Lucky call Sean with information about Simon's finances. The Lake Shore house had a second mortgage. Through public disclosure documents, Lucky found that six years earlier, Simon had invested a substantial sum in an oil venture in Venezuela. The solicitation prospectus sold the venture as "high-yield return" after five years. There were other American investors, including retired military men such as Simon. A change in Venezuelan government officials occurred, which raised concerns, but there was no recourse but to wait out the five-year period until the prospect came on-line. Things started to go wrong with the project, and the Venezuelan who headed the project and solicited the investors was assassinated. Shortly after the assassination, the government nationalized all the assets, and the American investors had no way to recover their money. Simon and others sought assistance from the U.S. government, but their efforts proved unsuccessful.

Lucky also discovered that Simon had acquired properties over the years in Montana and Wyoming, but they had not appreciated in value. He had been trying to sell the small ranch in Wyoming for two years. The property in Montana had recently been put on the market, but the asking price was not much above the price he had paid for it. Both properties were mortgaged to the brink, and based on current market prices in both of these areas, Lucky was skeptical Simon could sell the properties for close to the asking prices.

Lucky also answered the mystery of what had happened to Simon's cherished 1969 Dodge Charger Daytona. He learned that Simon had quietly sold it through a private auction to a buyer in California. Although he did not know the exact sales price, he surmised it was easily within the six-figure range.

"Sean, from everything I've seen, Montgomery is about tapped out. Those funds from the car sale bought him some time, but they are not going to last forever. If he can't sell his properties out west, and that looks doubtful, Simon is facing financial ruin. Based on his lack of cash flow, barring some miracle, Montgomery is likely heading toward bankruptcy."

Arlo Lopez was the most talkative of Sean's deputies. If there was a dispute between neighbors, he had a way of mediating disputes without them escalating. Being former military and an avid outdoorsman, he could be tough if the situation required, but his preference was to peacefully settle things. "Hey, Chief, got a minute?"

"Sure, Arlo. Have a seat."

"I told you the other day that the guard's log showed Mrs. Montgomery's car driving through Friday afternoon, and it was about the time she would have driven through after leaving Ms. Zimmstein's foundation. You know about Luca driving through later?"

Sean nodded.

"Well, something else. Flynn Taggart. He's the one who came to see you, right?"

Sean figured either Kim or Alex had told him about Flynn—department intrigue on an otherwise boring day. "Yes, that's him."

"I reviewed the log and video from the day Mrs. Montgomery died. Something kept bugging me, and I decided to look closer. Earlier that morning, the realtor, Jason Worley, came through. I went by and talked to him. He had a client with him that morning. The client was Flynn Taggart."

Sean arched an eyebrow in interest. "On the day she died?"

"Yep. The realtor told me Mr. Taggart said he had served in the military, really liked the area and was considering relocating here. Flynn asked specifically to look at Lake Shore. While they were driving around, Flynn told Jason he had served with the Brigadier and heard he lived there and wondered if Jason would show him where, which he did."

Sean asked, "So he saw where the Brigadier lived earlier the day when Mrs. Montgomery died?"

"That morning."

Sean thought out loud, "This is an interesting development. From what I know about Flynn's finances, he couldn't afford a place in Lake Shore, so I have to think his real reason was to see where the Brigadier lives. But why?"

Arlo shook her head, "I don't know, Sheriff, but is there any reason to think he killed Mrs. Montgomery?"

"I need to chew on this. Good work, Arlo. We need to know more about Flynn's schedule that day." He gave Arlo the name of the motel Flynn had been staying in and asked him to see what he could find out.

Chapter 55

While Syd was visiting people who had attended Harvey's weekend business meeting, Alex met with the manager of the hotel where Simon and the others had stayed. The manager checked the keycard records for Simon's room, and it showed that Simon had entered his room at twelve-sixteen on that Friday, and the next activity showed him entering late that evening after the dinner had concluded. The manager explained that there would be no record of him leaving the room, and that while there were surveillance cameras in the elevators, they did not have any in the halls or stairwells. Because Simon had opted to park his car in the adjacent parking lot instead of using the valet, there was no record or video of when, or if, his car had been moved.

Since a guest was not booked in the room, the manager showed Alex the room. It was on the third floor, so there was no way Simon could have exited from the room itself other than through the door. When they walked back into the hallway, Alex asked the manager if he could look around.

Alex looked in the small room that contained the ice machine and three vending machines. Other than the one elevator bank and the stairway, there were no other exits.

It would be easy enough for Simon to have left down the stairway, but how could he have gotten back into his room without there being a record? If he had driven to Bekbourg, was he dressed for dinner so when he returned to Columbus, he had no need to first return to his room? There was a back entryway that did not have a video feed, but a guest card was needed to access that entry. *If he had entered through the main lobby entry, he would have been videotaped, and there was not any evidence of that occurring. Maybe Simon had entered the back entryway when another guest was using that doorway.*

Before leaving the hotel, Alex asked the manager if a member of the staff might have let Simon into his room. He assured Alex that that was strictly against policy—that a guest could only be admitted to his or her room after being vetted by the manager on duty if they lost or left the room key inside the room. At Alex's insistence, he told Alex that he would inquire of the staff to see if anyone had allowed Simon entry. Since admitting to that would probably result in dismissal, Alex did not hold much hope that anyone would admit to letting Simon into his room even if they had.

Based on what he learned from people at the hotel, Alex concluded that there was no way to prove that Simon drove back to Bekbourg, killed Skylar, and returned in time for dinner. If he drove to Bekbourg, he could have evaded the video camera by another guest letting him in the back-entry door or by a staff unlocking his room door. Both seemed unlikely to prove. It could be that he returned to his room after lunch and stayed until dinner time—the key card suggested that. Credit card records would show if he used them outside the hotel that day, but based on Sean's statement about how savvy a planner Simon was, Alex doubted he would have left an evidence trail.

Chapter 56

"Simon, I've combed through the prenup agreement, and you have no claim on the investments and bank account that Skylar had before you and she married," said Simon's attorney. "If you remember when I wrote this up, you didn't want her to have any claims on your assets, so I wrote mirror provisions."

"Why in the hell did you do that? I never asked for that—just that she couldn't get my assets."

Simon couldn't see that attorney's scowl through the phone line, "You never told me anything about getting access to her assets, only to make it, and I quote, 'ironclad' that she not be able to make a claim on yours, except through the provisions of the will. Look, Simon, if I had tried to make either the prenup or the will one-sided, all in your favor, there might not have ever been a marriage. Her attorney would have objected that there weren't reciprocal clauses, but if I'd been in her shoes, I'd have raised red flags about what you were up to. Not a good way to start off a marriage."

"What about the new will she signed?" Simon was abrupt. "Have you looked into that?"

"Yes. I called Skylar's attorney right after you called me, and she sent me a copy. The will that Skylar signed when you all married is succeeded by her new will. Her attorney crossed all the T's and dotted the I's in meeting all the legal requirements. She left everything to her sister, Natalia Ramirez."

"She didn't have a right to change the will, damnit!"

The lawyer calmly replied, "That's not correct, Simon. She had every right to change the will, just like you did for yours."

"I don't buy that!" Simon paused, "Hell, her sister doesn't know anything about wills. You can file a claim against the will. She won't fight us. She'll roll over."

"It's not that easy, Simon. Skylar didn't trust her sister to handle things. Probably for the reasons you're thinking. I gathered from what little her attorney said, Skylar didn't trust Natalia's husband. Skylar had a trust set up with Natalia as the sole beneficiary. Skylar's attorney will oversee any litigation, and she knows what she's doing. My advice to you is to forget about contesting the will unless you want to spend a lot of money. The law is stacked against you."

"This is bullshit! It is not the way I understood it. It's not what we agreed to. I'm paying you to solve this problem. Look at everything again about breaking the will. And, I need an answer ASAP!"

"Okay, Simon. I'll give it another look."

Simon slammed down the phone. "Damn you, Skylar! You had *no right* to do this to me! Because of you, I'm going to be penniless. I won't be able to show my face! I've spent a lifetime to get where I am, and now *EVERY DAMN THING* will be flushed down the damn toilet! *Damn you to hell*!"

Chapter 57

Lilly saw Cheryl walking by and stood, "Hi, Cheryl. Could I ask you something?"

"Sure."

"Would you mind if I don't come in on Saturday? We need to do our final shooting for the video, and we're starting to run short on time. Everyone's available then."

"Of course. No problem. How's it going?"

"Actually, really good, except I'm a little nervous about getting it all edited. Reid and I have been working on the editing, but it needs some work, and we haven't been through the whole movie. He and I are going to get together early next week after school to hopefully finalize the editing. The deadline for turning in our movie is next Friday."

"Jake's still hanging in there?"

Lilly laughed. "I don't know if it was making him an assistant director, or if it's just that he is super competitive, but he *really* wants to win first place. If he sees something he doesn't like about the script or the acting or whatever, he makes suggestions. So, yes, he's into it."

"I know that is a relief to you. What is this movie about?"

Lilly described how Esther's ghost learns that her great-great granddaughter, Katrina, played by Clair, is engaged to be married to Russell. She has a request that Katrina try and find the jewelry that her beloved Anton lost on his way to propose to her. Esther's ghost tells Katrina that Anton was coming to propose to her before he left to fight in the First World War. On his way across the valley, two thieves started pursuing him, and he didn't want them to steal his mother's ring and necklace he was planning to give to Esther when he proposed. He knew the thieves were going to catch him, so he buried the jewels near a tombstone and rushed on. When they caught him, he only had money on him, which they took. Fortunately, they didn't kill him, but they roughed him up and left him unconscious.

When he finally got to the Krause's place and started up the hill, Herr Krause, Esther's father, met him with his shotgun and demanded he leave. Anton tried to explain that he was going off to war and that he loved Esther and wanted to marry her before he left, but Krause's mind was made up. Esther was only fifteen years old—too young to marry according to her father. He told Anton that if he still wanted to marry her when he returned from the war, he could come back and propose then.

Esther's ghost was emotional as she relayed to Katrina (Claire) how heartbroken she was that

303

day when her father turned Anton away. She pined for him for three years. They had met at a church dance, and it was love at first sight. He had been to see her twice after the dance, and their courtship consisted of them sitting on the front porch with her father sitting just inside the house. But their time together, as short as it was, gave them the chance to realize their love for each other was soul-reaching and that they were destined to be life mates.

Lilly told Cheryl how Claire/Katrina had real tears running down her cheeks as Esther's ghost/Lilly told the story. Because he was set to be shipped out, Anton didn't have time to search the cemetery to find where he had buried the jewels.

When Anton finally returned from war, they were married and lived a long life together. Esther's ghost explained to Katrina the life-time of love they held for each other. "This band of gold," she held out her wrinkled ghostly hand "was all I ever needed, but Anton tried several times to find the ring and necklace to give to me, but he never found them. He wanted me to have his mother's jewelry. Knowing how much it meant to him, I wish I had it to give to you for a wedding present."

Esther asked Katrina if she could locate the jewelry in the old cemetery, because she wanted her great-great daughter to have it on her wedding day. Katrina vowed to try and find the long-lost ring and necklace.

Katrina tells Russell the story. They make plans to take a metal detector and shovel to the cemetery, but as they discussed their plans, they are unaware that the handyman is eavesdropping on their conversation. The handyman villain gets to the cemetery ahead of them and is looking for the jewels. When he hears Katrina and Russell arrive, he hides. He watches as they search. What he doesn't realize is that he is being watched by the ghost of Anton. Katrina and Russell finally hear the metal detector pinging and start digging. Near a small granite tombstone, the inscription worn beyond reading, they find the leather bag and inside are the ring and necklace.

Anton had not been able to depart this world, because he was obsessed with never finding the buried jewelry and being unable to give it to his beloved Esther. During all these years, his ghost has hovered around the graveyard. Anton's ghost overhears Katrina talking to Russell and learns that she is Esther's great-great granddaughter and that they are attempting to locate the jewelry. He realizes to his joy that Esther's ghost is still around and that it is Esther's wish that Katrina wear the jewels on her wedding day.

Suddenly, the villain appears and startles Katrina and Russell. They fear for their lives as he points a knife at them and demands they give him the jewels. Anton's ghost sees what is happening and is determined that the villain not get away with the jewelry, so he uses a special ghostly power to distract the villain, which gives Russell and Katrina a chance to escape. The villain pursues them, with Anton's ghost fleeing alongside him, causing the villain to stumble and break his leg. Russell and Katrina escape and alert the authorities, who find the villain trying to drag himself out of the woods. He begs the police to get him out of there, claiming a ghost is haunting him.

Lilly concludes, "The scene ends with Esther's ghost watching Katrina and Russell getting married with her wearing her great-great grandmother's ring and necklace. Anton's ghost is standing behind Esther smiling with his hand on her shoulder. She puts her hand over his, and they smile and fade away."

"I love the story, Lilly!"

"Well, it captures the group's ideas—a love story, action adventure and ghosts," Lilly smiled.

"I am looking forward to seeing it. It's going to be sensational."

Chapter 58

Buddy's ears perked right up before he went barreling to the front door, which was followed by a knock. Buddy's whining and tail wagging left little room for speculation. "I know," cooed Cheryl, "it's grandma Kye," she said laughing as she opened the door. Kye had the treat ready as she greeted Buddy and Cheryl. "He always knows it's you before you knock," said Cheryl. "Let's go in the kitchen. I just make a pot of coffee."

"Thank you, dear. I hope I'm not disturbing you. I know your Sean is participating on that anti-drug program this evening at the high school and thought you might like some company."

As Cheryl poured their coffee, Kye sat at the kitchen table and looked at the old open shoe box. "What's this, dear?"

Cheryl explained about Hogan's sister bringing the boxes with her when she asked Cheryl to look into his death. She picked up a key that was lying on the table and showed Kye. "This was in the box, and something has been bugging me about it. I can't figure out why it would have been in Hogan's car. I'm going to take it to Joe's Key and Lock shop tomorrow and see what he can tell me about it."

"Can I see it?" asked Kye.

Cheryl handed the key to her and watched Kye's perusal as she sipped her coffee.

"Humm. This reminds me of a key that Cecil had that he used for his room at the railroad bunkhouse in Wheeling, West Virginia. That was their turnaround when he took the train east."

"Oh? I never heard about a railroad bunkhouse."

Kye chuckled, "The railroaders probably use motels today, but back then, in some smaller cities, the railroad arranged its own accommodations for the crew. I always liked hearing Cecil's stories about what went on there with the locals coming to eat at the buffet they served. Anyway, the bunkhouse was large enough that Cecil, with his seniority, was assigned his own room. He was given a key, and it looked a lot like this key here."

"Why would Hogan have a key for something like that?" Cheryl furrowed her brows.

"Well, I can't imagine he would have a key for a railroad bunkhouse. His dad didn't work for the railroad. But, this type of key was used by institutions that had their own keying system. See these letters." Kye pointed to the two letters stamped toward the top of the key's flat surface. "I suspect that stands for a specific wing or building. The number here is likely a room number."

"Do you have any idea who may have used this type of key around here?" asked Cheryl.

"No, dear. I can't think of any business around here forty years ago that would have used a key like this." Kye drank her coffee and continued to study the key. "It doesn't match the keys we used for our classroom doors at the high school. Hogan wasn't planning to go to college, was he?"

"No. Why?"

"It's the type of key that a college might use for its dorms. Hillsrock Community College doesn't have dorms, but maybe they use them for the classrooms."

"I wonder why he would have a key to the local community college. Do you think he might have found it and just tossed it in his car?" Cheryl asked.

"I don't know, but you might start there. They might have an idea about how to discover where this key came from."

Chapter 59

Following up on his conversation with Fritz, Sean called the police department in the small town on the outskirts of Jacksonville, near Camp Lejeune. Ralph Belks was the police chief. He told Sean that he was near retirement and had been the chief for just over twenty-five years. When Sean told him why he was calling, Ralph remembered the incident but wanted to see what he could find in their files. When he called Sean back, he told Sean something that left Sean questioning even more what actually happened in the Flynn Taggart investigation.

Flynn frequented a bar in an area to the southeast away from the Base. The bartenders and waitresses knew him. One of the waitresses liked to flirt with him and knew that he drove a red jeep with a scrape on the driver's side rear panel. The motel where Flynn and Caroline regularly met was along the highway about thirty miles north of the Base. On the night that Caroline was killed, the waitress was running late for her shift and saw Flynn changing a tire on the road heading to the bar. She figured he had things under control, and she kept driving. It was just starting to get dark when she saw him. The sheriff had not checked the mileage, but he estimated it was at least fifty miles between the location of where she spotted him changing the tire and the motel where Caroline was found. The roads between the two locations were mostly back roads.

Ralph explained how news about Caroline's killing was in all the newspapers and the talk of the area. When the waitress heard of Flynn's arrest, she called and told him about seeing Flynn changing his tire the same evening Caroline was killed. Ralph then called and talked to the MP who was investigating. His notes showed that was Fritz Marlow. He told Sean he never heard back about it, and then when he read they found the scarf in Flynn's jeep, he assumed they knew he was the killer, and that was why they never followed up with him.

Sean's former commanding officer, Tanner Bradford, had drummed into all his investigators' heads to never make assumptions and leave no stone unturned to unanswered questions. Tanner lived by his words, so when Sean had first called him and asked him about Flynn's court martial, Tanner decided to check into the case himself and see what he could learn. Believing his findings merited Sean's attention, he called Sean. "Sean, there's something I discovered that I thought I should pass on. I don't know how it fits into Flynn Taggart showing up in Bekbourg or even it if does."

Sean sat forward at his desk. Tanner wouldn't be calling with trivia. "Did you know Flynn had a younger brother who was a Marine?"

"No, Sir."

"About seven years ago, his brother was stationed at the Rota naval station in Spain. A military helicopter crashed in rugged terrain in Iraq, and a team of Marines was needed to fly into the area by helicopter. Once the chopper landed, the Marine team had to hike to the crash site and get the personnel to a secure location where they could be evacuated by choppers. The commanding officer needed a squad of Marines for the mission, and he asked for volunteers. Flynn's brother volunteered. Typical of our brave forces, several more volunteered than the number needed for the mission, so the commanding officer had to decide on the individuals for the mission. As it turned out, Simon Montgomery was at this base on a short stint, and the commanding officer decided to consult him and get his feedback on the team that would be deployed. Flynn's brother was one of those chosen. I have no way of finding out if Montgomery personally selected Flynn's brother, or how the final decisions were made, but there is a connection, if only a dotted line, between Montgomery and Flynn's brother. The significance is that Flynn's brother was killed on that mission along with two other Marines."

Sean's jaw tightened. "So, if Flynn believed that Montgomery was the one responsible for sending his brother on that mission, he could hold resentment against Montgomery."

"If Flynn believed that Montgomery held a grudge against him for killing his wife and retaliated by sending his brother on a dangerous mission where he lost his life, then, he could blame Montgomery. The commander would have made the final call, but if he relied on Montgomery's input in making that decision, like I said, there is a dotted line between Montgomery and Flynn's brother. It may be a stretch, Sean, but it's another data point. One other thing—I don't know if that information made it back to Flynn with him being in prison, but I would not rule out that possibility."

Chapter 60

Sean needed to question Flynn about why he wanted to learn where the Brigadier lived and whether he held a grudge against him because of his brother's death. Because he considered it a formal interview, he called the local sheriff and explained the situation. The sheriff arranged for a deputy to pick up Sean at the airport and accompany him to where Flynn was living.

A grass strip ran up the center of a gravel driveway leading to a small block house. An older model SUV was parked in a small patch of gravel off to the side of the driveway. A tree stump stood in the middle of the yard. From the dirt patch extending beneath the two front windows—it looked as though shrubs had been recently removed.

Flynn was mowing the yard when the deputy pulled up. He stopped when he saw the deputy and Sean get out of the cruiser. As they approached, Sean introduced the deputy. "Mind if we go in? There are some questions I have."

"You're a long way from Bekbourg, Sean," Flynn said as he wondered why they were there.

"We need to talk."

Flynn had grown up on the outskirts of Columbia, South Carolina. After his mother died, the attorney handling her estate sold the small house and its five acres and put the money in the bank for Flynn when he got out of prison. There was also a modest amount of savings—giving Flynn something to live off until he could get his life in some order. His mother's brother owned the small rental house nearby and was letting Flynn live there for as long as he wanted. Inside, the walls had dark paneling, and the furniture was old. If it wasn't for a shirt on the back of a chair and a newspaper on the small laminate coffee table, the place would have looked deserted.

After they were seated, Flynn asked, "Okay. What's this about?"

"Let's start by you telling me the real reason you came to Bekbourg," Sean volleyed his first question.

Flynn tilted his head. "I'm not sure what you're getting at, Sean. I told you why the first time we met."

"Okay, Flynn. Then, why did you have a realtor take you around Lake Shore on the pretense of looking for property? You asked him to point out where the Brigadier lived."

"So? What's so wrong with that?" Flynn looked at Sean and then at the deputy. "I told you I saw Montgomery in town. That surprised the hell out of me. Then, I got curious. Wanted to see where he lived. I was thinking I might ask him for his help. Hell, he might have some ideas about who killed Caroline. I had served twenty years. Why not help me? I thought he might."

"I heard there was a scene in front of the GilHaus between the two of you, and he told you he never wanted to see you again. So, you thought you'd ask him *again*?"

"After he cooled down, yeah, he might."

"I don't believe you, Flynn." Sean did not want Flynn to ask them to leave before he answered his questions, but he decided to push to gauge Flynn's reaction. "You've been lying to me from the first time you walked into my office, and you're lying now."

Sean watched as Flynn studied him. Flynn's words were measured, "I don't know why you think that, but I wanted your help. You obviously were not interested in helping. I did not mislead you, and I don't know why you think I did."

Sean looked hard at Flynn. "Where did you go after your joyride with the realtor?"

For his part, Flynn was curious why Sean had come from Bekbourg to talk with him. He dismissed the notion that it had something to do with Caroline's death when he saw the deputy, because there would be no reason to bring him along for a twenty-year-old court martial. If he continued talking, he figured Sean would get to the point of his visit.

"It's not any of your damn business, Sean, but after we got back to the realtor's office, I decided you weren't going to help me. I had second thoughts about again asking Montgomery to help me. So, I headed back here. No use hanging around Bekbourg."

"Just like that?" Sean probed.

"Yes. What's this all about, Sean? Let's quit playing games."

"Why didn't you tell me about your brother?"

Flynn jerked his head up, "Huh? What the hell has he got to do with anything?"

Sean paused and then shook his head as his chuckle carried no humor. "Are you telling me that you didn't know that Montgomery was at the base at the time your brother was sent on the mission where he was killed?"

Flynn looked at Sean like he had just landed from Mars, "What. In. The. Hell. Does. That. Have. To. Do. With. *ANYTHING*?" Flynn demanded.

Sean leaned forward, his elbows on his knees. "You're not telling me you didn't know, are you?"

"No, I knew." Flynn clipped his words. "Hell, it's a small world in the Marines—even in prison. Look, I don't know what you're getting at. My brother volunteered for that assignment. He knew the risks, but that's who he was. I don't know . . . wait. You think I somehow blame Montgomery for my brother's death?"

Sean didn't respond.

"Man, you are full of it, Sean. Other men were killed along with my brother." Flynn looked at the deputy, who sat emotionless and silent, and returned his focus to Sean, "Hell, even if I do blame him, which I don't, so what?"

"What do you know about Montgomery's wife's death?"

Flynn furrowed his brows, "Is this a trick question?" When neither Sean nor the deputy moved a muscle, Flynn's impatience escaped, "Hell, twenty years was a long time to think about it and how I ended up in the slammer for something I didn't do, so what *exactly* do you want to know?"

"I'm not talking about Caroline," Sean responded. "I'm talking about his second wife."

Flynn's jaw dropped. "What second wife? When did she die? Shit, I need a hallucinogenic drug to follow this conversation."

Silence filled the room. Finally, Flynn leaned toward Sean putting his elbows on his knees. "Sean, I don't know what in the hell you think you know, and I sure as hell am not connecting the damn dots. You're saying that Montgomery had a second wife who died?"

Sean was having none of his playacting. "Yeah, Flynn. On the day you checked out of the motel."

They sat in silence staring hard at each other. Flynn finally stood, "I don't know a damn thing about that, but you must think I do, or you wouldn't be here. You better go, Sean."

He walked over and opened the door. As Sean and the deputy walked by, Flynn said after him, "Don't you think it's *just a little* too convenient that two of Montgomery's wives died?"

Sean ignored Flynn, but on his short flight back, Sean replayed their conversation and considered the possibilities. Maybe it was a stretch to assume Flynn blamed Montgomery for his brother being selected for the mission. There was no way that Flynn would know if the commander consulted Montgomery and what his input was. Hell, for all Sean knew, Montgomery may have objected to his brother, but the commander made a final decision to include him.

Flynn acted surprised to learn that Skylar had died, but he was skilled enough to lie—and be convincing. She died later that afternoon after he allegedly left town. Sean did not think Flynn would kill an innocent woman for revenge against Simon. If Flynn suspected that Simon was complicit in Caroline's death, such as working with Keaton, maybe he wanted to kill Simon. Maybe, he went up there to scout out the place and ran into her and killed her to prevent her from telling Simon.

Sean was not even sure there was foul play in Skylar's death, but there was the bump on her head which suggested there might be. Maybe Flynn was innocent in Skylar's death. Maybe it was Luca, the brother-in-law. Hell, why did he keep coming back to it being a murder in the first place? Because, thought Sean, it didn't feel right to think she killed herself or would have accidently drowned. Sure, there was the possibility that she slipped, being inebriated, and hit her head, but why would she have been that close to the water's edge knowing she had been drinking?

Then, there was Simon. Sean pondered Flynn's departing words that both of his wives had died—one killed, and the other dead under mysterious circumstances. Simon had two motives. One was he needed money, and he was the beneficiary under Skylar's will, or so he may have thought. The second was that she was leaving him, but why was that a motive for murder?

If he had listening devices and knew she had changed the will, then money was not a motive. Perhaps he did not have listening devices, or she talked with her attorney where her conversations could not be overheard. The search after her death did not show any evidence the house was bugged. He needed to check if there was any record of Simon purchasing listening devices. So, money may or may not have been a motive, depending on whether Simon knew the will had been rewritten.

From conversations with Skylar's friend, Liz, from D.C. and Natalia, Sean was suspicious of some of the things Simon had told him, like they were working to save their marriage. Neither Liz nor Natalia had heard Skylar say they were trying to salvage their marriage. Just the opposite—she was leaving him. Also, Sean was skeptical that he did not know she was taking a job at the Pentagon. Maybe another motive was that he was the type who couldn't accept the idea that Skylar was planning to leave him.

As between possible suspects, Simon, Flynn, and Luca, there was evidence that Luca was there that afternoon. Was it possible that Luca and Simon conspired to kill Skylar since they both had a financial incentive to see her dead? Or did Luca kill her for his financial gain?

Sean decided to bring Luca in for questioning.

Chapter 61

Even though he was a senior football player whose name began with a B, Billy's youthful appearance in the yearbook seemed at odds with the "man" Rylee's diary referenced. On the other hand, she could check all the boxes when it came to Baxter Colbert. He was a senior football player, and from his yearbook picture as well as people's accounts of him, he certainly would have seemed like a "man" to an innocent sophomore girl. His name started with a B, and he was in town for both the Christmas and spring breaks. Another factor was that his father was a crony of Randall's, who could have easily influenced the sheriff to drop the investigation into Rylee's death. More suspicious was that he was speeding out of Bekbourg on the night both Rylee and Hogan died. Instead of returning to college for second semester, Baxter joined the army. Did he do so to escape something he did that night?

Cheryl decided she wanted to talk with him again. She pulled into the driveway and observed the farm house. While it could use a paint job, it looked structurally sound. The shutters were securely attached, and the gutter and roof were newer. She got out and looked around. It was around supper time, which she thought would be her best chance to see him. When she got to the porch, the door swung open.

"Baxter, I was hoping to talk to you again."

He stepped out on the porch and let the storm door slam. "My wife almost has dinner ready. This is not a good time. Actually, no time is, Ms. Seton. We don't have anything to talk about."

"Why is that?"

"I wondered why you came to see me and was asking about Rylee. I dropped by the library and looked at some recent publications of the *Tribune.* I found the article you wrote about their deaths. The fact that you're trying to talk to me tells me you must think I know something, but I don't."

"What about the car crash you had during spring break your freshman year?"

He narrowed his brows. "What about it?"

"I understand that you were lucky you weren't killed."

"So?"

"The passenger side of your car was crushed. Did you have a passenger that night?"

"No."

"Why were you speeding out of town? I understand you had been drinking."

"What in the hell is this all about? No one was hurt. My old man took care of the old people in the other car. No harm, no foul. Why are you dredging up ancient history about me?"

"Seems you were in a hurry to leave that night. There must have been a reason."

Baxter's eyes turned to steel. "You reporters are all the same. I'm between a rock and a hard place. If I don't answer, you take me as guilty of whatever the hell your story is about, and the alternative is for me to spill my guts about something that is none of your damn business just to get you off my back." He glanced around, and turned rage-filled eyes back on her as he gritted his teeth, "I don't want you hounding me or having your boyfriend show up here to harass me. So, I'm going to say this once, and I don't want you ever showing up here again. I had an argument with my old man that night about what his gambling had done to my mom and sister. It was no secret he was squandering everything. Mom had been crying because there wasn't enough money for my next semester's tuition. I wasn't worried about myself, but I was damn sure concerned about Mom and my younger sister."

Cheryl and Baxter looked each other in the eyes, neither breaking the connection. "I've got one more question. What was the name of your dorm at college?"

"You got to be kiddin' me. How the hell should I know?" he snarled with disgust. "This is bullshit. I want you off my property."

As he turned away, Cheryl said, "Mr. Colbert, I am just doing my job. Those kids' families have lived with questions for forty years. If I can find what really happened that night, regardless of where the facts take me, I intend to do it." She doubted he heard her final words through the slammed door.

Chapter 62

Cheryl slumped back in her office chair and pushed her hair away from her face. She looked at the ceiling and considered her next steps. Because she did not seem to be making much progress, she determined to approach her investigation from a different angle. The sheriff at the time had quashed the investigation into Rylee and Hogan's deaths, and someone with clout had caused that to happen. Given what Jack Rhodes told her, there were three boys, all football players, whose fathers had that type of influence: Baxter Colbert, Billy Abbott, and Simon Montgomery. Cheryl prepared a spread sheet to list the criteria that met with Rylee's description. She knew a fair amount about Billy and Baxter, but she did not know whether Simon's middle name started with a B and whether he was in Bekbourg during Christmas or spring breaks that year.

The following afternoon, she went to the high school to see if Annalee, a close friend and high school counselor, could help her. Annalee pulled the old records to see if there was anything that would connect Simon's name with a B. As she was looking, Cheryl was scanning the notes in the back of the yearbook that listed where each student was planning to attend college.

She said, "We know Simon went to a military academy for college. He doesn't have a B in his name, but maybe there's something else. I don't know if this might help, but look here," she pointed for Annalee to see. "Here is another boy who went to the same military academy that Simon attended, James Lofton."

"Mmm. You're thinking he might know something about Simon?" asked Annalee.

"I don't know, Annalee," Cheryl sighed. "Maybe it's a wild goose chase. Simon doesn't have a B in his name, and that was one of the things *clear* from Rylee's diary."

Annalee saw Cheryl's frustration. "Okay, but let's get back to where you were when you first came in today. We know from Jack Rhodes that three of the boys who happened to be football players had dads who were influential around here. Even though Simon's name doesn't have a B in it, why not still give him a look. There's no harm other than a little lost time. This James Lofton who was at the same college might at least know if he was in town during the school breaks. Then, you have something to put on your spread sheet."

They both laughed.

"So, my advice is to talk to him and see what you can find out about Simon. If you learn he wasn't in town on the college breaks, you can strike him from consideration. If you can eliminate someone, at least you will feel you are making progress."

Cheryl hugged Annalee. "Now I know why you've always been my best friend."

As Cheryl pulled back from the hug, she was somber. "I remember all those nights when we had sleepovers pouring our secrets out to each other. I feel sad for Rylee. She wouldn't even tell her best friend about B. She sounded so alone and frightened. I can't believe she didn't tell *someone*."

"If she had, things might have turned out so different," Annalee sighed. "At least she might be alive, and likely Hogan would be, too."

"Why do you think she didn't tell someone?" asked Cheryl.

"It's hard to say exactly. I can see where she was thrilled to be asked out by a boy she had long had a crush on. The excitement of being asked out by an older boy—someone who was in college— was something she acted on impulsively. You said she seemed naïve."

Cheryl nodded.

"But then, after they were intimate, she probably just didn't know what to do. All of the kids at school knew she and Hogan were engaged. Paige was going to be her bridesmaid, and they double dated. You know how concerned teenage girls can be about their image and reputation. Maybe she thought Paige wouldn't understand? She may even have thought Paige would turn against her—especially if Paige also considered Hogan a friend since they double dated."

"It's too bad she didn't tell her sister or mother."

"Well, she just couldn't bring herself to reach out to anyone for help. It's really too bad," said Annalee. "It hurts me too to think about how isolated and confused she must have felt."

"I know. Sean brought up some good points. He said that it's possible that when she told Hogan, that he just lost it and hit Rylee like the police concluded. That may be where I end up on this, but I'm not ready to give up." Cheryl smiled, "So, with that said, do you know if James Lofton lives here?"

Annalee started typing. "I don't know, but if he's kept up his alumni information, it will be easy enough to check."

While Annalee was reviewing the database, Cheryl looked up James' picture in the yearbook. He also played football for the high school.

"He lives in Cincinnati, Cheryl. It shows that he served in the military after graduating from the military academy and then moved to Cincinnati—where he is a partner in a financial investment firm."

"Thanks, Annalee."

Chapter 63

When he walked into the precinct, Kim told Sean that Arlo had Luca in the interrogation room, but that the sheriff, Ralph Belks, from the small town near Camp Lejeune, wanted Sean to call him back. Sean decided to call him back and let Luca cool his heels in the interrogation room.

"Hi, Sheriff Belks. Sean Neumann. How are you?"

"Doing good. Planning on taking my grandson fishing later."

"I sure enjoyed spending time with my grandfather. I'm sure he's looking forward to that."

"Yeah, and me, too. He's eleven. We always have a good time. Say, after we talked the other day, I got curious—bad habit of mine. But, I got to checking into things. That woman who was killed, Caroline Montgomery? Her husband was Simon Montgomery. Well, on the night she was killed, about ten o'clock, there was a Simon Montgomery, address Camp Lejeune, who got a speeding ticket driving north on Interstate 95."

That was the interstate between Camp Lejeune and D.C. Sean pursed his lips before asking, "You sure about this? Are you sure it's the same night? Maybe it was a couple days before when he drove up to D.C. for the conference he was attending?"

"Well, it definitely shows the date to be the same night she was killed. It could be a wrong date got entered. I called North Carolina state police, and they are going to look back in the files and see what they can find. Anyhow, I wanted to let you know."

"Well, I appreciate this. Let me know what you find out."

"I sure will."

"Enjoy your fishing trip. Maybe you both will reel in some big ones."

Sheriff Belks laughed. "That'd sure thrill my grandson."

Sean swirled his chair to face the window. If Belks was right, Simon was driving from the Base to D.C. on the very night Caroline was killed. She was killed during the evening, so he could have murdered her and got back to D.C. before anyone noticed. Hell, he bet the MP never followed up with people in D.C. to validate Simon was there when the murder happened. This possibly shed new light on Caroline's death.

However, Sean now needed to go talk to Luca about the death of Simon's second wife, Skylar.

Arlo and Luca sat in the interrogation room waiting for Sean. "What is this all about?" demanded Luca.

"Can't say, Amigo. We're waiting on the Sheriff."

"Does this have to do with Skylar?" Luca snarled.

"You can ask the sheriff when he comes in."

"Damnit. She's haunting me from the grave."

"How's that?" asked Arlo.

"Never mind. Where's the sheriff? I have things to do," Luca huffed.

They both turned as Sean walked in.

Arlo said, "Mr. Ramirez was just saying that he is looking forward to talking to you, Sheriff."

Luca smirked, "It's not like you gave me a choice, *Amigo.*"

Sean leaned forward, taking an aggressive posture—his eyes hard, and his lips firm. "We have some questions, Luca. What did Mrs. Montgomery ever do to you to get you to dislike her?"

Anger flared in his eyes before he remembered who he was talking to.

When he didn't respond, Sean leaned closer, "I know you didn't like her, Luca. I've heard that from multiple sources. Did you hit on her and she refused?"

Luca nearly came out of his seat. "You're crazy, man! She never thought I was good enough for Nat." It was like a dam broke the way Luca went off. "Not only that, she didn't give a shit what me and Nat were going through back here. Hell, we raised her, and then when their mother was sick, she didn't lift one damn finger—not even to come back and help or send money. Nat had to do it all, and I was working my ass off to pay for everythin'. She didn't even bother to show up for her own mother's funeral. You know what that did to my wife?" When Sean and Arlo didn't respond, Luca continued, "Then, when she did move back, that's all Nat wanted to talk about 'til she knew I didn't want to hear no more. She'd take Nat to that expensive restaurant in town and buy her stuff that Nat had no need for. I could tell she was tryin' to turn Nat against me. No man would like that."

Arlo was thinking, *The sheriff knew how to pull his string.*

"What about Simon Montgomery? Did you like him?"

Luca exhaled and rubbed his fingers through his hair. His outburst had robbed him of further emotion. "I don't know nothin' 'bout him—except he didn't want nothin' to do with me or Nat. Nat wanted to go there for Christmas and Easter. Skylar was nice, but he spent most of the time in his office or watching sports shit on TV. He acted like he was better than us. He sure as hell wasn't friendly. Whatever, it's no skin off my ass."

"Did you talk to him without Skylar or your wife around?"

"Huh?"

"Did he ever ask you to help out around the house or call you or meet you for a beer or something?"

"No, I never talked to him like that. He never asked for my help around the house. Skylar did a few times, but not him."

"Did you ever talk to him on the phone?"

"No. I didn't have no reason to. Hell, I don't even know his phone number."

"Let's talk about your financial situation."

Luca blinked, "What financial situation?"

Sean opened a file. "To start with, I understand that the bank is about to foreclose on your house."

Luca narrowed his eyes but did not respond.

"Nothing to say about that?" Sean pressed.

"No."

"You need funds to keep the bank from foreclosing, right?"

"No shit."

"How much does your wife stand to get from the life insurance policy that Mrs. Montgomery had?"

Beads of sweat broke out on Luca's forehead as he looked between Sean and Arlo.

"Cat got your tongue?" Sean probed with steel in his eyes.

When Luca didn't respond, Sean's voice amped up. "You didn't like your wife's sister, Luca. Hadn't for a long time—isn't that right?"

Luca stared at Sean.

"You told me that you went up there to offer to let her spend the night at your house that Friday night, but that wasn't true, was it?"

"It is true."

334

"Your wife didn't know you were going. Why not tell her?"

"Why bother, man? She would know if Skylar showed up at the house."

Sean was harsh. "That was your chance, wasn't it? You knew about the life insurance policy! You thought she owed your wife! That was your way out! Kill her and get the insurance money!"

Luca's eyes were wide and perspiration beaded down the sides of his face. "You're crazy, man!" Luca yelled. He looked at Arlo for support, but Arlo's expression did not change. He turned back to Sean, trying to restrain himself, "This is a lie! I never saw her! She wasn't there!"

"You know the property is isolated—no one around. You dragged her down to the pier and threw her in. You drowned her so you could get the life insurance money! Hell, you were bragging at Knucklepin's about getting that money, Luca! I know all about it. You said you might buy you a new vehicle!"

Arlo had asked around at Knucklepin's, and some men had heard Luca bragging.

The flicker in Luca's eye did not go unnoticed by Sean. Luca shook his head, "That means nothing! I did not kill her, Sheriff."

Luca sat like stone refusing to say anything else. Sean asked Arlo to take him home but instructed Luca not to leave the area.

Chapter 64

Alex, Syd and Arlo sat at their desks around Sean.

"Chief, what are you thinking?"

Sean firmed his lips in concentration. "Luca had a motive, and he was there that evening. The coroner can't give us the exact time of death, but he knows it was Friday afternoon or evening or maybe even that night."

"What about Flynn Taggart? You said he had a motive, and there's no alibi for him Friday p.m." said Alex.

"What we know is that he filled up his gas tank Friday afternoon after he checked out of the hotel. He knew where the Montgomerys lived—he had the realtor show him. But, the guard at the entrance into the Lake Shore development has no record of him coming in after the realtor showed him around that morning. The Brigadier's house is at the far end of the development. If he climbed the fence somewhere, Syd talked to people there, and no one saw him walking around."

"Our only other suspect is the Brigadier," Alex said. "No one saw him on Friday between around twelve-thirty and seven o'clock. He had plenty of time to drive from Columbus and back. If he knew Mrs. Montgomery was leaving him, he had a motive."

Sean agreed, "Yes, and he also had a financial reason, because I don't think he knew she had changed her will. Flynn didn't go back through the guard gate later in the afternoon, and there is no record of the Brigadier coming back through until he arrived Saturday afternoon."

Sean noticed Arlo's brows furrowed and his eyes narrowed in concentration. Sean tilted his head, "Arlo, you seem in deep thought. What's on your mind?"

"You were talking about how no one would have seen Flynn walking through the Lake Shore development. Something just occurred to me. Thing is, I don't see how he would know about it, because he's not from around here."

"Know about what?"

"The western side of that development, up on the end where the Montgomerys live, is on an old farm that has not been occupied or farmed in years. When they were developing that subdivision, for a while, the utility trucks used an old road on that farm."

Arlo had Sean's full attention. Alex asked, "How do you know about this?"

"It's one of the areas I hunt on. No one is ever there. I knew all about the farm when I was a kid. Me and some friends used to camp out there. Like I said, it's been abandoned for years."

Sean asked, "Who would know about this?"

"Well, the utility companies. Maybe the people who surveyed the property. Harvey Bennett might even know. The builder might know."

"What about Montgomery?" asked Sean. "Is this close enough to his property that he might know of it?"

"I think so. I'll grab a map and show you." Arlo said as he stood.

They all looked at the map and concluded that Montgomery could be aware of the old road. "See, it's off at this far end past his property. It's rough. Lots of potholes and rocks, but a SUV or truck wouldn't have any problems clearing the ruts and rocks," explained Arlo.

Alex said, "Flynn's not from here, so he couldn't know about this, but what about Luca?"

Arlo nodded, "He grew up around here, so he might know."

"But if he did, why would he use the main entrance where everyone would know, when he could have used this back road?" Syd questioned.

"Good point." Alex conceded.

Sean leaned back in his chair. "So, it's possible that Simon and Luca knew about it. But, we should not rule out Flynn. He was in the Marines' recon special forces." Arlo let out a low whistle. "He was teaching recon at Lejeune when he was charged with Montgomery's first wife's murder. If anyone could find out about something like that, Flynn could."

"Maybe that's why he wanted to know the exact house where the Brigadier lives. He already knew of the back road," said Arlo.

"And they all three drive SUVs," added Alex.

"There is still a lot we don't know. We have to keep in mind that there may not be a murder here—the evidence isn't clear on that. But, I don't want anyone outside this room to know about this development. We need to go there and walk it and see if we can find any evidence. The good news is that the access point is off of this back road so no one will see us. If we find anything, I'll call in Ronnie Vin's forensic team."

Chapter 65

Cheryl was at a loss of where to go next with her research. Her experience told her to keep talking to people and following leads. With that mindset, she decided to take Annalee's advice and called James Lofton, the man who had attended the military academy with Simon Montgomery. His secretary scheduled an early-morning meeting to work her into his schedule.

James' office was on the ninth floor of a bank office building in downtown Cincinnati. The secretary showed her to a small conference room where she could look out the large window into other tall brick office buildings and watch pedestrians and vehicles moving about their purposes below. Shortly, James entered, and Cheryl moved from the window and set her coffee down and shook his hand. Their exchange of pleasantries was brief. When he realized she was not there as a potential client, that she was a reporter, he was eager to end the conversation. "Mr. Lofton, I know you are very busy, but I just have a few questions."

"Okay, Ms. Seton. What are they?"

"I understand that you attended a military academy after graduating from Schriever High School. You and another graduate in your class attended. Simon Montgomery."

He knitted his brows. "That's right."

"Was it just you two that attended that year from Schriever?"

"Yes."

"Did you graduate from there?"

"Yes, we both graduated. I enlisted for one term, but Simon made a career with the Marines."

"Have you stayed in touch with him?"

Suspicious as to where this was leading, he was getting slower in responding with each question asked. "Not really. I saw on the alumni announcement from the academy a few years back that he had retired, but we've not stayed in touch."

"During your breaks, like Christmas, spring break, summer breaks, do you know if he returned to Bekbourg?"

"The only year we roomed together was the first year, so I don't know about after that. We weren't really friends, but we knew each other from school, so we kind of hung out then, but after that, we branched off with other students."

"What do you remember about him going home that first year?"

"Ms. Seton, I'm not sure I'm comfortable talking about Simon."

"I understand that you haven't kept in touch all these years. I just have a couple more questions."

"Well, I know he went home at Christmas. His mother's health was failing, and his father wanted him to be there for the holidays."

"Did you see him while in Bekbourg for the Christmas break?"

"We met at Frau's once or twice with a couple of guys we graduated with from high school, but that's all."

"What about for spring break?"

"He and I and two other guys went to the beach."

"His mother was doing better?"

James paused. "Wait. Now that you ask, he told us that his dad had called and that his mother wasn't doing well. Simon told us he would drive home Friday night and try to catch up with us at the beach early in the week."

"And he did?"

"Yeah, he didn't miss much. He caught up with us on Monday."

"You didn't go to Bekbourg for spring break?"

"No."

"Do you remember any women calling him in your dorm room?"

"Not his mother. She never called. Sometime after we returned from Christmas break, a girl called a few times. He never said who, but that didn't last long. Simon was funny about that. He didn't like girls calling. I think he thought he should do the calling, not the girls."

"Do you know if a girl named Rylee Flowers ever called him?"

James furrowed his brows. "That name sounds familiar."

"She was two years behind your class in Schriever."

His eyes widened. "The girl who was killed?" When Cheryl did not respond, he continued, "Ms. Seton, I don't know who called him, and frankly, I'm not in the habit of talking about other people."

James stood, "I need to prepare for my next meeting."

Cheryl gathered her purse. As they walked down the hall, she asked, "Did he ever talk about Rylee Flowers?"

Up until then, James had been communicative. "Mr. Lofton," Cheryl probed at his silence, "Did he ever mention Rylee Flowers?"

"Not that I remember."

Cheryl had additional questions she hoped he would answer before they got to the exit. "What building was your dorm in?" When he didn't respond, "Do you remember your dorm room number?"

"Ms. Seton, you're asking questions about things I don't remember off the top of my head. I'm sorry I can't help you."

As they neared the exit, Cheryl asked him if he knew of anyone on the football team besides

Billy and Baxter whose name started with a B. She noticed him stiffen.

"You could look at the yearbook."

"I did."

"Well, I don't know what else to say," he replied as he leaned to open the exit door. He was through being communicative and politely bid her a safe trip back to Bekbourg.

Cheryl drove back to Bekbourg feeling she had wasted a morning. Yes, she had learned that Simon was in town during both breaks, but that did not advance the ball in learning who Rylee was meeting. *So much for being able to eliminate Simon from my spreadsheet. Oh well. I have other things at the office that require my attention this afternoon.*

Chapter 66

Simon opened the door to see Harvey Bennett. Harvey was glad his sunglasses concealed his shock at Simon's appearance. He was unshaven, and his face was flush and puffy. Harvey quickly recovered thinking the old sweat pants and faded T-shirt were his yard-work clothes. "Hi, Simon. I know this must be a difficult time, but there is something I need to talk to you about, and I couldn't reach you on the phone. Mind if I come in?"

At first, Harvey thought Simon was going to turn him away, but he finally opened the door wider. "Sure, come in. I haven't checked my voice mail in a couple of days. There've been a lot of things I've had to attend to. You want something to drink?"

Harvey was not one to turn down a good scotch, but ten o'clock in the morning was early for him, but apparently not for Simon. There was a half-full bottle sitting on the bar, and the glass in Simon's hand was nearly empty. "Thanks, but I'll pass this time." Harvey was rethinking his assessment that Simon was doing yard work.

"Let me know if you change your mind. I was just getting ready to refresh this."

After Simon poured a glass, he motioned for Harvey to have a seat. Harvey wanted to break the ice before he got to the purpose for this visit. He nodded toward the large window. "I always liked this part of the development. It's private, and you have a nice view of the lake. This was one of my favorite building sites. That's the reason we decided on all these windows."

After taking a drink, Simon mustered a "Yeah."

Harvey decided he'd best hit the topic straight on. "I guess you know that's not why I came here—to admire your view. We are almost to the point of no return on the development. We have to move forward, or the other investors are going to move on to other opportunities. I know you want to be in on the project, but I have to have your part of the investment nailed down this week. You have to sign the papers and transfer the funds, or I'm going to move on and find other investors. I don't want to lose the ones I've got."

Simon swirled the liquid in the glass before looking at Harvey, "Skylar's death has really made a complicated financial situation nearly impossible for me. I was hoping you could explain to the other investors what I was going through and buy a little more time. I just don't know when this all will resolve itself, but I am still committed to this project."

Harvey looked at Simon. "I understand what you are going through, but we can't hold off any longer. So, talk to your lawyer and see if you can't come up with funds that show you are still in the game. I'll give you five days, but if I don't have the funds in escrow by then, I'm going to have to move on."

After Harvey left, Simon cursed as he lumbered to the bar. He ignored the glasses and drank from the bottle.

Chapter 67

"Chief, it looks like a vehicle may have been through here lately. Some of the grass appears flattened, but it's hard to tell. There aren't any large limbs lying across any of it which would obstruct a driver. The hard rains from the other night marred any tire impressions that would have been here," observed Arlo.

Sean and the three deputies had walked the almost mile-and-half stretch of the old road.

Sean looked up the old road. "Yeah. I don't think forensics could find anything helpful, but you were right, Arlo. This isn't far from Montgomery's house, and no one would see him or anyone else if someone drove this way."

"If someone came this way, they were careful not to leave any trash or other evidence," Alex added.

"Simon and Flynn would be too smart for that," Sean said almost to himself. "Even Luca probably would think of that." They continued to look for any evidence as they made their way back to the main road. Sean told them about Sheriff Belks finding a speeding ticket issued to Simon the night of his first wife's murder. The deputies stopped and looked at him.

"So, it's possible that he drove back, and no one at the conference knew he was missing?" Alex asked.

"It's certainly possible. Everyone assumed he was in D.C. at the conference, and I'm not sure anyone followed up with the attendees or staff."

Syd spoke up, "He may be using a similar M.O."

"What do you mean?" asked Alex.

"Let's assume he killed Caroline. He got away with it by not leaving any evidence and making sure he had an alibi of being at a conference in D.C. He led everyone to believe he was in D.C., drove back, killed Caroline, and made it back to D.C. Here, he may have driven back to Bekbourg, killed Skylar and returned to Columbus without being detected."

"Yeah, if he did that, he was careful to cover his tracks between here and Columbus. But something I've been wondering about is why frame Flynn in Caroline's death, especially since he felt he had an alibi?" asked Arlo. "Another thing—he hasn't framed anyone here."

Syd's eyebrow arched. "Not yet, or at least we don't know about it yet. But another difference is that his first wife was strangled—so there was a murderer. Here, we still don't know if it was an accident or suicide. Also, in his first wife's death, framing Flynn was belt and suspenders. If someone did check and his presence in D.C. during the time she was killed couldn't be validated, he had a fallback—setting up Flynn."

"So, what you're saying, Syd, is that he has used the same game plan for both murders?" asked Alex.

She shrugged, "If he killed Skylar, then yeah."

"If this is murder, we haven't found any direct evidence," said Alex. "So far, everything is purely circumstantial. If I had to rank them as suspects, Luca would be at the top of the list because he was there that evening, and he had a financial motive. Simon had a financial motive, and the sheriff mentioned maybe a motive is that he didn't want her leaving him, but we can't tie him to being there."

"That's true," said Arlo, "but we can't say for sure he was in Columbus, and this road gives him a way to get to the house unnoticed by the guard at the front gate."

"Then, there is Flynn," said Sean. "I don't think he would have killed Skylar unless she found him on the property scoping out a way to kill Simon. Like Simon, he could have used this road and gone unnoticed. We need to dig deeper and see if we find something. No one knows we know about this road, and we need to keep it that way. I'm going to talk to Montgomery again. Arlo, identify any car washes between here and Columbus along the road. It had not rained a few days before Mrs. Montgomery died. If it was Simon, he may have had some weeds in the grill or in the hub caps or dust. Let's see if he stopped anywhere to wash his car. One more thing. Syd, talk with the businesses and see if anyone saw Flynn after he left the realtor that morning. Talk to the motel, gas stations, stores, places like that."

Arlo and Syd nodded. Sean turned to Alex, "I want you to go with me to visit Montgomery."

As they continued walking, Arlo asked, "If the Brigadier killed his first wife, what would have been his motive?"

"It could have been that he was tired of her unfaithfulness, but I think it was more than that. I think he knew she was planning to leave him, and he may have been concerned that his military career would take a hit. I don't think we'll get anything from talking to him, but we'll see."

Sean pressed the doorbell three times before Simon answered. Sean had never seen Simon look anything but impeccably groomed and dressed and a specimen of health and vitality. His face was slack, and he had not shaved in days. "Simon, you know Deputy Ogle. Can we come in?"

"This is not a convenient time, Sheriff."

Even at their distance, Sean could smell alcohol. "Mr. Montgomery, we have some questions we need to ask you. I would prefer to do it here, but if necessary, I'm prepared to take you to the station."

Scorn swamped Simon's red face. "You can talk to my attorney. I don't have anything else to say to you."

He stepped back to close the door, and Sean shot out his foot to stop the door. Simon glared at Sean. "We can do it your way, but just so you know, I know you weren't at the hotel in Columbus the afternoon that Mrs. Montgomery died." Sean couldn't be absolutely sure of that, but he gambled he was right. "And, I've been looking into the death of your first wife, Simon. You had her followed. You knew she was seeing Flynn. There are other questions about your behavior back then."

Simon pulled back his shoulders, "If you were still a Marine, I'd have you brought up on a number of violations. You'd be lucky if you escaped with a dishonorable discharge. I expected more from you, Sheriff. Making false accusations is beneath you. I am going to lodge a complaint with the county commissioners as a starting point. The state police and attorney general may have some things to say, too."

"You do that, Simon, but I also have proof that on the night of your first wife's death, you were given a speeding ticket heading toward D.C. as you drove through North Carolina."

Simon's grin was contemptuous. "Neumann, you are a disgrace to the sheriff's uniform and a disgrace to the uniform you wore as a Marine." Alex mustered all his willpower not to respond to the tirade. No one should talk to Sean that way. "Let's be clear," berated Simon, "You don't have a damn thing on me. My first wife died twenty years ago, and the vermin responsible was convicted. You have absolutely *nothing* to tie me to the death of Skylar—*nothing!* Now, if you think my wife was killed, then do your damn job and find the killer. But don't harass me again. Move your damn foot and get off my property before I call the state police."

"Just remember this, Montgomery," Sean said with steel in his eyes and words. "There is no statute of limitations for murder."

Simon slammed the door and stomped to the bar. He picked up his nearly empty scotch glass and sent it shattering against the wall across the room. Sean and Alex would have heard his guttural roar as he wildly sent the contents on the bar flying with a swiping arm—had they not already walked out of earshot.

As Alex followed Sean back to the cruiser, he was furious. He'd never seen anyone talk to Sean, or anyone for that matter, with such venom. As Sean pulled away, he glanced over at Alex and calmly said, "He's right about one thing. We don't have any concrete evidence to tie him to Skylar's death. It's all circumstantial. Unless Arlo can find that he stopped by a car wash or a credit card transaction of him buying gas or stopping somewhere between here and Columbus, it will be hard to convince the prosecutor to bring a case." As a side, Sean added, "I'm not holding my breath that we'll find anything. He's an expert in detailed planning."

"What about the evidence of him driving back to D.C. the night of his first wife's death?"

"Even with that, it's all circumstantial, and twenty years later. It would be hard, in not impossible, to get the case reopened. Hell, Flynn was found guilty of her murder," said Sean.

"I've been thinking about that. Flynn was nowhere close to the motel where she was killed. How did the Brigadier know Flynn would not have an alibi?"

"I don't think he cared. With her being murdered, Flynn's career was over since he was sleeping with her. If Simon planted the scarf in Flynn's car, it may or may not have worked, but Keaton wasn't going to look closely. Hell, Keaton could have planted the scarf. So, even if Flynn came up with an alibi, no one was really going to focus much on someone trying to frame Flynn. He'd escape the murder charge with an alibi, but the damage to him was done."

"How did Keaton fit into all this? Could he have killed her?"

"That's a possibility. I think it more likely that Simon used Keaton to railroad Flynn. Caroline had fallen in love with Flynn. Maybe Simon wanted Flynn to pay for destroying his marriage. Simon knew about Keaton's fling with Caroline, and he held that over Keaton's head to ramrod the conviction. Keaton being an officer certainly would not have wanted it to become public that he had slept with Simon's wife."

"Mmm. Does that mean that he may get away with killing both wives?"

"First, all of this is speculation. I keep harping on the point, but we don't know that Skylar was killed. We also have two other suspects, Luca and Flynn, who look equally suspicious. We don't have hard evidence; everything is circumstantial. If she was murdered, whoever did it was careful, and again, any of the three men could have pulled it off. I'm not giving up. We keep digging."

They were interrupted by Sean's phone ringing. It was Arlo. "Hey, Boss. I stopped in at Frau's to get some coffee, and when I came out, I saw a SUV drive by, and I swear, it looked like Flynn was driving it."

"What color, Arlo?" When Sean went to Flynn's house in South Carolina, he had seen a dark green SUV sitting in the driveway.

"It was a darker green."

"Mmm."

"You want me to drive by the motel he stayed at before and see if he's checked in?"

"No, let's let it ride for now. I may stop by myself, and if he's there, see what's up."

After they disconnected, Alex asked, "If that's him, why do you think Flynn would be back in town?"

Sean couldn't think of a good reason.

Chapter 68

"Geeze, Reid. The first shoot at the old Shiloh Ridge Cemetery doesn't do a good job of catching Jake running through the cemetery and hiding the jewels." Lilly was sitting behind the computer slowly reversing the images and then viewing them as they were forwarded.

"Here, let me see." He pulled his chair close and started looking at the film. "Wait, this is the afternoon when Jake left to get Brian the shoulder pads and one of his flannel shirts. We shot this again after he got back, because we wanted to experiment with how it would show up with it being later. Go forward and see if there isn't more footage."

Lilly started to move the video forward. "*What is this*?" She was frazzled with the upcoming deadline, and seeing a video of something that was unrelated to their project was annoying.

"Huh. Oh, that was when Brian and I went down the hill to check out the features on the camera while we waited for Jake. Keep going. You'll come to the right footage."

"Okay. Sorry if I'm cranky."

"It's okay, Lilly. You have been burning the midnight oil on this project. We all know that you have put a *lot* more time on this than any of us."

"Well, everyone has done a great job and worked hard. I've always wanted our group to win first place, but knowing how much that means to Jake just makes me want to push harder."

"I know. He's had some good ideas."

Lilly was watching as the video played. "You guys got some good shots here experimenting with the lighting."

"Yeah, Brian and I have been talking about doing a special video this summer if Mrs. Janacek will let us use this camera. We are going to get some other students involved. Claire is on board even though we're going to make a scary witch or zombie type movie with special effects. Maybe we'll become famous."

Lilly had quit listening. She was rewinding and replaying the video. "Oh. My. God!"

Cheryl was in her office when Lilly and a boy she didn't recognize materialized at her door. Lilly was pale, holding a video tape, and the boy was clutching a video camera to his chest. Lilly didn't wait for a greeting, "Cheryl, we need to show you something right away. Let's go to the conference room where the video player is." They didn't wait for Cheryl to say anything before they headed down the hall. Lilly was already setting up the player when Cheryl arrived.

"Lilly, what is going on?" she asked looking at both of them.

Reid walked in behind Cheryl and closed the door so it was just the three of them.

"Here, Cheryl. Watch this." Lilly pushed the power button as Cheryl moved closer to view whatever it was they wanted her to see.

All three were crowded around watching. Creases formed in Cheryl's forehead as the video played on. Her face was grim when she rewound and replayed the video again, and then one more time. Pausing it and looking at the somber teenagers, she asked, "What is this?"

Between Reid and Lilly, they explained how they were shooting their first scene at the Shiloh Ridge Cemetery a few weeks ago and how Reid and Brian had gone off to experiment with the high-definition camera while they waited for Jake to return with his football pads. Reid's eyes were bright when he told her that he and Brian were planning on doing a horror film over the summer if Mrs. Janacek would allow them to use the new camera, and they wanted to see what the film would look like in the woods as it got later in the day. "We were just taking random shots in the area. We've been so busy trying to get our class video ready, I hadn't gone back to look at this. I even forgot we shot it until Lilly discovered it today trying to find the second video shot we took that evening of the thieves chasing Jake through the graveyard."

"Where was this taken?"

"There on the lake in Lake Shore."

"Let's sit down. I need to know everything."

Reid told Cheryl that his parents lived in the gated Lake Shore community. "There is an old graveyard up on the hill. You can't see it from the lake. It's not all that big. No one has probably been buried there in seventy years. That's why we chose it, because it has old tombstones and even rocks as tombstones for some graves. Brian and I walked down the hill to where there are more woods. I know the area well. He and I did some filming in the wooded part which borders the lake. We taped across the lake. I was showing him how to use the lighting and Zoom controls."

Cheryl thought she knew the answer to her question before she asked it, "When was this taken?"

Sure enough. The date coincided.

"Okay, stay here. I need to call the sheriff."

When she returned, she could tell Lilly was rattled, and Reid was pacing the room. When she closed the door, "Ms. Seton, that was the woman who was killed, wasn't it?" asked Reid.

"I'm afraid it might be."

Shortly after that, Sean walked in. The three grim faces told him something was amiss. Cheryl explained how the video came to be and how it had just been discovered. Reid was periodically nodding to confirm Cheryl's statements. Lilly sat like a statue. Cheryl then played the video.

Sean's face was impassive, and his lips had thinned. Only the sound of the video player could be heard as Sean watched the video a couple of times, having Cheryl slow the speed and replay the pertinent clips. Satisfied he knew the essence of what he had viewed, he looked up, "How did you know about this location, Reid?"

"As I told Ms. Seton, we live in the Lake Shore subdivision. This part where we filmed is up at the upper end. Our house is in the first stage of the development, which is closer to the main entrance. Me and my dad used to go up there, and me and my friends went there fishing and swimming before they started building houses up that way."

He looked at the teenagers. "When was this filmed?"

Lilly told him the date.

"How can you be sure?" he asked.

"We've only been up there twice to film. It was the first time that Reid and Brian went down there to experiment with the camera. I know the date."

Sean asked, "Is this the original?"

Reid spoke up, "No. Lilly and I made the tape here to show Ms. Seton. The original tape is in this video camera," he pointed to the camera they had brought with them. "We also have a copy that we downloaded onto the editing computer at school so we could edit it."

"Who else had access to this camera?" Sean asked.

Lilly said, "Only us. The school has enough for each team to have their own camera. This one is checked out to me. It has to stay with me except for when we are filming, but every night, I have it. No one but me, Reid or Brian has used it for filming."

This was the break Sean had been searching for.

Sean did not want to scare the teenagers, but his look underscored the importance of his words. "Lilly, Reid, this is very important that you not tell *anyone* about this. No one outside this room can know. *No one.* What about the computer at school. Can anyone see this on that computer?"

Lilly and Reid shook their heads. "Well, our teacher could if she wanted to, but there is no reason. We have it saved in a file for our movie, and none of the students can see it."

"Let's keep this between us. Don't mention it to anyone until I say it's okay." After Sean was certain they understood the importance of his words, he continued, "What about your friend who was with you when this video was made, Brian McCrosky? Does he know what is on this?"

"I was the one using the camera, showing him the different controls and settings. He wouldn't have seen what we filmed that day. No one has seen it until Lilly saw it this afternoon."

"Okay. I need to take the camera and tape with me."

"What about the camera?" Brian squeaked. "Lilly is not supposed to let anyone outside our group have it."

Lilly and Reid eyed Sean. "He's right, Sheriff Neumann. I will get in trouble if something happens to the camera."

"I will take good care of the camera, and I'll work out any issues with your teacher if that's necessary. If your teacher asks about it, do *not* tell her why I have it. Just tell her to call me. Is that understood?"

Both teenagers nodded.

As Sean walked out the door, he overheard Reid say, "Lilly, we're going to be famous."

After leaving Cheryl and the teenagers, Sean called Lucky to arrange to take the video to Columbus the next day to have the FBI specialists enhance the video's frames. He hoped the video would provide a clear picture.

Chapter 69

Cheryl's sleep had been fitful. When Sean left for Columbus, she headed to the *Tribune*—hoping the video was conclusive about who was responsible for Skylar's death.

Cheryl leaned back in her chair twirling a pencil between her fingers. Other than confirming that Simon had been in town for both the Christmas and spring breaks, she had not leaned anything helpful from James Lofton. She didn't know why she was even thinking about him, because there was not a B anywhere in his name, including his middle name. The only reason he was on the spread sheet was because his father had influence around Bekbourg at the time. She needed to think about boys whose names began with a B.

She thought back to her conversation with Baxter. There was no way to verify Baxter's claim that he had an argument with his dad that night—unless she tracked down his sister. Even if she could locate her, Baxter had not said whether she was there that night to witness the argument.

Just before lunch, Milton called her and said that he and Martha were arriving home later that day. He told her that they had really enjoyed their time away. After hanging up, she thought about Milton and how happy she was for him and Martha. They both had been through so much, but they had found each other and were off on a wonderful life together.

The phone's ring jarred her from her musings. It was a call from a representative from one of the colleges she had talked to about the key she had found in Hogan's belongings.

After her previous conversation with Kye, Cheryl met with a security official at the local community college and got information about how their keying system worked. Although the key did not come from Hillsrock College, the employee explained how each of its keys contained letter markings to identify the building to which it belonged and the classroom number.

The local locksmith, whose father before him had made and maintained keys for most of the local businesses, did not recognize the key as used by his commercial clients. Because the old downtown hotel used the old-fashioned keys before it ceased operations, it could not have come from it. He explained that it did not look like a motel or hotel key, because they typically only put the room number on their keys. Cheryl's key looked like one used by a business or institution that had multiple buildings. The locksmith confirmed that it could have been used in a college or university.

On a hunch, Cheryl reached out to both colleges attended by Baxter and Simon, and after talking with the managers responsible for each of their keying systems, she had emailed photos of the key to see if they recognized it as being used around campus.

Cheryl could not believe her good luck when the caller now told her that the key had indeed been part of his college's keying system. The initials stood for a dorm that had since been demolished, and the number on the key indicated a dorm room. Cheryl did not know how the key came to be in Hogan's car, but she felt this information was significant.

Shortly after she hung up, she received another call. "Ms. Seton. This is Austin Towman. My wife and I have been traveling around the country in our RV the past several weeks, and we just got home yesterday. You said you are checking up on some of my high school classmates?"

"Yes, thanks so much for calling me back. I understand that you and Hogan were close friends in high school."

"Yes, we were."

"What can you tell me about Hogan?"

"Like what do you want to know?"

"He was dating Rylee when you and he were seniors. What was their relationship like?"

"Well, if you're asking me if I think he killed her, I categorically don't. He was very happy when they got engaged. He thought she hung the moon. The police suggested that he hit her hard enough to make her fall. First of all, Hogan did not have a temper *at all*. In all the years I knew him, he never got angry. If he got miffed about something, he quickly shook it off. He was just an all-round good guy. More than that, it would have gone against his code to ever hit a girl. He had enough self-control that he would have walked away before he hit Rylee—in my opinion."

"How well did you know Rylee?"

"I have to say—not all that well. My girlfriend and I double dated with them, and we'd always have a good time. I liked her. She was a sweet person, and every time I saw them together, they were having fun."

"Did you ever hear any rumors or suspect that Rylee was interested in anyone else after she and Hogan started dating?"

He was silent before responding, "No, I never heard anything like that."

Cheryl felt deflated. It did not appear he could add to what she already knew. She suddenly heard him say, "Now that you mention it, there was something odd that I saw. I never mentioned it, because—like I said—when I saw them together they seemed happy, and she was a cute girl, very friendly. The reason I thought it was strange was that she was talking to a boy who had graduated the year before. Buck was already in college.

Cheryl jerked forward in her chair—the name started with a B. "Who is Buck? What did you see?"

"Well, it was around Christmas, and you know the annual Christmas parade there in Bekbourg? I assume they still have it. The football team went to regionals that year, so we were being pulled on some floats. We were tossing candy to the crowd. I know it was Rylee, because I did a double take. She was standing back along one of the buildings away from the jam of people laughing at something Buck was saying. She even reached over and touched his arm. Hogan was on the other side of the float, so he didn't see it, and I never said anything, because it didn't seem important."

"Who was Buck?"

Austin laughed, "That was a nickname the football team gave him when he was a sophomore. He was a rough kid, not afraid of things. When it came to football, he plowed his way right through the line. During one football game, there was this big senior lineman who didn't like Buck's aggressiveness, so he started taunting him and trying to get to him. One of the things he did was start calling him 'Buckboy.' The teams almost ended up in a fight. After that night, we started calling him 'Buck.' It stuck with the whole football team. Even the cheerleaders called him Buck."

"What was his real name?" Cheryl repeated. She caught her breath when he told her.

After they hung up, Cheryl reclined in her chair, dazed. It was surreal, but the pieces of the puzzle seemed to fit. Cheryl turned to gaze out the window, thinking about everything she knew. She finally shook herself. Since Sean had driven to Columbus, she figured he would be late coming home, so she pulled together all her notes and outlined the string of events. It was dark by the time she finished. She knew who killed Rylee and needed to tell Sean, but it could wait until tomorrow, because he would be consumed with whatever he had found out today about the video from Lucky.

Chapter 70

Cheryl turned off the lights and walked outside. Everyone else had left for the evening, so she locked the main door and headed toward the sidewalk to walk home. The duplex was in the downtown area, allowing her and Sean the luxury of walking to work. She heard something behind her, but before she could react, someone grabbed her and smothered her mouth with something having a faint odor. She struggled against his strength, but she couldn't budge him, and before she knew it, she lost consciousness.

As she started to wake, she was disoriented. She had no idea where she was or what had happened. Everything was dark. Pain was searing her arms and wrists. Something was tight across her mouth—tape or a gag—that made breathing difficult. Cheryl's body ached as she was tossed around as she lay on her side. The haze started to recede, and her memory began to return. She remembered coming out of the *Tribune's* building and walking toward home when someone had grabbed her from behind. Some chemical had been used. Was it chloroform? She heard the hum of an engine and knew she was in the back of a vehicle. The good news was that she was not dead, but that was not totally comforting since she did not know who had her, where they were taking her, and what they intended to do.

Chapter 71

Martha was busy doing laundry, and Milton was bored. While he and Martha were away, he periodically called into the office to check on how things were going at the *Tribune*. Patti Richards, the receptionist, had a list ready with phone messages, mail notices and office updates, but only shared those after scolding him for checking in while on his honeymoon. So, while he felt fairly up to speed, he decided to go to the *Tribune* and check his inbox. At least when he showed up tomorrow, he would be up-to-date and ready to hit the ground running.

As he approached the front door, something caught his eye. The street light was reflecting off something. He picked it up and held it where he could see that it was Cheryl's keys. "This is odd," he thought. He dialed her cell phone, but no one answered. He entered the building, which was empty. Milton walked back to her office and turned on the light. Nothing looked out of place, but he walked around her desk. A writing pad was lying there on top of an open file of papers. Some wording grabbed at him, because the letters had been retraced several times and stars were drawn at the top of the page. Milton's heart started to race, because he knew what Cheryl had been working on. Cheryl had identified B.

He rushed to his office and called Kye to see if Cheryl was there. She told him that she had not seen Cheryl or Sean all day and that Buddy was staying with her. He told Kye to lock the door and pull all the shades and to not open her door under any circumstances. If she talked to Sean, she was to tell him what Milton had found. He urgently repeated, "Kye, I'm going to locate Sean. Keep Buddy with you. Call 911 if anything happens there. *Don't hesitate.*" Kye did not know what this all meant, but she understood that Milton was concerned, and that worried her.

Milton called Sean's direct cell line as soon as he hung up with Kye. Sean had just walked into the station from his return from Columbus when he saw Milton was calling, but he did not answer. He needed to talk to his deputies who were waiting on him, and then he would call Milton back.

Alex, Arlo, and Syd stood when Sean walked into the room. He had called on his drive in from Columbus and asked that they meet him at the station. Although they would wait until early in the morning to execute the warrant, he wanted to map out the details with them tonight. He explained what the FBI's enhancement of the video revealed. They were in the process of outlining each deputy's role when one of the dispatchers rushed up to the doorway. It had been a long day, and Sean was

372

impatient when the dispatcher tried to interrupt. His terse words were meant to rebuff the dispatcher, "We're busy. If it's important, contact Darrell."

Sean could not have been more emphatic, and the look on his face *almost* made the dispatcher turn away. "I'm sorry, Chief, but Milton Grant is on the phone in the dispatch center. He says it's *urgent* and he needs to talk to you *now*."

Sean looked quizzical and told everyone to hold up and went to take the call. Milton asked if Cheryl was with him or if he had talked to her recently. Sean's stomach started to turn. "No. Why?"

Milton told him what he had found. Sean hung up and tried to call Cheryl, but there was no answer. A cold sweat soaked his body. The only explanation was that she was with him, and that meant she was in grave danger.

He rushed back to the deputies, and they stiffened when they saw Sean's expression. Sean had a plan, and he hoped to god it worked. In rapid fire, his words detailed everyone's assignments. The deputies shook their heads with understanding and grabbed their gear and bolted to their individual cruisers.

Chapter 72

Simon opened the back of his SUV and peered down at Cheryl. He ripped the tape from her mouth, causing Cheryl to yelp in pain. The flood light above shone in her face. All she could see was a dark figure looming over her. He grabbed Cheryl's hair and yanked her so hard she thought her neck might snap. "You scream, and I'll kill you right here. Where's the damn key?" he demanded.

Cheryl's mind was still foggy—but not so much that she failed to recognize the import of his question. He knew the dorm key found in Hogan's car could implicate him in Hogan's death. The call earlier from the military institute he had attended confirmed the key was part of their key system and that the initials represented one of the dorms and the number a specific dorm. Her instincts to deny knowledge of the key kicked in. She did not want Simon to know anything about her leads. "Whaat key?" she groaned.

The slap jarred her vision and would have forced her head sideways if he had not had the tight grip on her hair, "Don't lie to me. Where is the key?"

She shrieked in pain, "I don't know what you're talking about."

Yanking her hair, "James Lofton called me yesterday. Why were you asking about our dorm?"

"I wanted to find out about phone records, and I needed the dorm room," she lied.

Although she could not see his face, she envisioned its fury.

When Simon had returned to college after spring break, he realized his dorm key was missing. For months after that night, he worried if the Bekbourg police would find it. When nothing came of it, he figured either they had found it and did not pursue its origin or it was lost that night or over spring break. When James tracked him down yesterday, he panicked hearing what Cheryl was asking. She wanted to know their dorm number, so he jumped to the conclusion that she had found the dorm key. That coupled with her asking James about a football player whose name started with a B alarmed him that she was on to him. That damn Rylee girl always called him by his nickname, "Buck."

He had been thinking about a plan B if Cheryl started to get close. He had no idea that she had made so much progress. Had he known, he would have followed through with his plan to frame Baxter to get her off the scent. Unfortunately for her, she had learned too much too fast, and he could not risk her disclosing her findings. He had to find out who else knew.

He considered Cheryl's response about the phone log and was satisfied she was telling the truth. He jerked her head again—forcing her to cry out in pain. "How'd you find out about me?"

The torture racked her breathing as she panted out her words, "The story didn't fit about Hogan. The coroner's report said she was pregnant, and the police report showed they didn't do a thorough job. So, I figured whoever was the baby's father had the ability to get the investigation stopped. As I researched, I found that you and Baxter's dads had ties to Randall Thompson."

Cheryl hoped she was persuasive. He stood still and then demanded, "Why were you asking about a name that began with a B?"

Cheryl's moan at the increasing pain caused by his tightening grip gave her the seconds she needed to fabricate another lie. "The police report said they found a B written with an ink pen with a heart around it on her left palm. That's another lead they didn't pursue."

"Ahh. Only the football players and cheerleaders knew my nickname. That's why you talked to Baxter. That SOB called me after you talked to him." His fist tightened in her hair.

If he killed her, Cheryl did not want him to know about the diary. Hopefully, Sean could figure out the trail since he knew parts of what she had learned, but she certainly did not want Simon to know that Sean or Milton knew, because he might kill them.

"You saw my newspaper story?" she squeaked.

He continued his tight grip on her hair. "Yes. I figured you would run into a dead end, but you didn't." He jerked her head so hard Cheryl thought he might pull out her hair. "Who else knows?" he gritted.

"No one," she screamed out. She could not lead him to Sean or Milton. "I didn't even know for sure it was you. If I solved it, I wanted the headline for breaking the story," her words leached through the pain.

He threw her head back on the floor. She grunted as pain singed her shoulders where her hands were bound behind her back.

"After you killed Rylee, you put Hogan on the railroad track, didn't you?" her voice was weak. "Someone must have helped you. Who?"

"My dad. When I realized she was dead, I didn't know what to do, so I went home and told him. It was his idea to target Hogan, because Dad knew they would discover she was pregnant. I didn't tell Hogan who I was when I called. I told him she had a flat tire, and that I'd stop to help, but she asked that I call him. When he got there, he got out and looked around, but he got suspicious when I walked up. He jumped back in to take off, but I was able to drag him out of his car. We killed him and put him on the track. That damn train was late, but it finally got there."

"Your dad stopped the sheriff's investigation."

"He told me to leave for spring break, that he'd handle things. He never told Randall about my involvement. He made up some story he was intervening on behalf of the families, that he didn't want their names dragged through the mud, and Randall made that happen."

"You framed Hogan like you did Flynn Taggart for your first wife's death."

His humorless laugh sent chills up Cheryl's spine. "Yes, and Taggart got to think about all those years in prison how he had turned Caroline against me. So now you know. Not that it's going to do you any good."

"The guard will know you drove in and then left. You've left a trail."

"You're wrong! There's an abandoned road I found one day hiking. No one will *ever* tie me to your disappearance!"

Cheryl saw him move to reapply the tape, so she blurted, "Sean will find out about everything."

He pushed her face hard as he taped her mouth. He stood back and sneered. "You're going to disappear. Even if he tries, I've got a plan. You see, you outsmarted yourself. After you talked to Baxter, it caused him to think back, which is too bad for him. He called me and said he saw me with that girl one night at the Shopper's Pavilion during that Christmas break. I made up an excuse that I had given her a ride back home to get a key because she had locked her car key inside the car, but he is a loose end that I can't afford, just like you are. I'm going to kill Baxter Colbert and then frame him with that ring on your finger. His name starts with a B. He'll be a perfect patsy. It worked in Caroline's murder, only this time the suspect dies. As smart as your boyfriend thinks he is, he'll never find any evidence. He can rattle all the sabers he wants. In the end, I have enough pull to make him look desperate. Hell, if he crosses the line, his ass will be mine. I got lucky tonight when everyone left except you. I didn't have to go to my plan B.

"I'll get a shovel and some plastic bags." He slammed the back. Cheryl tried to kick, but there was no way to get out. She was trapped, and that monster was going to kill her. She waited, hoping something would intervene. When he didn't immediately return, she prayed something had happened—maybe a miracle.

Her hopes were dashed when she heard him open the back door and throw things into the back. He was cussing about the "damn guard" telling him that the sheriff was at the gate and wanting to come see him. He yelled through the back-seat area, "That damn boyfriend of yours is deluding himself if he thinks he can find evidence about Skylar. He will never find anything. I told that guard to tell Neumann to call my attorney—if they want to show up here, they better damn well have a warrant. I'm tired of Neumann's shit. By the time they get things straightened out, you'll be dead and buried, and I'll be back here," he vowed as he slammed the back door. When Cheryl heard that Sean was at the guard's gate, she squealed through the tape with relief that maybe he would arrive in time. She then remembered that Simon was taking her out a back way, and hope began to fade. Simon closed the front door, and she heard the engine roar to life. Cheryl's head was throbbing as she felt the vehicle lung in motion.

Chapter 73

Simon needed to get this done and get back to his house. Even if Sean had discovered Cheryl missing, he would not have any reason to think of Simon, but Simon did not want to risk being gone if Sean returned. He did not see him getting a warrant, at least not this late. His SUV was bumping along the rugged road when his headlights caught two cruisers blocking the road up above.

"What the hell?" he bellowed. He slammed the SUV to a stop. *How the hell did they know about this road and what are they doing here?* Realization smacked hard that Sean had figured it out. Options to evade capture raced through his thinking. It would not work to try using Cheryl as a hostage. Reversing course and trying to escape through the subdivision was futile. He had to ram past them and escape. He had a "flight bag" with cash and an altered passport in a safe deposit box in Athens. If he could get there in the morning without being detected, he could find a way out of the country. They would never find him once he left the country. He just needed to disable their cars and elude them long enough to get to Athens, a larger Ohio city several miles away.

Pain jolted through her as Cheryl smashed into the seat back as the SUV screeched to a stop. The engine was idling. Something was happening, but the privacy cover above her prevented her from trying to sit up and look out the windows.

Cheryl heard something. At first, she couldn't decipher what it was, but then she heard a man's voice booming through a loudspeaker— Sean! Tears welled in her eyes. "Oh, God, please let me see him alive again. Please."

Sean was saying, "Simon, it's over, Simon. Step out of the car with your hands up."

Simon boiled with contempt as he glared through the front window.

Sean kept going, "Simon, the state police are on the way. The front gate is already blocked. You cannot escape. Face this like the military officer you are. Step out of the car with your hands above your head."

Sean had hoped like hell all his assumptions would be right and his trap worked. After talking to Milton, Sean's instinct was that Simon had her. Sean was struggling to remain calm, because he did not know where Cheryl was. He did not even know if Simon knew of the back road, but it seemed likely that he would. Sean had called the guard on his way here who told him that Simon was out earlier in the day, but he had not seen him leave during the evening. He assured Sean he would have noticed Simon's "big shiny SUV with his initials on the front license plate." Sean told the guard to call him and tell Simon that Sean was at the gate. He wasn't, of course, because Sean was hoping that if Simon had Cheryl, he would panic and try leaving via the back road—thinking Sean was at the front gate.

The guard called Sean back and told him that he had reached Simon and told him the sheriff was at the front gate and wanted to see him. Simon screamed at him not to let him pass and to tell him to get a warrant. "Sheriff, I told him you were here even though you're not."

"Good. Listen. A deputy will be there very soon. He's driving through without stopping. If you see or hear from Montgomery, call me back immediately."

Sean hoped his hunch was right. A few minutes later, Arlo called and told Sean he was at Simon's but that Simon's car was not visible through the garage window. Sean and his other two deputies were waiting, hoping like hell that Simon drove this way, and he did.

God, if she was in the SUV, her life was in danger. He hoped to God she was still alive. He needed to get Simon to surrender. He did not think Simon had thrown her in the lake—how would he explain her drowning near his house?

Simon was watching to make sure that no one was trying to come up from behind. The police were behind their two cruisers, which were blocking the road. Sean had said the state police were on the way. If he could get by those two cruisers, he might stand a chance. As he saw it, he didn't have much choice. They wouldn't shoot at him if they thought Cheryl was in the car. His car was big and fast enough to ram the end of the cruiser sitting on the right, which—if he was lucky—would bounce into the other cruiser, disabling both. They would not be able to pursue him. All he needed to do then was get on a back road and stay out of sight of any law enforcement. Of course, he had to stop somewhere and dispose of the reporter's body, but he would not let that delay him.

He revved the motor. Cheryl heard and thought, "Oh, God!" Sean heard it and yelled at his deputies not to shoot just as Simon pushed the gas pedal to the floor, and the SUV took off barreling toward them. The deputies scrambled as Sean jumped at the last minute behind the car out of Simon's path. As Simon rammed the end of the cruiser, the wheel dipped at a large rut at the road bed's edge, and he lost control. The SUV rolled a couple of times until it crashed into a tree.

The SUV came to a violent rest on its side, and the flashlights from the running police showed steam boiling from beneath the hood. They sprinted toward the vehicle, thinking it unlikely he would be in any position to shoot and not sure if the vehicle might catch on fire. Simon's body was partially protruding through the windshield, his body mangled and bloody. Sean shined his flashlight on Simon and then checked for a pulse—not finding one.

As Sean was checking on Simon, Alex was calling 911, and Syd had circled around to the back of the SUV. She was shining her flashlight through the back window but could not see what was below the privacy shield. What she did see laying up against the window was a shovel. "Sheriff! Alex! Help!" she screamed as she started trying to force open the back-door lift. Sean quickly saw what she was trying to do but realized there was no way to get it opened. "We need to get inside," he yelled.

They ran around to the front where the windshield was cracked. He started hammering with his flashlight until the opening was clear enough to pass through. Syd gently pushed past him, "Let me." As she climbed past the back seat to get to the back, he was calling Arlo for more assistance. Alex raced to get a crowbar.

Syd yelled for the crowbar to pull back the privacy cover. Alex pushed through the front windshield to hand her the bar. She strained as she pried and pulled, but it finally gave enough for her to shine her light. Cheryl's limp body was lying like a ragdoll at the bottom. "Alex!" she shouted, "Find the door release and pull it! Chief, try to force the door open! I'll try from the inside!"

Arlo came speeding up, bumping all along the path and screeched to a halt near them. He jumped out and started helping Sean with his crowbar. Alex rushed around to help. With all four straining, the door finally started to give. They finally opened it enough to see Cheryl's crumpled body.

"Oh, God!" Sean choked as he lunged toward Cheryl. Arlo helped him gently extract her and carry her a short distance. Alex ran to his cruiser to get a first aid kit and blanket. Syd knelt down to cut the bindings. Sean was cradling Cheryl. Sirens sounded in the distance.

Arlo rushed up and grabbed Alex's keys as he was running back. "I'm going to meet the ambulance to make sure they know how to get back here!"

A nightmare engulfed Sean. Except for random flashlight beams, darkness surrounded them, but another form of darkness was enveloping Sean—the kind that blinds awareness to everything but fear and torment. Sean had withdrawn from all around him, except for the woman he loved cradled in his arms. His fingers lightly plucked hair from her face as flashes of her face were suddenly conjoined with streaking visions of his best friend Mike dead in his arms and flashes of an explosion that had taken another close friend, Clint. The mental bombardment of these horrors threatened to pull him into a dark pit. Someone was easing Cheryl from his hold and laying her flat. Sean needed to wipe the blood that was marring her beautiful face. He jerked out his shirt and gently blotted as he urged in whispers for her to hang on, stay with him, she would be alright.

Syd gently worked with Sean to release his grip as she helped lay Cheryl on the blanket. Tears were running down Sean's cheeks as he tenderly wiped the blood from her face, and Alex looked grim as Syd checked her pulse and put her ear near Cheryl's mouth. "Chief, I found a pulse."

Arlo figured he had damaged two cruisers by the time he led the ambulance back to where it was needed, bouncing and scraping along the rutted road. The EMS personnel rushed down to help Cheryl, and a second one pulled up for Simon. Alex told Sean they would handle things at the scene, for him to go to the hospital with Cheryl.

Chapter 74

Silence filled the hospital waiting room. Milton's head rested on the wall. Martha held his hand as she watched the clock. Sean had his elbows on his knees holding his head between his hands. They were the only ones left and had been at the hospital for several hours waiting to hear from the doctor. The stillness was broken when Kim came rushing in. They all three looked up, thinking it was the doctor. She sat down beside Sean, "Chief, is there something I can do? Do you need anything?"

He shook his head. She glanced at Milton and Martha, and they shook their heads. The four had just settled into another soundless interlude when the doctor walked in. Sean sprung from his chair, as the other three slowly approached to hear the doctor's report.

"Sean. She is stabilized. We ran a number of scans and tests. The scan to her head shows there is swelling on her brain. She has a concussion as a result of severe trauma to the head. Her right shoulder was dislocated, and there are a number of abrasions from the trauma of being thrown around in the back of the vehicle. The vehicle's privacy cover protected her from greater trauma and injury. We were relieved to find that there are no injuries to her internal organs. There is substantial bruising to her face and her upper body in particular. She has suffered major trauma, and it's going to take time, but I think we are looking at a complete recovery. I'm going to keep her in the ICU for at least the next twenty-four hours. Once we've moved her to a room, she'll be in the hospital for a few days before we release her."

Except for the shadow cast by his whiskers, Sean's face was tight and pale. He still wore the bloodstained uniform shirt he used to wipe her blood from her face. "You said she is going to make a full recovery?"

The doctor had kind eyes and spoke with compassion, "We can never guarantee a hundred percent recovery, Sean, but I have every reason to believe that she will fully recover. We are going to closely monitor her and take good care of her."

"When can I see her?"

"In about three or four hours, you can see her for ten minutes, but Sean, she will be sleeping. She needs her rest right now." The doctor asked if there were any other questions. Sean looked at the other three, but no one said anything. Sean thanked the doctor.

After he walked away, Milton wiped his eyes, "That's about as good a news as we could expect—given everything." Sean nodded. Milton continued, "If you don't need me and Martha, we're going to run by and tell Kye. She wanted to know what the doctor said. Is there anybody else you would like for us to contact?"

"Well, there are a lot of people, but for now, I need to call Mom and Dad. I didn't want to tell them until I heard from the doctor."

"Are you going to stay here?" Milton asked.

"Yeah, until I can see her."

Kim spoke up, "I'll run by the station and get you a fresh change of clothes." Sean kept an extra uniform for unexpected occasions. "It won't take me long to bring those back. I'll bring you something to eat and some coffee."

"Thanks, Kim. I guess it will be daybreak in a couple of hours. Give the deputies an update on Cheryl and tell them you'll let them know when I get back to the station."

"Sure will."

Chapter 75

Sean did not recognize the old model car sitting in Luca and Natalia's driveway. He and the three deputies walked up to the front door, and Arlo knocked. Luca came to the door, looking defeated. Sean introduced him to Alex and Syd and told him that they needed to come in, that they had a warrant.

Luca opened the door without saying anything, and they followed him into the living room. Natalia sat on the sofa beside Father O'Brady, a local priest. Luca slumped into a chair and rubbed his hands over his face. Father O'Brady greeted the officers and put his hand on Natalia's.

Luca then looked up at Sean, "You were right, Sheriff. I drove there that evening. She was down at the pier. I walked down to see if I could talk to her. We got in an argument, and she slipped and hit her head and fell in. I couldn't save her."

Natalia jumped up, screamed, and wrapped her arms around Luca. "No! No! It was me! Me!" she wailed. "I just confessed to Father O'Brady. I wanted Luca to take me to the police station."

Luca started to protest, but Sean interrupted, "We know what happened, Luca. We have proof."

Chapter 76

Over the next two days, Sean was busy with paperwork and the aftermath related to Simon's kidnapping of Cheryl, but he was a frequent visitor at the hospital. Cheryl was in ICU for two days before being moved into a private room. Although she had gained consciousness, she mostly slept. Sean would sit by her bed and hold her hand and think about his love for her and the brightness she brought into his life. Both wrists bore red ugly evidence of the bindings Simon had used.

As he held her hand to which the tube was taped, he felt her stir. He looked up and, despite the dark bruises and a couple of bandages, her eyes focused on him. Her mouth couldn't form a smile, but her eyes did. She whispered, "Hi."

Sean smiled and leaned closer, "Hi."

As she gained her strength over the following days, she managed to tell what had happened, and that Simon had admitted to killing Caroline, Rylee and Hogan. She told Sean how he had admitted to framing Flynn and intended to kill Baxter and plant evidence on him to make it appear that Baxter had killed Rylee and herself.

392

He told her what happened to Skylar. Skylar was overwrought by the time she unexpectedly arrived at Natalia's after leaving Mary's foundation and insisted that Natalia go help her pack before Danny arrived with the rental truck. Natalia could tell something was off, and Skylar told her she had taken two anti-anxiety tablets because of the stress of everything. She couldn't reason with Skylar about waiting until Saturday morning to pack and leave, so Natalia called Luca and asked if he would pick her up later that evening. Since Skylar could drive through the resident lane, the video did not pick up that someone was in the passenger seat, and there was no record of Natalia's presence. When they arrived at her house, Skylar insisted that they have some wine and chocolates and go to the pier and enjoy the lake one final time before packing. They sat in the chairs where the pier was wider and met the property. According to Natalia, Skylar had three glasses of wine.

Natalia knew how close she and Luca were to losing their house and asked Skylar if she might cash in the insurance policy and give her the cash. She said that Skylar erupted and started bad-mouthing Luca—calling him a loser, lazy, a bum—several other names. Natalia told her to forget she had even brought up the insurance policy, but Skylar was acting strange and started saying that Luca was just like their mother and that Natalia let herself be used by them. Natalia was at this point crying and stood to walk back up to the house, but

Skylar jumped in front of her and would not let her pass, so Natalia rushed toward the end of the pier. Skylar stalked and cornered Natalia. Natalia did not know how to swim and panicked she was going to fall in. Her hysteria of falling in caused her to push Skylar to get past her, but when she did, Skylar lost her balance and hit her head on the post and fell in. Natalia was too afraid to jump in the water. She tried to reach for Skylar, but she was under the water, and Natalia froze.

When Luca arrived a while later, he found Natalia kneeling at the edge of the pier—shattered with grief. He finally got enough of the story from Natalia that he understood what had happened. He put Natalia in his truck. Natalia had not been in the house since Skylar told her to go on down to the pier and that she would bring the wine glasses and bottle. Since Natalia had not wanted any chocolate, Skylar had left the chocolate box in the kitchen. He took Natalia's wine glass, cleaned it and put it in the cabinet. He carefully carried Skylar's glass and the bottle so his prints would not be present and set them on the counter. He had Natalia lay in the floorboard as they drove out of the subdivision.

Sean told Cheryl that the video confirmed Natalia's story about her rushing to the end of the pier, Skylar following and crowding her, the push, and Skylar falling in. The district attorney was deciding whether to file charges. Before Sean could say anymore, Cheryl drifted to sleep.

To meet the demand, the *Tribune* printed extra editions with the coverage of Simon kidnapping Cheryl. While Milton left it for Cheryl to finish her story about Rylee and Hogan when she was strong enough, he wrote that Cheryl's kidnapping was related to her discovery of Simon's culpability in two other deaths. The paper also reported on the death of Skylar. At Sean's request, they did not print the story about Caroline's death at the hands of Simon until he could work the proper military channels.

Chapter 77

Milton had just wrapped up interviewing Sean for an update on stories about Skylar's death and Cheryl's kidnapping. "Sean, do you mind if I ask you a question, off the record, about something that has been on my mind?"

"No. What is it?"

"I'd like your thoughts on why in the hell he kidnapped her. For Christ's sake, he was going to kill her."

Sean tapped his pencil on the desk a couple of times before responding. "I think he cracked. Simon needed to be in control, and his life was spiraling out of control. He couldn't tolerate anything that stood in the way of what he wanted or would jeopardize his social standing. His personal life was in shambles. He was headed into bankruptcy. His marriage was falling apart. Skylar was through letting him control her. She wouldn't give him the funds he desperately needed to try and stay financially afloat. She was also leaving him, and to add insult to injury, he knew she was thinking of going back to the Pentagon where he was well known. Hell, I think he probably knew she had taken a job. Anyway, he couldn't take the idea of financial ruin and Skylar leaving him. So, all that impacted his frame of mind.

"That was part of it, but then there were the investigations. I think the tipping point was when his former college roommate called and told him the questions Cheryl was asking. First, he thought she had his dorm key, which he feared he had lost when he and Hogan tussled to get Hogan out of his car. The second thing was his realization that Cheryl had narrowed down a person of interest to a football player whose name started with a B. He thought she was on the verge of pointing an incriminating finger at him."

Milton shook his head. "Hell, I can see how he felt things were falling apart. The murders he committed were unraveling at a rapid-fire pace. You were coming at him with Caroline's killing, and then he must have believed Cheryl had hit the mother-load in those teenagers' murders."

"In addition to being concerned that Cheryl had uncovered incriminating evidence, I think he thought if he killed her and framed Baxter, then he could bluff his was through any new allegations into Caroline's murder by claiming Flynn had already been convicted and it was a smear campaign against him. Although he knew I had come across evidence that shattered his alibi for the evening his first wife was murdered, and new facts about Caroline's death were surfacing, let's face it, that happened twenty years ago.

"Yeah. I see that," agreed Milton. "He'd cornered the market on ego. That's why he wanted people to call him the Brigadier."

"Right. Unfortunately, he developed a mindset of murder—that was his fallback to solving his problems. While killing Rylee may have been accidental, let's face it. Her death eliminated any threats to his ambitions. Murdering Hogan solved any concern that his involvement in her death would be discovered, or so he thought, and he did get away with both of those for nearly forty years. I think he killed Caroline because he was concerned that her leaving him and any scandal associated with that could derail his military career. Killing Cheryl and Baxter would have, in his thinking, preserved his reputation. If he was concerned about being convicted for killing the teenagers, then he also may have thought he was possibly saving himself from going to prison.

"So, he had the mindset that murder was a solution, but he also had the arrogance he could outsmart the police and prosecutors. He had gotten away with killing his first wife. He had gotten away with killing Rylee and Hogan. As crazy as it sounds, I think he thought he could kill Cheryl and frame Baxter and he'd get by with that."

Do you think he would have been convicted in Caroline's death?"

"I can't say with certainty, but it's unlikely. He may have not even been charged. Keaton was dead, so he couldn't be questioned. Hell, the private investigator he used to spy on Caroline was dead.

My findings were circumstantial, and it would be like finding a needle in a haystack to find the proverbial smoking gun with the passage of twenty years. But if it came out that he was suspected of also killing the teenagers, the public suspicion of being accused of three murders at two different times would always follow him."

Milton finished off his coffee. "All those things were hitting him like a tsunami. Like you said, his financial collapse would be aired for everyone to see. Hell, he would have lost his house—everything. Then, with the murder scandals, I can't see anyone ever wanting to partner with him in any kind of business deal, and he'd be treated like a pariah in his social circles because of the murder suspicions. He probably thought there was no way to rebuild his life."

Sean agreed. "He just couldn't allow all that to happen. He had to know the distinction he had built over his lifetime, particularly among his military colleagues, would be irrevocably destroyed."

"He certainly was delusional. Do you think he thought about killing Skylar?" Milton asked.

"That's a good question. One thing that has bugged me is that we could not account for Montgomery's whereabouts on that Friday when she died. I've wondered if he came back here with that intent but couldn't find her. He had to get back for the dinner so he couldn't wait around. The scheme he used for Caroline's murder would have been similar for Skylar's. When he was in Columbus, he didn't know Skylar had changed her will, but it's just speculation that he might have tried to kill her."

"Mmm. Well, I guess since I came so close to losing someone I think of as a daughter, it's been on my mind a lot. Anyway, thanks for talking to me about it. I know that Cheryl wouldn't want me to dwell on it." He stood, "I'd better get back and get ready for our next edition. Thanks for the interview."

"Anytime, Milton. Once Cheryl is home, you and Martha come by often. She loves you both," Sean smiled, "and she will want updates on what is happening with the newspaper."

Milton chuckled. "That she will."

Chapter 78

Cheryl had a steady stream of visitors while she was in the hospital. When Sean arrived one evening, Max and Bri were just leaving. He leaned over and lightly kissed her forehead. "How's your day been, Honey?" he asked with a grin.

Cheryl was sitting up in bed. A sling protected her arm. "Great. Need to add on to our kitchen. Very soon."

"Why's that?"

Her voice was weak, and pain from moving her lips caused her words to be muffled and choppy. "All the food. Bri and Kim. Won't need to cook for weeks, maybe months."

Sean laughed. "Kim told me yesterday that people keep calling the station asking about you. Milton told me that the *Tribune* has been besieged with well-wishes and cards and flowers. We are lucky to have so many people thinking of us."

Her cut and swollen lips prevented a smile, but Sean saw warmth in her eyes. She nodded her concurrence.

"So," he said as he scooted his chair closer and took her hand in his, "I've been thinking."

She mumbled a tease, "Is that a warning?"

He laughed, "Could be. We have made a life here, and have lots of people we care about and who care about us. So, I think it's time to call in the chips."

Cheryl's eyebrow tried to arch, "You want people to bring food for a year?"

Sean's laugh rang out around the room. "Not quite. I'm talking about the chips you owe me."

Cheryl's eyes were bright, "What chips?"

"You promised to marry me, remember?"

Her eyes lit with amusement, and she nodded.

"Good. I'm calling in the chips. Now, being the sheriff and all, I have some pull at the county. We can apply for a marriage license while you're in here, and I can get the preacher to come here and marry us."

He sat there with that expectant gaze she knew so well. She smiled as much as she dared, "That's the most romantic thing I've ever heard."

Chapter 79

Jorge and Gabe were waiting for Jake when he pulled into the school parking lot. "Hey, man. Is that true what they said on the TV last night that your team recorded how that woman died?" asked Jorge.

Jake grabbed a book and closed his truck's door. "Can't comment. Matter of national security," he said as he hustled toward the school.

"Bullshit," huffed Gabe as they scurried to keep up. "Come on, man. What happened?"

"I don't want to be late."

Jorge howled, "Since when have you given a shit about being late for class? What happened?"

As Jake pulled open the door, he asked, "How's your Oscar-winning video coming?"

"Huh?" asked Gabe. "Why you askin' about that?"

"If I were you, I wouldn't spend too much time practicing walking down the red carpet. Gotta go, guys."

Jorge and Gabe frowned as he jogged toward the classroom. "Wonder what's up with him?" murmured Gabe.

A few days after Cheryl had been released, she and Kye were sitting on the front porch of the duplex enjoying the warm spring day. A truck pulled up, and Buddy stood to watch. A man exited the truck and walked toward them. Buddy leaped down the stairs and sniffed at him. "Hey, boy," he said as he patted Buddy's neck and approached the porch.

Kye was the first to speak, "Baxter Colbert. Well, well. I don't think I've seen you since you were in high school."

"You're Mrs. Davis, aren't you?" he asked after looking at her.

"Yes. We're enjoying this beautiful day. Is there something I can help you with?"

He looked at Cheryl, who still wore an arm sling and bandages on her face. "Actually, I was hoping to talk to Ms. Seton for a few minutes."

Kye looked at Cheryl who nodded, "Okay. I need to check on some wash. Come on up and have a seat."

"Thank you."

After Kye walked inside, he turned to Cheryl, "Ms. Seton, I read the articles in the *Tribune* about what happened. They didn't mention Rylee or Hogan, and I assumed they were leaving that story to be told by you. Because you talked to me about them, I was able to tell from the articles that Simon had killed them and planned to frame me, even though my name wasn't mentioned either.

"I know you were nearly killed by him and that was because you were doing your job. Because you didn't give up, once your story is published, everyone who knew Rylee and Hogan will know Hogan didn't kill her, and that's something. Anyway, I want to apologize for how I treated you and what I said."

Cheryl smiled the best she could. "Thank you, Mr. Colbert. I appreciate you coming here today and saying that to me. I was just trying to get at the truth."

"I know that, and I'm glad you did." He stood. "That's all I had to say. I hope you get over your injuries soon."

Cheryl watched him leave. His visit had been uplifting. She had already been working on the rest of story about Rylee and Hogan. She wanted to talk to Rylee's sister and Paige as well as Hogan's sister before she published it. With each day, she was gaining her strength and looked forward to returning to work.

Chapter 80

When Sean pulled into Flynn's driveway, Flynn was planting shrubs along the front of the house. His short-sleeve white T-shirt was smudged with dirt and damp from his exertions; the old pair of jeans had gone without washings for other outdoor projects before today. Perspiration beaded his forehead and dripped down the sides of his face. He looked up and saw the car and squinted. Sean exited from the driver's side, and a man in full military dress stepped from the passenger side.

Shit! What the hell is he up to now? Last time he accused me of murder.

He leaned the shovel against the wall and wiped his brow with his arm and walked toward them as they approached him. When they were within about twelve feet of each other, Sean yelled, "Attention!"

Flynn jerked up and saluted the officer, who in turn saluted him. After relaxing, Flynn's brows slightly narrowed in suspicion as he looked at Sean.

"Flynn, this is General Tanner Bradford. General, Flynn Taggart. Flynn, is there someplace we can talk?"

"Let's go inside."

After they were seated, Sean said, "General Bradford was my commanding officer when I retired."

Flynn didn't respond, so Sean continued. "Flynn, we're here about Caroline Montgomery's death."

Flynn's eyes trained on Sean's as he listened.

Sean then told him everything he had learned. He explained about the witness who told the local sheriff about seeing him changing his tire, about Simon knowing Caroline was planning to leave him, and about Simon's speeding ticket heading toward D.C. the night of Caroline's death. "He admitted everything to Cheryl Seton, the owner of the local newspaper, when he kidnapped her. I don't need to go into those details, but the bottom line is that she has provided an affidavit to his admissions."

Tanner then explained that a JAG officer would be in touch with Flynn. A board was going to be assembled to review the file, interview witnesses who Sean had spoken with and possibly others, and consider Ms. Seton's affidavit. They could never make right for the twenty years he had spent in prison, the general told him. He could not promise anything, but if Flynn was exonerated, under consideration would be a full reinstatement of his rank and pension and compensation for his years in prison, which would mean that Flynn would be retired as a full Colonel.

407

It was one of the few times Flynn had been speechless, Sean thought.

Flynn looked at Tanner, "Sir, it was always my goal to see my name cleared."

"Well, I wouldn't be here but for Sean. It was his investigation that led to the evidence being discovered. Of course, Montgomery's statements to Ms. Seton when he thought they would never be repeated confirmed Sean's findings."

Flynn looked at Sean. "When I walked into your office that day, I hoped my gut feeling about you was right. However, you gave me reason to question myself, especially when you showed up here with that deputy all but accusing me of murdering Montgomery's second wife. It's good to know though that I was right about you. I appreciate everything."

"Speaking of which, did you come back to Bekbourg after that?"

"Yes, I sure did. After you left, it came to me that Simon's newest wife had died, and that you were investigating her death. What burnt my ass was that it appeared you might suspect me. I'd been on that merry-go-round once before, and no way was I going to sit on my ass and hope you didn't screw up. So, I went there and went to the library and read up on the case and everything I could find out about them. I knew where they lived, so I also looked up all the maps of the area. I found out about that old road the day that all that shit with Simon happened. I was going to call you about it, but after

I read about everything in the newspaper, I decided you had things in hand, so I drove back here."

"Okay, Flynn. We wanted to tell you in person. One other thing. I regret like hell what happened to you twenty years ago. I am very happy that you've been vindicated. I hope you understand why I couldn't tell you what I was finding out during the past few weeks. Fortunately, the truth finally came out."

"Yeah, Sean. I know how you CID guys like to play things close to the vest. I'm grateful you didn't give up on this."

Sean nodded.

"Sir," Flynn looked at Tanner as a glint danced in his eyes, "When Sean called that he was coming, he didn't mention a general would be with him. I'd dressed up if I'd known that."

Tanner hid a smile as he stood and dryly replied, "So your state of dress is a result of Sean's dereliction to inform you that I was coming, too?"

"Yes, Sir. I would never have worn a dirty T-shirt and jeans for this meeting, Sir."

Sean arched an eyebrow as he eyed Flynn, and Flynn's mouth twitched.

"The JAG will be in touch, Mr. Taggart."

"Thank you, Sir."

Lilly's team won first place in the video contest at the high school's art night, which took place soon after the school year ended. They each won a gift certificate for a dinner at the GilHaus.

After the ceremony, Jorge and Gabe hustled up to Jake as he was walking toward the door. "Hey, Jake, congratulations, man. You have a future in Hollywood," Jorge ribbed.

Gabe jumped in. "Yeah, so we were thinking you might want to share your new-found celebrity with us. Maybe we could all share your gift certificate and then chip in for the difference." Gabe was looking at Jorge, who was nodding.

"That right?" asked Jake.

"Yeah, man. With you getting ready to leave for football camp, it'd be a good way to celebrate."

"Yeah?" asked Jake looking at both his friends.

"Sure, man. What do you say?"

"It might be fun. I'll let you know. I gotta move. I'm heading to meet my video team to get an ice cream. See you bros later."

Cheryl and Sean got married in church surrounded by family and friends. Bri and Max hosted a reception that went late into the night. Toward the end of the party, Sean pulled Cheryl to him when they found a private moment. He kissed her deeply. "I sure am glad I called in my chips," he smiled as he gazed into her eyes.

She wrapped her arms around his neck and kissed him back, "And I'm sure glad you did, too."

He laughed as they embraced into a loving kiss.

ABOUT THE AUTHOR

Sherrie Rutherford lives on Florida's Gulf Coast and has ties to Ohio, East Tennessee and Houston. She and Larry love traveling, hiking (especially in the Great Smoky Mountains), and playing Bridge. She is a retired attorney. Her passion for Appalachia and railroad history inspired the Bekbourg County Series.

Sherrie's website
http://www.sherrierutherford.com
Follow Sherrie on Facebook
Sherrie Rutherford – "Author"

Sherrie Rutherford